Dark Voyage

MATTERS OF THE HEART

THE CHILDREN OF THE GODS
BOOK SEVENTY-SEVEN

I. T. LUCAS

Frankie

Frankie regarded her boss with a wide-eyed stare and a sinking sensation in the pit of her stomach. "Are you serious? You're not even giving me two weeks' notice? You want me to leave right now?"

Who fired people on a Monday afternoon, right after the lunch break?

Scumbags like Vernon. That's who.

He nodded. "I've found that it's best to make a clean cut and not drag things out. I will pay you for the next two weeks, of course." He gave her one of the fake smiles he usually reserved for customers. "Consider it a paid vacation."

The finality in his tone didn't leave room for argument.

"Can I at least know the reason for my termination?"

Frankie had a feeling it had to do with the 'niece' he'd brought to the office the other day and paraded around like a prize horse, introducing her to everyone. What was her name?

Was it Ashley?

Frankie couldn't remember and didn't care.

The thing was, no one's niece looked like that or clung to her uncle's arm like a panda to a tree branch.

Did Vernon need to set his mistress up with a job?

The guy was so cheap that he couldn't even be a proper sugar daddy.

Vernon sighed dramatically. "Where should I start?" He braced his elbows on the desk and steepled his fingers. "Let's see. You are often late, you make typos in the emails I dictate to you, and you don't bother to run them through a spellchecker. Do you know how embarrassing that is for me? People assume that I wrote those emails myself."

Frankie squirmed in the uncomfortable chair. Everything he'd said was true, but it didn't happen as often as he'd made it sound. Everyone was late once in a while, and everyone misspelled a word here and there, and the spellchecker didn't catch every mistake.

His 'niece' wouldn't do any better, that was for sure.

Well, at least Vernon hadn't told her that she had a big mouth and an attitude. That was the reason Frankie had been fired from her previous job.

The problem was that if he fired her for a cause, she wouldn't get unemployment benefits, especially if he exaggerated her supposed misconduct, which the scumbag would certainly do.

"What if I promise to do better?" She was fighting tears. The money in her bank account wouldn't cover next month's rent. "Can you give me another chance?"

"It's not conducive to a good office environment to have a disgruntled employee spreading discord." Vernon leaned forward, giving her a surprisingly earnest look. "You are not happy here, Francesca, and you let everyone know that. You might be happier somewhere else."

So, that was supposed to be the reason for her sudden and totally unprovoked termination?

But, no one working for Vernon was happy. He and his partners expected each of their employees to do the work of two or three people, and on top of that, the pay sucked. Still, the others might have been better at keeping their discontent to themselves, while Frankie had a big mouth and no filter.

She might have blabbed to the wrong person.

Was it the barista at the coffee shop across the street?

Or maybe someone had overheard her talking shit on her lunch break about Vernon and his sleazy partners?

At least he was going to pay her for the next two weeks. That might be enough time to find another job with less stress and better pay.

Heck, she could probably make more money taking care of kids and cleaning houses, and she might even enjoy that, but Frankie had a college degree for Pete's sake. Her parents would be mortified if she didn't use it after all the effort and sacrifice they had made so she could get the education they never had.

Besides, Frankie liked dressing elegantly and working in an office.

That said, the office attire at the dream job Mia had promised her was probably super casual. Beta testers for the Perfect Match Virtual Fantasy Studios couldn't wear anything form-fitting while performing their duties, and they had to take their shoes off.

Mia had promised her the job months ago, but nothing had come out of it so far. Supposedly, the machines weren't ready because of production delays, but Frankie had a feeling that Mia might have promised something that she couldn't deliver.

"Will you at least write me a reference letter?" she pleaded, hating herself for having to beg Vernon for anything.

But what else could she do?

If he wrote her a reference, he couldn't later claim that she was a horrible employee and wasn't entitled to unemployment benefits.

"Of course." Vernon Hoffesommer III looked relieved. "In fact, you can write whatever you want, and I'll sign it."

That was better than Frankie had expected, but knowing Vernon, she'd better write it and get his signature before she left, or he would later claim he'd never promised to do it. Right now, he obviously wanted to get rid of her as fast as possible, and she needed to take advantage of that.

"Thank you." She gave him a dazzling smile. "I'll type it up right now, so I don't need to return for it."

Vernon's expression soured, confirming her suspicion that he was desperate to get rid of her, but he nodded. "Make it short."

Was his 'niece' in the waiting room? Ready to jump into Frankie's seat or onto Vernon's lap?

Probably.

"I'll be right back." She rose to her high-heeled feet and walked out of his office holding her chin up, even though she was faking it big time.

After typing up a glowing reference letter, she actually checked it for spelling mistakes before printing it out and striding back into Vernon's office.

He read through the letter with a grimace, twisting his fleshy lips, and when he shook his head, Frankie held her breath, but then he reached for his pen and signed it.

"Good luck, Francesca."

Unbelievable.

Frankie hadn't thought he would actually sign the thing. She'd made herself sound like the best assistant an executive could ever hope for.

To sign that, Vernon must have felt guilty for kicking her out to make room for his 'niece.'

Relief washing over her, she took the printed page from his hairy fingers and offered him her hand. "Thank you, Mr. Hoffesommer."

In exchange for his signature on the letter, she was willing to suffer his gross touch one last time.

Vernon had never done anything more than put his sweaty paw on her shoulder or her upper arm while passing by her desk, so it wasn't enough to sue his ass for sexual harassment, but to say that it had been unwelcome was to put it mildly.

Dreading his slimy touch, she'd stopped wearing outfits that exposed her shoulders or arms to the office.

Back at her desk, Frankie collected the one picture of her family and the tiny cactus she'd brought to decorate her space. Lifting her eyes, she scanned the rest of the staff working in the office's main room. She searched for one face that she would miss, but none of them even bothered to look up.

Hell, she'd made some friends during the eighteen months she'd worked there. They could at least wish her luck.

Turning around, she saw why no one dared to lift their heads.

Vernon stood at the doorway with his arms crossed over his chest and resting on his large belly.

Was he worried that she would steal a pen? Or maybe a book of stamps?

Plastering on a smile, she waved at her former coworkers. "Goodbye, everyone." She turned to Vernon with that smile still affixed to her face. "Goodbye, Mr. Hoffesommer. I hope your 'niece' will like it here better than I did."

Dagor

"What do you think?" Negal pointed with his chin at the two women walking through the door of the coffee shop that had become their refuge over the weekend.

The females were pretty, for young humans that is, but neither had the poise, elegance, and self-assurance that Dagor appreciated in his companions.

Sneakers and jeans just did not do it for him, and neither did all the skin decorations that were so fashionable among the young humans in this city.

Gods couldn't get tattoos because their bodies healed the punctures faster than the artists could make them, and Dagor was thankful for that. Who wanted to be stuck with crappy artwork for eternity?

Or even great artwork, for that matter?

"Not my type." He closed his lips around the paper straw and drew up more of the delicious Frappuccino that had become his favorite drink since he'd discovered it.

"You are too picky." Negal leaned closer to him. "You won't find goddesses here, and you need to compromise. For humans, those two are not bad."

"I'm not picky." Dagor put the Frappuccino down. After spending five years on Earth with him, Negal should have known what type of females interested him. "The attorneys the other day were very pleasant company."

Neither had been beautiful or even pretty, but the conversation was stimulating, and they had been immaculately dressed.

Negal grinned. "Yeah, those two were superb in more ways than one, or at least the one I picked. It's a shame we can't see them again."

After spending the night with them in the hotel, the ladies had been more than eager to provide their phone numbers, but Dagor and Negal had a rule about being with human companions more than once.

Before meeting Gabi, Aru had obeyed the same rule, but he'd broken it for her without giving it a second thought. At the time, Dagor couldn't understand their commander's odd behavior and his fascination with the human, but as it had turned out, Gabi had not been fully human. She had godly genes in her, which explained the attraction.

Still, Gabi was not a goddess, only an immortal—a hybrid who was considered an abomination in their home world.

Not that Dagor believed in that nonsense. Gabriella was a lovely female, but even more importantly, she was Aru's fated mate. Nevertheless, the union was problematic in the sense that Aru could never take her back to Anumati with him and could never introduce her to his family and friends back home. The resistance would have welcomed her, but there was no way to smuggle her onto the patrol ship, or any other ship for that matter. All the stasis pods were accounted for, and their occupants' biometrics were monitored from Anumati.

If only the resistance could build its own ships somewhere away from Anumati's watchful eyes, but that was impossible. Humans thought their privacy was being eroded, but they had no idea how much worse it could get.

The one good thing about being on Earth was the freedom to do and say whatever he wanted without worrying about the censorship that possibly extended even to thoughts. There was no proof, but there were rumors about the king employing telepaths. Most of them couldn't read actual thoughts, but they could sense intentions, which was dangerous for the resistance.

Rebels had learned how to shield their thoughts and emotions.

The problem was that it didn't mean much when there was so little that he could do with this planet's primitive technology.

Leaning back in his chair, Dagor groaned. "I need something to do that involves using my head for more than people-watching. I'm bored out of my mind, and I'm not even a century old yet."

A guy sitting at the table next to theirs turned to him and nodded. "I get it, bro. Sometimes I feel ancient, too."

Forcing a smile, Dagor lifted the plastic cup and saluted the guy.

He'd found out that humans responded well to noncommittal gestures that could mean many different things.

Negal glared at him. "You need to keep your voice down."

"I know. My bad."

That was another human expression Dagor had adopted that worked very well for a variety of situations.

Leaning even closer to him, Negal whispered in his ear, "You are too young to suffer from the affliction of boredom. Perhaps you should contact the ship's counselor."

Dagor wasn't losing his mind, and he had no intention of talking to the counselor, but to get Negal off his back, he had to acquiesce.

"Perhaps I will go to see her after this mission is over. You know that empaths need skin-to-skin contact to be able to provide real help. She can't do much for me through the communicator."

"By the time we get picked up, it might be too late," Negal said in their native tongue. "A hundred and fifteen years is not long in the life of a god, but if you are already showing signs of mental fatigue, you should not delay seeking help. Even talking with the counselor might be beneficial. She might give you advice on how to combat these early signs of decline."

Dagor didn't wish to offend Negal, but he'd had enough of the insinuations that he was going insane. It was a major concern for Anumatians, but he was too young to be showing even early symptoms.

"My mental faculties are intact. It's just that we are stuck here doing nothing while Aru takes care of his mate. I am tired of sitting in this blasted coffee shop and watching humans come and go." He lifted the venti Frappuccino cup. "That's the only saving grace of this place."

Arching a brow, Negal leaned back. "I quite enjoy the respite we have been given. Sitting here and hunting for suitable bed companions is far more enjoyable than trekking through Tibet and sleeping on the cold ground. I am not looking forward to the day Aru decides that Gabriella is strong enough to travel, and we will be back on the road, searching for the missing Kra-ell pods."

Sometimes, Dagor wondered whether Negal's linear way of thinking was an inborn tendency or a product of his many years in the service.

"The pods are not the only thing we should be searching for."

The immortals were hiding gods among them, and Aru knew about it. He just didn't seem to think that his teammates were trustworthy enough to tell them about what he had discovered.

No matter how Dagor tried to excuse his leader's motives, the insult stung.

The smirk slid off Negal's face. "We are not supposed to know about the gods, and I feel conflicted about not telling Aru that we do."

The guy at the other table looked at them with curiosity in his eyes. "What language are you two speaking?"

"It's a dialect of Hungarian," Dagor said. "We are from a small village high up in the mountains, and our people are the only ones who speak this particular form of the language."

The guy nodded sagely. "I thought that it sounded European."

Dagor wasn't sure whether Hungarian sounded like their native tongue or even if the country had mountains, but this explanation had worked before, so he used it again.

Negal shook his head. "If you want to keep talking, we should get out of here."

"And go where? To the penthouse where Gabi and Aru might be frolicking amorously on every available surface?"

He didn't begrudge Aru his happiness, but he wished the guy would get over the honeymoon phase so they could get moving again.

They had a mission to complete.

Negal released a sigh. "We could go to a museum or to a library. There is so much we still don't know about these humans, and we can use this idle time to learn more about them."

"The humans are of no interest to me. I want to find out who the gods are that Gabi's brother talked about. Perhaps we should just confront Aru and tell him that we know."

The conversation between Gabi and her brother had been recorded by the spy bug they had attached to the brother, and Aru had later erased it. Their leader wasn't familiar enough with human tech and didn't realize how primitive it still was. He couldn't have guessed that deleting the recording wouldn't do the trick.

Dagor's intention hadn't been to spy on their leader when he'd checked the trash folder. Suspecting that Aru had messed with the laptop, he had checked it just to make sure that nothing important had been deleted by mistake.

Listening to the recording, he'd realized what Aru had been trying to hide, but not why he had done it. They were supposed to be a team, and they were all members of the resistance.

Aru should have trusted him and Negal with the information, and it was disturbing that he hadn't.

What else was he hiding from them?

Annani

After spending the weekend in atypical solitary contemplation, Annani had a little more clarity about the information they had learned from the three gods who claimed to belong to the resistance. Regrettably, it was not enough to help Kian form a strategy regarding the threat of the Eternal King.

Her paternal grandfather.

Her greatest nemesis.

It was funny how inconsequential Mortdh and Navuh seemed in comparison.

Mortdh had been a bully with delusions of grandeur, a powerful compeller, but a mediocre politician at best. He had not been difficult to outmaneuver, but in the end the law of unintended consequences had prevailed, resulting in a disaster that had eclipsed anything Mortdh had in mind for her and the future of the gods.

Perhaps things would have ended the same way regardless of her role in shaping the events, but Annani would always carry the guilt of inadvertently being responsible for her people's demise.

For Khiann's death.

His murder at the hands of Mortdh.

If she could have seen the future, she would never have pursued him. It would have been better to have never known the great love they had shared than to mourn his death.

Mortdh was dead, and his successor, her current arch-nemesis, was not as delusional and not as powerful as his father, but Navuh was smarter and a better politician. It took more than his incredible compulsion ability to lead an army of immortal warriors dedicated to the cause and eager to do his bidding.

Her clan could deal with Navuh and his Brotherhood of murderers, but just barely so, while the Eternal King was in a league of his own.

He had been ruling over the gods, the rulers of the galaxy, for hundreds of thousands of years, and according to Aru, a large number of his subjects were not opposed to his rule. They were satisfied with their lives on Anumati.

Her grandfather was brilliant, a true master of propaganda, but then even the gods were easy to manipulate. As long as there was prosperity and something to strive for, people were willing to overlook things like the gradual erosion of their personal freedoms, especially when such things took place ever so slowly over eons.

So what if saying things that did not agree with the official line could get them in trouble?

Remaining silent was easier than becoming part of the resistance and actively doing something against the censorship.

Not everyone had what it took to be a rebel, but she must have inherited her father's rebellious character because no one could accuse her of being complicit.

Annani was an idealist and a fighter.

Or had been.

Now that she had a clan comprised of her descendants, their chosen mates, and two other groups of people to protect, she was much less hasty to rise to the challenge than she had been in her youth.

Still, she was keenly aware that Earth was uniquely positioned to host the rebellion against her grandfather. Come to think of it, her father had laid the groundwork, either anticipating this or just as a result of following his moral compass and building a community based on the ideals he had pursued on Anumati.

Had Ahn envisioned Earth becoming the place where gods, immortals, humans, and Kra-ell, both purebloods and hybrids, could coexist in harmony and equality?

Had he foreseen that Kra-ell and immortals could someday form fated bonds and produce uniquely gifted hybrid children?

The tapestry the Fates had woven on Earth was unlike anything else in the universe. Had they done it to show the gods a model of a civilization that did not discriminate between the different species?

A society that did not place taboos on mating between gods and Kra-ell, immortals and humans?

Had they foreseen the new species of hybrid children that would be unlike anything the galaxy had seen before?

Right now, Earth was far from utopia, and humans overwhelmingly outnumbered all the other alien species living among them, but that was just the beginning. It could become the crown jewel of the resistance, the place they could point to for people to see what was possible.

The problem was protecting this precious jewel from the Eternal King and also from self-destruction.

Thanks to technology, the world's economy was so interconnected that it did not make sense for one superpower to launch a military attack against another, but humans did not always do what made sense, and the threat of a third world war was not as far outside the realm of probability as many believed.

Regrettably, the vast majority of the world's leadership was not concerned with the well-being of its citizenry. The elites looked after their own, filling both their pockets and those of their associates, while the young died in senseless wars and families died of plagues and famines that could have been avoided.

There was nothing new under the sun. Generations came and went, but the dynamic never changed.

With a sigh, Annani walked over to her favorite armchair and sat down.

Would things ever get better?

She had spent her entire life, over five thousand years, working on improving the human condition, and the fruits of her labors were evident, but there was still so much to do, and now it seemed like she was running out of time.

Lifting her arm, she examined her luminous skin and wondered whether it looked dimmer because of her melancholy mood or if it was her imagination.

The mystery of the commoner gods on Anumati lacking glow still had not been satisfactorily answered, and perhaps the simplest and easiest explanation was lack of energy. Perhaps they lacked luminosity because they were suppressed and their freedoms were limited. Maybe positive energy was needed to fuel the glow, and the commoner gods on Anumati did not have enough of it, while all the gods she had known on Earth had a healthy glow, and not all of them had been nobility.

Annani shook her head.

That could not be the explanation.

She had not met Aru and his friends yet, but if finding his fated mate did not make Aru burst with positive energy and activate his glow, then he did not have the ability.

When her phone rang, Annani pulled it out of the pocket of her gown and smiled at Kian's handsome face filling the screen.

"Hello, my darling son," she answered.

"Good evening, Mother. Are you busy?"

"Not at all."

"Are you in the mood for receiving guests?"

Annani chuckled. "That will depend on who the guests are."

"Syssi and I would like to share a vision that Syssi had and ask your opinion about it."

Excitement bubbled in Annani's chest, and as she lifted her arm to look at her glow, it was much brighter than before. Perhaps there was a connection between mood and luminosity after all.

"I would love a visit from you whatever the reason." She had to admit that the vision added a level of excitement. "Are you bringing Allegra along?"

"She is asleep. I'll leave Okidu to watch her, and if she gets fussy, he can bring her over."

Annani laughed. "Am I a bad grandmother for wishing her to get fussy just so I can see her?"

"You are the best grandma," Syssi said in the background. "We will put her in the stroller and bring her over."

"She is sleeping!" Kian protested. "You know what happens when we wake her when she doesn't want to be up. She becomes a terror."

"I'll be careful," Syssi said. "Perhaps she should be there when I share my vision."

To Annani's great surprise, Kian agreed.

"Yeah, you might be right."

She could not stifle her curiosity. "Why would you need Allegra with you to tell me about your vision?"

"Syssi will explain when we get there," Kian said. "We will be on our way shortly."

Kian

"**Y**ou're incredible," Kian whispered after Syssi had somehow managed the impossible and transferred Allegra from the crib to the stroller without waking her up.

"I know." Smiling smugly, Syssi packed several bottles and pacifiers in the baby bag.

Allegra wasn't a great fan of pacifiers, mostly using them as projectiles to throw at people when she wanted their attention, but occasionally they helped her fall asleep.

The soft pink blanket she had gotten from Anita was also a necessary sleeping aid. It was surprising that Syssi's mother even knew how to knit, let alone found the time to knit a blanket for her granddaughter.

Which reminded Kian. "Did you talk to your parents about the cruise?"

"I did." Syssi transferred the command of the stroller to him. "Surprisingly, my mother was excited about joining and said that she would try to get a replacement. If she finds a doctor to take over for her, she'll let me know so we can make the flight arrangements." She smiled. "It's not like we are giving my parents ample notice to plan. You only decided to go ahead with the cruise yesterday, and we are sailing in two and a half weeks."

It wouldn't have mattered if her parents had months to prepare. Most of the time, Anita just didn't want to leave her clinic, and not being able to find a replacement was always a convenient excuse for why she couldn't come to this or that event.

And yet, Syssi never made a fuss about it or showed her disappointment, and it wasn't because she didn't want to see her parents. She was just selfless and accepted that her mother's work always came first.

His wife was the most understanding person on the planet, and he was the luckiest guy to have her.

"Let's take a little stroll up the street," Syssi said.

It was only a few paces to his mother's house, and it was a pleasant evening for a stroll, but he had promised that they would be there shortly.

"Just for a few minutes." He passed his mother's house and kept walking. "Are you excited?"

Syssi shrugged. "I'm excited about Alena and Orion finally getting married and all the other weddings that will take place on the cruise. As for my parents, I will hold off my excitement until their flight is booked, and even then, I won't allow myself to celebrate until I see them boarding the ship."

"That's a wise attitude." He wrapped his arm around her and pushed the stroller with his free hand. "But then everything you do is wise."

She arched a brow. "Really? Says the guy who was upset about me chasing visions."

"In your infinite wisdom, you convinced me of the futility of my worries."

Syssi's frown deepened. "Who are you, and what did you do with my husband?"

"I am a reformed man." Kian winked. "Most of the time."

"Oh, yeah? And what are you at other times?"

He chuckled. "Sometimes I'm still the alpha-hole you fell in love with and married."

She didn't smile. "I've never called you that. Where did you even hear that expression?" She narrowed her eyes at him. "Have you been reading my romance novels again?"

He pretended to look guilty. "You leave your books in my office, and it's easy to pick one up and start reading a paragraph or two." He smiled. "I need to know how to keep things fresh, and those books are a great source of inspiration." And also a few laughs, but he kept that part to himself.

Sometimes, when he had to work late into the night, Syssi sat on the couch in their home office and read while he worked. He loved having her there and seeing the relaxed expression on her face while she was immersed in the story. She read romance novels to relax at the end of her day, and those types of books guaranteed happily-ever-afters, where nothing truly terrible ever happened to spoil her mood.

There was enough of that in the real world.

Letting out an exasperated sigh, Syssi put her hand on his arm. "Please don't. Those are someone else's fantasies, not mine. If you want inspiration, my Perfect Match scenarios are a better source."

"You haven't written anything new in a while."

"I know." She sighed. "Between taking care of Allegra, working at the university, and dealing with one crisis after another, I don't have the bandwidth left to think creatively." She lifted a hand to her temple. "I used to be able to tune everything out and concentrate on the scenarios, but lately, I can't even bring myself to read through the Perfect Match financial reports or do anything productive at the end of the day."

"You need a vacation." He kissed the top of her head. "That's one of the reasons I accepted my mother's suggestion and made compromises regarding the cruise. The Kra-ell will stay behind with most of Kalugal's men."

Syssi tilted her head. "I hope Jade doesn't feel left out."

He snorted. "I would love to reenact her response for you, but I'm not a good enough actor to do it justice. The gist was that she called me nuts for thinking that her people would ever want to get on that ship again. The Kra-ell hate deep water, and some are still traumatized by the swimming lessons Phinas forced them to take in the ship's freezing pool."

"Yeah, it occurred to me that they might not be overly enthusiastic about going on the cruise. Your mother will be disappointed, though. Knowing her, she thought seeing her presiding over the weddings would be the best way to introduce her to the Kra-ell without making it formal."

Annani had met with Jade and several of the other main Kra-ell players, but there hadn't been a formal meeting with all the newcomers.

Kian trusted Jade, but he didn't yet trust all of the Kra-ell. That was one of the reasons he hadn't lowered the security alert level even after the crisis with the new gods had been resolved. A team of Guardians watched over his mother twenty-four seven.

"I just hope she won't demand a formal meeting with the Kra-ell before we sail."

Syssi arched a brow. "I thought you trusted Jade."

"I do, and she also vowed to protect the village to her last breath, but I'm not sure about all the others, and I need more time to get to know them."

"Did she give you the life vow? You said that you didn't want her to do that."

"It wasn't the life vow per se, and I tried to stop her, but it was no use. Jade is an incredibly stubborn female."

"And yet you like her."

He nodded. "I see a lot of myself in her."

"I'm okay with you admiring Jade, but don't overdo it." Syssi pouted. "You are making me jealous."

Kian stopped and turned to his mate. "You are the person I admire most in the world. You are everything to me." He took her hand and brought it to his lips. "You and our daughter own my heart."

Perhaps he could have come up with something more eloquent, but that was how he felt.

"I know." Syssi smiled. "I was just kidding about Jade. But you can't admire me more than your mother. That's just not right. She's the Clan Mother, the only legitimate heir of the Eternal King, and therefore, the second most important person in the galaxy, or perhaps even the most important one if the resistance takes the Eternal King down."

Syssi

K ian's steps faltered for a moment, but then he let out a sigh and continued walking. "For some reason, hearing you say that has driven it home, and it scares the shit out of me. I was always apprehensive about my mother's safety, paranoid even, but that is mostly because of how reckless she used to be. She and Alena would fly to a random destination with just their Odus for protection, and she wouldn't even tell me. I never knew where she was or what she was doing. Thankfully, she hasn't been doing that lately, but then new worries surfaced. The sanctuary is the safest place for her, but I can't force her to stay there and not go anywhere."

"Right." Syssi nodded. "I don't think it's a good thing. It worries me that your mother seems to have lost some of her mojo. Not having a companion to travel with is the main reason she doesn't go on excursions anymore, but she might also be a little depressed."

That wasn't healthy for the goddess on several levels. She needed adventure and excitement to keep her positive attitude and sharp mind, but as important as that was, it wasn't as critical as the knock her sex life must have taken.

No son wanted to think about his mother's needs as a female, but Annani needed the excursions to pick up bed partners. She couldn't do that while cooped up in the village or the sanctuary.

After losing Alena as her companion, Syssi had hoped Annani would choose a new one from the immortal females in the sanctuary or even in the village or Scotland, but she hadn't, and she wasn't the type who enjoyed hunting for companions alone.

If Annani had lost her libido, it meant that she was depressed, and that was not good.

"Did you notice anything specific?" Kian turned around, heading back toward his mother's house.

"It's nothing major, and there isn't one thing I can point to. It's just that I don't think she is as happy and exuberant as she used to be. It's not like her to be satisfied with her roles as the head of the clan and its matriarch. She needs to get away for at least a little bit, and she hasn't done that in a while."

"I've noticed." Kian let out a breath. "I was happy that I could finally sleep at night without worrying about her shenanigans, but you are right that it's not good for her. Perhaps I need to talk to her."

He looked like he'd just bitten into a lemon.

"I think that your sisters are better suited for that kind of conversation. We should talk with Alena."

The best and safest solution for Annani would be to bring human lovers to her and then thrall them before returning them to where they'd been picked up from, but Annani wouldn't agree to that. Syssi had never spoken to her mother-in-law about matters of the heart, or rather of lust, but given the goddess's personality, she enjoyed choosing her bed companions herself, and she loved the seduction part.

Not that she ever had to work hard on that.

Annani was the most beautiful woman in the world, even when she used shrouding to make herself look more ordinary.

When they were a few feet away from the goddess's front porch, Kian stopped, scanned the area again, and nodded at the Guardians stationed nearby to protect her.

He'd thought Syssi hadn't noticed him doing that when they had passed the house before, but he should have known that there wasn't much he could hide from her. "Your mother doesn't need the extra security. These Guardians can't stop anyone or anything that she's incapable of stopping herself."

"I know." Kian lifted the stroller and carried it up the three steps leading to Annani's front porch. "It's for my peace of mind. Besides, she's as defenseless as any of us when she's asleep, and she can't be constantly alert and scanning for danger when awake. The Guardians are there twenty-four seven, but they rotate, and they are on high alert." He knocked on the door.

It was opened immediately by one of Annani's Odus, who bowed deeply. "Good evening, Master Kian, Mistress Syssi, and Mistress Allegra. Please, come in."

Syssi wanted to point out that the Odus never slept and that they were the best defense for the goddess, but she knew it wouldn't change anything. Kian had admitted that the Guardians were there mainly for his peace of mind, and she could understand that.

He needed to have an active role in his mother's defense.

Annani smiled from the couch. "Please, join me. I have tea and an assortment of desserts ready."

The spread was on the coffee table, and as Syssi eyed the elegant teapot, she thought about her vision of the luminous goddess and the modern art she'd had in her receiving room.

Details of that vision were starting to fade, but she remembered the golden vase vividly. Or did she?

She was unsure whether it had been a vase or a statue, but given the spotlight above it, the piece was artwork and not something that had utility beyond the beauty of its form.

"Syssi, my dear." The goddess's voice cut through her musings. "Are you having another vision?"

"No, Clan Mother." She dipped her head. "I was thinking about the vision I had before the last one. It was also about a luminous goddess, and although I don't think it was the same one as in my latest vision, I think that the two are connected somehow."

The goddess inclined her head imperiously. "You will tell me all about it after we have tea." She patted the couch cushion next to her. "Come sit with me."

"Yes, Clan Mother."

"Mother or Annani will suffice, dear. I have told you so many times."

Syssi smiled sheepishly. "I know, and I apologize for having difficulty addressing you informally, but can you blame me? No human or immortal can be in your presence and treat you casually."

"Is it the glow?" Annani lifted her arm and looked at her luminous skin. "I can do away with it." The glow disappeared before the last word had left her mouth.

"It's not just the glow. Your power is palpable whether your skin is luminous or not, and you are the second most important person in the galaxy." Syssi smiled. "Possibly, the most important."

Annani

ᏀᏇᎧ

Unmoved by Syssi's declaration, Annani put her hand on her daughter-in-law's thigh. "Semantics, dear. I am just as important today as I was yesterday or a month ago." She smiled. "I admit to having a big ego, but not so big as to think of myself as the most important person in the galaxy."

"But you are," Syssi insisted. "You're the Eternal King's only legitimate heir."

"So what? That only puts a target on my back. Besides, even if my grandfather did not want me dead, I would not want to be in the position of one day having to step into his shoes. They are too big for my tiny feet."

Annani had always been embarrassed by her child-like feet, but since the idiom fit so aptly, she lifted her leg and let the skirt of her floor-length gown slide up and reveal her foot.

Kian chuckled. "Your feet might be small, but they leave big impressions."

Syssi laughed. "That was a good answer, Kian."

He looked very satisfied with himself. "The thing is, we don't know the size of the Eternal King's shoes. Perhaps he has tiny feet as well. But the size of the impressions they leave, now those are awe-inspiring. I have to keep reminding myself that he's a despicable person who had no qualms about killing his own children, and to stop admiring him."

"Can we change the subject, please?" Annani lifted the teapot and poured tea into the three cups Ogidu had prepared. "I would rather hear about Syssi's visions than talk about my grandfather and his shoes." She handed a teacup to her daughter-in-law.

Syssi glanced at Kian. "Should I start with the first one?"

He nodded. "It's relevant to the second one."

After taking a sip of the tea, Syssi put the cup down. "In the first vision, I saw a goddess of such brilliant glow that I couldn't discern her features. Still, I knew she was exquisitely beautiful in the way dreams tell us things that we don't actually see. She was tall and had long white hair that shimmered like diamonds. Her gown was silver with some delicate pattern on it. Another female entered the room, who was also a stunning goddess, but since she bowed, I figured she was a servant or an underling. She told the other goddess something that I couldn't understand, but the impression I got was that she was delivering exciting news. They were both smiling. I thought she might have been your mother, but Kian told me she was petite, so it couldn't have been her."

And while her mother had also been luminous like the other gods in their community, her glow had not been blinding.

Was it possible that instead of receiving a vision, Syssi had been remote viewing someone on Anumati?

That could be even more valuable than the visions.

"Did you see any details of the room?" Annani asked.

Syssi nodded. "It wasn't large." She waved a hand around the living room. "About this size, and it was decorated in a soft, feminine style. At first glance, I thought I was seeing the past, but then I noticed a gold vase or piece of artwork with an abstract, modern shape. Later, when I thought back on the vision, I also realized that there had been no windows in the room and no torches, but it was well-illuminated and not just because of the glowing goddess. There was overhead lighting, with a spotlight directly over the modern art piece."

"You must have viewed Anumati," Annani said. "If the vision was in real-time, you were remote viewing rather than seeing into the future or the past."

"That has occurred to me." Syssi leaned down and picked up her teacup. "I've never remote viewed before, so I don't know how it differs from a vision."

Annani smiled. "I have never had a vision, so I cannot tell the difference either. I can only describe my experience while remote viewing. It feels like spying—a camera-view lens that allows me to peek. My remote viewing is not strong and usually only allows me to see people I care about. Other remote viewers can see locations and spy on their enemies, but that is not my talent."

Syssi frowned. "Do you get impressions? Like you know what is happening even if it is not part of what you are seeing?"

Annani shook her head. "It is no different than seeing someone through a video call."

"That's the difference." Syssi put her empty cup down. "You see things as they are. I see things as my mind makes them seem. It's kind of like the difference between watching a movie and reading a book. My mind fills in the blanks."

Syssi

It felt awkward to have a talent that seemed superior to Annani's, and Syssi had to remind herself that the goddess had many talents that were more powerful and useful than her vague visions.

Annani could thrall, shroud, and compel immortals, which only gods could do in varying degrees of power. Compulsion was a rare ability, though, even for gods, and Annani's dislike for it meant that she hadn't tested her full powers yet and had probably utilized only a fraction of what she could do.

Could she be as powerful as her grandfather?

Syssi was reluctant to even mention the possibility. Annani seemed determined not to step into the Eternal King's shoes even if they were offered to her on a golden platter.

Hey, maybe that was the symbolism of the golden vase she'd seen in her vision.

Right.

Visions were so damn tricky.

Annani lifted a plate of cookies and offered them to her. "Is there anything else you want to add about that vision?"

Squinting, Syssi tried to remember if she'd forgotten to mention anything of interest. "I can't think of anything, but maybe something will come to me later." She took a cookie and bit a small piece of it.

"It's delicious. Who made it?"

Annani smiled. "Ojidu, but the recipe is courtesy of Lusha." She turned to look at Kian. "She is such a lovely young woman. I wish we could keep her in the village. From what I hear, a certain young pureblood is interested in her."

"It was Lusha's choice to return to Safe Haven." Kian snatched a cookie off the plate. "There is no future for her and Pavel. Not unless we figure out how to activate her recessive Kra-ell genes. He has another thousand years of life ahead of him, while she has less than a century."

Annani sighed. "That is regrettably true." She turned to Syssi. "What was your second vision about?"

Syssi put the teacup down. "What impressed me the most about this vision was its clarity. It was much more cohesive than my other visions, and I think Allegra had something to do with it. I was in her room when I induced the vision. She was asleep, but perhaps her presence was enough to enhance my ability."

Annani smiled proudly. "My granddaughter is special. I have no doubt that she will do great things for the clan one day."

Kian groaned. "I just wish she could have a normal life. I don't want to place the burden of leading the clan on her shoulders."

Annani arched a brow. "Are you angry with me for putting this burden on your shoulders?"

He shook his head. "I accepted it willingly. This is what I was born to do."

"Precisely." Annani nodded. "When Allegra comes of age, she will decide whether she wants to lead. It might be what she was born to do as well."

"I think I know what she will decide, and I'm not happy about it."

Syssi leaned over and put a hand on his knee. "There is plenty of time to worry about that. She might decide to be a musician for all we know."

That got a smile out of Kian. "I hope she does that."

"That would be lovely." Annani turned to Syssi. "Now, tell me about your vision."

Syssi nodded. "The second vision took place in a large reception hall, and by large, I mean cavernous. I estimate it was an area of about three thousand square feet, give or take a couple of hundred, and the ceiling was at least forty feet high. It was supported by thick pillars with fancy capitals but not in any style I'm familiar with. Again, there were no windows, but the illumination came from torches this time. Three torches were attached to each column, so there was plenty of light. A goddess sat on a throne-like chair on top of a low dais. She was as bright as the one from the previous vision, but she wasn't the same female. Her bearing was different, although also regal. She wore a toga-style pure white dress, gathered at the shoulder and secured with a golden clasp."

"Were there any other people with her?" Annani asked.

"A scribe sat next to one of the columns, recording what the petitioners asked for and the goddess's replies. I couldn't understand the language, but I got the impression that they were asking for a blessing. The goddess gave the first couple some good news and put her hands on their heads. I forgot to mention that they had been on their knees in deep obeisance. They seemed very happy with what she told them, but the next petitioner wasn't. Another thing that I forgot to mention was that the petitioners were all gods. I couldn't see the scribe, but I assume she was also a goddess."

Annani tilted her head. "Perhaps this vision was about the past. What did the scribe use for writing?"

"Something that looked like a stylus or a quill, but I didn't see ink. She sat on a pillow on the floor and had a little wooden table to write on. It was the size of a lap desk. She wrote in a book, though, not a scroll. It was bound in some material I didn't recognize and was big."

"What about the gods' glow? Did the petitioners emit any?" Annani asked.

"No, and thank you for reminding me. I forgot that part. All three were exceptionally beautiful, which was how I knew they were gods, but the couple didn't have a glow at all, and the god that came after them had a little. If the vision was from Anumati, then the couple were commoners, and the guy was some minor noble."

"That is possible," Annani said. "Although I still do not understand why the commoners on Anumati have no glow. Are they all depressed?"

"That is not likely," Kian said. "Perhaps it has something to do with nutrition. The nobility might have access to some elixir that the commoners do not."

Syssi chuckled. "Perhaps the stories about the special foods that the gods consumed and humans were prohibited from touching were not myths any more than the existence of the gods."

"I am not aware of any such elixir," Annani said. "But then, I was not privy to most of my father's secrets."

Leaning back, Kian crossed his arms over his chest. "Syssi's visions might be vague, but they usually try to tell us something. We were hoping that you would help us make sense of this one. Anything else you can think of that will make its meaning clearer?"

Annani pursed her lips. "The lack of technology could signal that it was a place of worship, which means that the goddess you saw was a priestess. That would also correspond to her giving the couple a blessing."

"Maybe the shrine was on one of Anumati's colonies," Kian said. "And that was why there was no artificial lighting."

Syssi shook her head. "I doubt the gods living in those colonies would have agreed to forgo such conveniences. They are not exiles like the rebel gods sent to Earth."

Annani

As Kian and Syssi looked at her, Annani shrugged. "My guess is as good as yours as to the location of your vision and what it tried to show you. Do not forget that I was born on Earth, and as I said before, my father did not share information about Anumati with me." Annani leveled her gaze on Syssi. "You said that you induced the second vision. Did you induce the first one as well?"

"With the first one, I meditated and asked to be shown things that might help us with the newcomer gods. I don't know what the vision was trying to tell me, though."

"And the second time?" Annani prompted.

"I wanted an explanation for the first one." She scrunched her nose. "I just remembered something that I forgot to mention about the first vision. The goddess wore a gold necklace, a medallion with a design I couldn't see, probably because of her intense glow. I wonder if the two goddesses are really as luminous as I saw them or was it the nature of the visions to obscure their features."

"There is obviously a connection between the two goddesses." Annani refilled her teacup and took a sip. "I also think their luminosity in real life is not as bright as in your visions. Since you are not remote viewing, and what you see is not like a movie but an interpretation of the information the vision is feeding your mind, you might have created the glow to symbolize something. Maybe the two goddesses are sisters, or both are royalty, or maybe they are both rebel sympathizers. The only ones who can provide us with any clarity are the three gods currently residing in Kian's old penthouse." She turned to her son. "I want to talk to them."

He shook his head. "That's a very bad idea. What if you look like your grandfather, and they immediately recognize you as his heir?"

She smiled. "Why would that be a bad thing, my son? Only mere moments ago, you and Syssi wanted me to pick up the banner and challenge my grandfather's rule. To do so, I must first be recognized as the legitimate heir."

Kian opened his mouth, closed it, and opened it again. "I didn't say that. I don't want him to know that you exist."

"Of course not. You are always worried about my safety. I appreciate that, and most of the time I humor you, but not this time. I need to speak with these gods."

"Why? You can make a list of questions, and I'll ask them for you. You can even speak with them on the phone and ask them yourself."

She smiled. "I want to see their response to me and my glow. That cannot be done via a phone call or a messenger. It is also why I want to meet all three, not just their leader. Negal and Dagor might be less guarded than Aru."

Kian shook his head. "The moment your grandfather learns of your existence, he might choose to eradicate the entire planet just to get rid of you. Even if Aru and his teammates are trustworthy, they will get picked up in a hundred and fifteen years, and there is very little chance that they will be able to keep you a secret."

Leaning back, Annani regarded her son with an indulgent smile. "You are overthinking everything, Kian. If I had done that when I started out on my mission, there would be no clan, and humans would have been centuries or even thousands of years away from developing the technologies they have today. Sometimes, you need to follow your gut and take a risk. Aru, his teammates, and an entire patrol ship housing thousands of warriors, scientists, and other crew members are part of the resistance, and yet they managed to fly under the radar of the Eternal King."

"We only have Aru's word for that. What if he lied?"

"Andrew can talk to him," Syssi offered. "I don't know whether his gift works on gods, but it's worth a try. You can also get Edna to probe him."

Annani nodded. "Please do both and schedule a meeting. I am sure that Onegus needs time to prepare, and I want to meet them before we sail in two and a half weeks."

Kian was so pale that Annani feared he would faint, but she had to draw a line in the sand somewhere. It was not that she thought his fear for her was exaggerated or uncalled for, but she had not gotten to where she was by living in a panic room.

Well, that was not entirely true.

The sanctuary was the most secure panic room on the planet, but Annani refused to spend her entire life there.

She would perish from boredom.

Unlike Kian, Syssi was grinning. "After the meeting, we can invite Aru, Gabi and his friends on the cruise. It would be a wonderful opportunity for them to meet everyone. I'm so excited."

Kian groaned. "I'm starting to regret this whole thing. The ship is fully armed now and can defend itself from Navuh but not from the might of the gods."

Leaning forward, Annani tried to reach for his hand, but he was sitting too far away and had to meet her halfway. "The Eternal King is many light years away, and by the time any of his forces could get here, our beautiful ship will probably be rusting in the junkyard or wherever they retire old ships to. In the meantime, I refuse to live in fear. I will meet with these three gods and invite them to join us on the cruise myself."

Kian

"Thank you for meeting me here." Kian shook Edna's hand and then Andrew's.

"I'm excited," the judge said. "After hearing so much about these gods, I can't wait to meet them."

Kian had informed the council about the latest developments, and most of them had expressed a wish to meet up with the gods, but he hadn't been ready to do that yet.

His mother had twisted his arm.

"I'm curious about them too." Andrew smiled good-naturedly. "It seems like you and I are here every other week, testing this or that person. It's never boring in our world, so it's all good. I don't mind missing lunch with Tim to come help you out."

The forensic artist was incredibly talented, maybe even paranormally gifted, but his personality left much to be desired.

"How is our dear Tim?" Kian led them toward the elevator. "Weren't we supposed to test whether he's a Dormant?"

His brother-in-law smiled sheepishly. "You didn't seem overly excited about Tim potentially joining the clan, and I couldn't blame you, so I pretended to have forgotten about it. Do you still want to test him?"

Kian motioned for Edna to go ahead before following her into the elevator. "If you can arrange for it to be done away from the village, then sure. I don't want a wasted potential Dormant on my conscience."

"We don't know that Tim is a Dormant, and his case is weak. The only thing that makes him a suspect is his supernatural talent to render almost lifelike portraits of people just from how others describe them. No one, human or immortal, ever felt an affinity with Tim, and according to Amanda, that's a stronger indicator than a paranormal talent." Andrew chuckled. "The guy prides himself on being a pain in the ass." Wincing, he glanced at Edna. "Forgive my language, judge."

She chuckled. "I'm mated to Rufsur. I hear much worse."

Kalugal's second-in-command was a little rough around the edges, but he was a good guy, and Kian liked him. If not for him and Edna, the accord between the clan and Kalugal and his people would have never been signed.

"Did you tell Aru that we were coming?" Andrew asked as they got out of the elevator at the penthouse level.

"I told him to expect us, but I didn't tell him what it's about." He let out a breath. "I'm walking a thin line with these gods. On the one hand, I want to establish friendly relationships with them because they are our only link to Anumati and the Eternal King's plans, but on the other hand, I can't bring myself to trust them. They are too powerful, and the story they told us is too convenient, and now my mother insists on meeting them, and I'm desperate for any excuse to tell her that it's not possible."

Andrew patted his shoulder. "I get it. I can't compare my parents to your mother, but I get frustrated with them too. I only want what's best for them, but our opinions differ as to what that entails."

Edna chuckled, which was uncharacteristic of her, but then she had changed a lot since mating Rufsur, who was her exact opposite. "From what I gather, dealing with parents is more difficult than dealing with children. I don't have children yet, but I do have a mother, and she is not easy."

Kian didn't know Edna's mother well, but if the judge said that about her, he had no doubt it was true. Edna was not prone to exaggeration.

"No earpieces?" Andrew asked when they stopped in front of the penthouse door.

Kian grimaced. "My mother had a few things to say about my paranoia, and I decided to take a page out of her book and just go for it. No earpieces and no Okidu to guard me. Anandur and Brundar are already there, though, and they have their earpieces in." There was a limit to how reckless he would allow himself to be, but perhaps it was too much for the judge. He looked at Edna. "Are you okay with that?"

She shrugged. "Even with your new resolution regarding the level of risk aversion you are comfortable with, I know you wouldn't have forgone these safety features if you believed they were needed."

"You know me well, judge."

"Indeed, I do."

This time Kian remembered to knock instead of just walking in.

Anandur opened the door with a big grin on his face. "Hello, boss. We have everything ready."

"Meaning?" Kian asked.

"Come in and see." He threw the door open.

Dagor

As the redhead opened the door for his boss, Dagor emptied the rest of the Snake Venom down his throat and put the bottle down.

The beer was growing on him, and it seemed to please Kian's bodyguards that they had managed to make a convert out of him.

It was funny how alcohol was truly a universal equalizer. Gods, immortals, and humans loved to socialize while drinking. Barriers went down, people felt more at ease with each other, and tongues loosened up.

When Aru pushed to his feet, Dagor and Negal followed, and even Gabi rose to greet the clan leader.

He hadn't arrived alone. One of his companions was a female who looked like an attorney, given her attire and the severe expression on her face, and the other was a male whose posture and confidence spoke of a past in the military.

Was he another guard?

"This is the clan judge, Edna," Kian introduced the female. "And this is my brother-in-law, Andrew."

So Dagor had been right about the female, and he was probably right about the male, but confirmation of that would have to wait.

Aru offered his hand to the judge first. "I'm Aru. Are there any legalities involved with our temporary residence in the penthouse?"

She offered him a barely-there smile. "No, and I'm not here in my capacity as an attorney and a judge."

"Edna is also a council member," Kian said.

The judge turned her eerily penetrating gaze to Dagor and offered him her hand. "Hello."

She had the eyes of an oracle. Was Kian lying about who she was?

Just in case she was one, Dagor bowed his head respectfully. "I am Dagor. It's an honor to meet you, councilwoman."

The smile she gave him was warmer than the one she'd given Aru. "It's nice to make your acquaintance, Dagor."

The greetings were repeated with Gabriella and Negal, and then everyone sat down on whatever piece of furniture was available.

Naturally, the males had waited for the ladies to be seated first.

Kian rubbed the back of his neck. "This is awkward." He let out a breath. "There is no polite way to do this, so I'm just going to say it as it is. Andrew is a truth-reader, and Edna can read your soul. I brought them both to reassure myself that you can be trusted. Please don't take it as an insult. I'm known for being super cautious, and I've used Andrew and Edna's services to test all newcomers."

"What do you mean by reading our souls?" Aru asked the question that was on Dagor's mind.

"She can't read thoughts, so don't worry about that, but she can read intentions and emotions. I need to make absolutely sure that you mean no harm to any of my people."

Dagor stifled a derisive snort. Kian was no doubt concerned about the gods within his clan, the gods that Aru thought he should hide from his companions.

"I understand," Aru said. "But I have my own secrets that I need to keep, and I'm not a hundred percent sure that I can trust you, so we are at an impasse because I don't want Edna inside my soul." He cast her an apologetic look. "No offense, judge."

She dipped her head. "None taken."

"You can test me," Negal volunteered. "I have nothing to hide."

"Neither do I," Dagor said with a pointed look at Aru.

If she discovered that he resented Aru for hiding things from him and Negal, it would be a good thing. It would save him the trouble of confronting their team leader about it.

Kian didn't look happy. "What about Andrew? Do you mind if I ask you a few questions and have Andrew verify the veracity of your answers?"

"I don't mind that, but if you ask me questions I don't wish to answer, I won't."

"Understood." Kian turned to Edna. "Can you take Negal and Dagor to my old home office and test them there while I ask Aru a few questions?"

She hesitated. "I'd rather take one at a time. I need to concentrate, and it's difficult to do with another person in the room. Besides, I thought you wanted Andrew to verify their answers as well."

Dagor would have preferred to stay in the living room while Kian interrogated Aru so he could hear the answers, but he didn't like that the judge seemed afraid to be alone with him and Negal.

Dagor put his hand over his chest. "You have nothing to fear from me or Negal. We mean you no harm." He turned to Kian. "We mean no harm to any of your people, no matter whether they are immortals, Kra-ell, or others."

"Truth," Kian's brother-in-law said.

Kian regarded Andrew for a long moment before returning his gaze to Dagor. "Are you happy here, Dagor?"

"Sure. Why wouldn't I be? The bed is very comfortable."

Andrew chuckled. "That was a lie."

Kian frowned. "The bed is not comfortable?"

Andrew chuckled. "I don't think he meant the bed."

Aru

Aru had no intention of letting Edna into his mind, and he hoped she couldn't do that without touching him.

In fact, he regretted shaking her hand.

His secrets were too important to fall into even the friendliest of hands.

"What did you mean?" Kian asked his brother-in-law.

Andrew shrugged and tilted his head toward Dagor. "Ask him."

Dagor cast a quick look at Aru before lowering his eyes. "The penthouse is very comfortable, but being around a honeymooning couple is not easy."

Aru was aware of that, but there wasn't much he could do about it. He and Gabi tried not to act overly amorous in front of Negal and Dagor, but every look they exchanged was laden with the love and desire they had for each other.

"Truth," the brother-in-law said.

The wife was a seer, and her brother was a truth-reader. That was a lot of paranormal talent in one family. Were they related to the gods living in Kian's community?

Syssi and her brother possessed impressive abilities. They were both good-looking but did not possess the near perfection that Kian exhibited, meaning they were not direct descendants of gods. Their godly ancestor must have been formidable, though.

"Okay." Kian let out a breath. "I'm glad that your talent also works on gods." He turned to Aru. "What about you? Can you repeat Dagor's words?"

Aru had no problem doing that, but he was getting tired of Kian second-guessing him. "The bed in the primary bedroom is very comfortable, thank you."

"Truth," Andrew said. "Even though the answer was sarcastic."

"Come on, Aru." Gabi nudged her mate's arm. "Tell them that they have nothing to fear from you."

"I already did, and it's annoying that I was not believed."

"They only want assurances." She took his hand and gave it a squeeze. "It's not personal, Aru. They are facing an existential risk, and they have to take security seriously." She shook her head. "We, not they. I am now part of their community, and my safety is tied to theirs. Remember what they did to me so I couldn't tell anyone about immortals? They are super cautious not because they are paranoid but because it's necessary."

"Thank you," Kian said. "I'm glad to have at least one person understand why I have to be so careful."

"I mean you no harm," Aru said. "Not to you, not to the Kra-ell, and not to anyone else in your community. I'm racking my brains trying to figure out how to keep you all hidden from the Eternal King for as long as possible."

"Truth," Andrew said.

"Is everyone on the patrol ship really part of the resistance?" Anandur asked.

"They are." Aru looked directly at Andrew. "But since it's always possible that someone could be a spy for the Eternal King, we don't talk freely among ourselves. Everything is compartmentalized and on a need-to-know basis."

Dagor snorted. "Yeah. But somehow, you know more than anyone else, including the commander. I wonder why that is?"

Aru gritted his teeth not to reprimand Dagor for saying stuff like that in front of others. He would have to talk to him later.

"It just seems like that to you because I know more than you do. I'm sure other team leaders know as much, if not more, than what I was entrusted with."

"Truth," Andrew said, but he did so with less conviction than the other times.

Was he trying to be helpful? And if so, why?

Dagor let out a breath. "I should not have said that. Apologies, sir."

The guy never called him 'sir' unless they were in the presence of higher-ranked commanders.

"Accepted." Aru nodded.

"Do you really know more than others?" Kian asked.

"I can't answer what I don't know. I'm not privy to what everyone on the patrol ship is entrusted with."

Andrew shrugged. "That was an Igor-style answer. Evasive. Neither truth nor lie."

Kian cast Aru a calculating look, and there was understanding in his eyes. Perhaps he had finally realized that there were things Aru couldn't reveal in front of his teammates.

He pushed to his feet. "Join me in my old office for a few minutes." He glanced at Gabi, who looked worried. "I won't keep him long."

"It's okay. I'll stay to chat with Edna." She gave him a dazzling smile. "She can examine my soul. I have nothing to hide."

Edna cleared her throat. "Perhaps some other time. Today, I need to reserve my energy for the gods. I don't expect it will be easy to probe them."

"That's a shame." Gabi pouted.

The judge turned to Negal. "We can do this in your room if you're comfortable inviting me in."

"I will be delighted to host you in my room, judge." Negal pushed to his feet and offered Edna his hand. "I have not entertained any ladies there yet. You will be the first."

She gave him a polite smile. "Just so there is no misunderstanding, I'm happily mated."

Negal's eyes widened. "My apologies, judge. I did not mean it like that. I know that you are mated. I can smell him on you."

"Gross," Gabi muttered. "That's the one thing I don't like about gods and immortals. Talk about lack of privacy."

Kian

As Kian led Aru and Andrew to his old office, unease churned in his gut.

There was a reason Aru had refused to be probed by Edna, and it might have nothing to do with ill intent toward the clan, but it left a void in the security blanket Kian was trying to form around his stubborn mother.

It wasn't even that he disagreed with her. She was right about refusing to live in fear, but she was a hypocrite. It was much easier to gamble with her own life than with the lives of her loved ones, which was why she insisted that Kian never leave the village without taking two bodyguards with him.

In his bachelor days, Kian had been much the same as her, and hadn't hesitated before walking into danger. Since he'd mated Syssi and they had Allegra, he was mindful of the pain and suffering his death would inflict on his mate and daughter.

There was also the memory of being helpless under Igor's control. That experience had shaved off a significant portion of Kian's bravado.

"Please, take a seat." He motioned for Aru and Andrew to sit on the couch while he pulled out one of the chairs and turned it around to face them.

Letting out a sigh, he pinned Aru with a hard stare. "You are making it difficult for me."

"It can't be helped. All I can say is that the information I'm protecting has nothing to do with nefarious intentions toward you or any of your people, including the gods living among you."

"Truth," Andrew said.

"I assume you haven't told your teammates about the gods yet."

Aru nodded. "I have not."

"Why not?"

"Because you asked me not to. What is this all about, Kian? Why the sudden paranoia attack? Have you learned something new that bothers you?"

"It's nothing new." Kian groaned. "It's the same as always. My mother is making my life difficult."

Aru arched a brow. "Your mother?"

"She wants to meet you and your friends, which means the cat will be out of the bag very soon."

Light shone in Aru's eyes as he realized what Kian was implying.

"Your mother is a goddess. I should have known. You look more like a god than an immortal because you are a demigod."

Kian grimaced. "I don't think of myself that way. It sounds so bombastic. My mother wanted to meet you and your teammates as soon as possible, but I convinced her to wait a little longer."

The light in Aru's eyes dimmed a little. "In that case, I need to tell Negal and Dagor about the gods living among you."

Kian lifted his hand. "I want to test them before you do that. I need Edna and Andrew to question them and give me the green light or tell me that they are not to be trusted. If that's the case, I'll tell my mother she can meet you but not the others."

"I can vouch for Negal and Dagor's trustworthiness."

Kian chuckled. "Then why are you keeping secrets from them?"

"I told you. We keep each other safe by compartmentalizing. Every member of the resistance only knows what she or he has to. That way, if any of us are discovered, we don't take down the entire organization with us."

It sounded logical, and Kian agreed that it was good practice given who they were dealing with, but it could also mean that Aru himself was not trustworthy.

"Even if Edna and Andrew clear them, don't tell them yet. Wait until I give you the green light."

"When is the meeting going to take place?"

"Two and a half weeks."

Aru frowned. "Is there a reason for this timeline? Does it have anything to do with Gabi's recovery and our stay in this penthouse?"

"No, but it's a happy coincidence. You, Gabi, and your teammates are going on a vacation with me and my family."

He didn't want to tell Aru about the cruise yet or that most of the clan would be there. As the god himself had said, compartmentalizing information was a prudent safety precaution.

Aru seemed taken aback, but he was a skilled politician who plastered an amiable smile on his too-handsome face. "Thank you for inviting us. I'm sure it will be a wonderful opportunity to get to know each other and perhaps develop more mutual trust, but may I inquire about the destination and duration of the trip?"

"Mexico," Kian said. "Ten days round trip."

"I've never been to Mexico. I'm looking forward to it. Will formal attire be required for any part of the trip?"

That was an incredibly good guess. Had Anandur blurted something about the cruise weddings even though Kian had warned him not to?

The rest of the clan hadn't been given the exact sail date yet, and Amanda was still working on the itinerary, but it had to be done soon. People had work obligations they needed to rearrange. Come to think of it, new clothing for the trip and evening wear for the celebrations would need to be purchased. After all, they would be attending several weddings, and the ladies would no doubt want a different gown for each night.

It would be difficult to keep the cruise a secret from Gabi.

Kian nodded and leaned back in his chair. "I wanted to keep the details a secret for a little longer, but your question about formal attire made me realize that it wasn't the best idea. We are going on a cruise, and each night is reserved for a different couple's wedding. So yeah, you will need a tux or two, and Gabi might want to get several evening dresses."

The light in Aru's eyes intensified. "Gabi will be thrilled. She'll probably want to get married on the ship, too. Are there any nights still available?"

"Not as far as I know, but you can have a lunchtime or morning wedding."

The light dimmed. "I don't think Gabi will want that. I'd rather wait and give her the wedding of her dreams."

Aru seemed entirely enchanted with the idea of a wedding cruise, and unless he was a superb actor, he wasn't thinking about it as an opportunity to do harm.

Since Andrew was already there, Kian might as well ask a question or two to make sure.

Frankie

F rankie waved at the waiter. "Another round of margaritas, please."

Mia regarded her with concerned eyes. "It's your third one. You're gonna puke."

"I'm going for passed out." Frankie glanced at Tom, who was pretending not to have heard the puke remark.

It was embarrassing to get plastered with her besties around, but it was doubly embarrassing with a hot guy at the table, even if he belonged to Mia.

Tom had offered to leave and come back later to collect his girl, but Frankie had invited him to stay in the hopes that the Perfect Match job would come up, but so far, he pretended that he hadn't connected the dots.

Men. Even the smart ones were stupid.

Frankie had invited her besties to a night of drinking to lament the job she'd lost. Couldn't he have figured out that she desperately needed a new one?

She'd filled out a bunch of applications, but so far, she hadn't gotten an answer from any of them. There was no reason to panic yet, and she had only been unemployed for a total of four days so far, but given that no one had bothered to even acknowledge her application, her prospects weren't looking good.

There wasn't much she could do with her worthless college degree in English other than teach or go to grad school and become a lawyer. Her minor in performing arts was good for nothing, as well. She'd taken it for fun and had enjoyed every moment. Still, she wasn't a great actress or singer despite what her family kept saying.

After she'd told her parents about getting fired, her mom suggested grad school, but Frankie didn't want to accumulate even more student debt, or at least that was what she had told her parents. She didn't want to go back to school and put her life on hold again.

As the waiter arrived with their drinks, Margo removed the paper umbrella and added it to the other two she'd collected. "It's not the end of the world, Frankie, and getting fired from that dead-end job is no reason to drink until you pass out."

"Words of wisdom, as always, but it's not just about the job, and you know it."

Margo grimaced. "I'm not having any more luck than you in that department. There are no good men to be found these days." She cast Tom an apologetic glance. "Except for you, of course."

"What about the gentlemen Mia's grandparents introduced you to?"

"What about them?" Margo asked. "None of them asked either of us on a date." She looked at Mia. "Your grandma is awesome, but she's a bit of an airhead. The guys she found for us were all gorgeous but talk about awkward. Frankie and I felt like we'd stepped back in time."

Mia grimaced. "Yeah, that wasn't the best idea. I'm sure they wouldn't have been as awkward if my grandparents weren't there."

Possibly. Or maybe the guys hadn't found her and Margo attractive, interesting, or smart enough, or whatever they had been looking for in a girl.

Talk about a blow to the ego.

"So, Tom." Margo leaned back with her margarita in hand. "What about those Perfect Match jobs you and Mia were talking about? It would be great if at least one was available for our Frankie."

Thank you, Margo. Frankie could have kissed her on both cheeks.

"There have been some delays." Tom gave Frankie an apologetic look. "The tech department was busy with another project that took precedence, but now the parts are in, and they are working on it. The machines should be ready in a couple of weeks, so if you can hold off until then, I can see what I can do about a job for you."

Mia cleared her throat. "You are forgetting about the cruise. No one will be there to train Frankie."

"Right." He smoothed a hand over his enviably silky dark hair. "I forgot about that."

Margo looked at him with incredulous eyes. "Are you taking everyone in the company on a cruise?"

"Not everyone," Tom said evasively.

His answer could have meant he was taking only a few or almost everyone.

Mia uttered a little gasp, which usually meant that she'd thought of something that could be amazing. "Maybe Margo and Frankie can join us on the cruise? We could bring the machines onboard for everyone's entertainment."

"That's not feasible." Tom gave her a stern look.

"Why not? It's only ten days, and the memories created in a short time are easily... you know, forgettable."

What the hell was Mia talking about?

Frankie lifted two fingers up to check how drunk she was, but they still looked like two and not three or four, so she wasn't drunk enough to misunderstand Mia's strange comment.

"When is the cruise leaving?" Margo asked.

"Two and a half weeks. We are going to cruise down to Mexico and back to Long Beach. It's not so much about the excursions as it is about the ship and spending time with family and friends. Several couples are getting married on the cruise, so it will be fun."

"I don't know if we have room," Tom said. "I need to ask."

Mia waved a dismissive hand. "There is plenty of room. I bet not everyone who was invited will come."

"Thanks for the invitation, but I can't go." Margo made a miserable face. "Lynda is having a bachelorette party in Cabo. I have to be there even though I would rather have consecutive dentist's appointments. She will make my brother suffer if I bail for any reason."

"Oh, right." Mia's face fell. "Their wedding is in a month." She looked down at her legs. "I'm still not going to be able to walk on my own. It's taking so long."

Frankie leaned over and patted her friend's shoulder. "It's a miracle that you are regrowing your legs at all. It doesn't matter how long it takes, as long as it happens, right?"

Toven

Mia's legs were progressing beautifully. Her body had just started regenerating her feet, but since those were the most complicated parts of the reconstruction process, they would take a while.

That was one of the reasons why the two of them were not getting married on the cruise. Mia wanted to dance at her wedding, and she also wanted her best friends to be there. If the two proved to be Dormants, moved into the village, and transitioned, the wedding would occur either in the village square or on another cruise. However, if Margo and Frankie were fully human, Mia had suggested a small wedding in Zurich.

Toven liked the idea of a smaller wedding with just the close family attending, but at the end of the day, he knew that he would do precisely what Mia wanted and how she wanted it.

"I know," Mia sighed. "I'm so grateful." She turned to Toven with so much love on her beautiful face that he would have given her the moon if she had asked for it. "Can Frankie come?"

Or at least tried.

He had a feeling that convincing Kian to let Frankie join the cruise might be more difficult than getting her the moon.

"You know it's not up to me, love."

"Aren't you the boss?" Margo asked.

"I have partners, and they are very reclusive."

"Oh." Frankie's face fell. "So, they are the ones organizing the cruise." She turned to Margo. "There is no chance in hell they will invite us. Remember how secretive they were when Mia and Tom first met them?"

Margo nodded. "I can't come anyway, but I'm sorry you can't."

"We can pick you up at Cabo," Mia said, as if her friends joining her on the cruise was a done deal.

Margo winced. "It's a week-long thing, and Lynda is not the compromising type. I have to be nice to her because she's about to become family, and I will be stuck with her for as long as she and David are married."

"Excuse me, ladies." Toven pushed to his feet and put his hand on Mia's shoulder. "I'll be back in a few minutes."

A secretive smile blooming on her face, she nodded and lifted a hand with crossed fingers but only as high as her thighs so her friends couldn't see it.

Of course, she'd guessed that he was going to call Kian.

It was after working hours, but he knew Kian would take a call from him. Lifting Frankie's mood might not be high on Kian's list of concerns, but she was a potential Dormant, or at least Toven hoped she was, and it was time to put the suspicion to the test.

It was a shame that the girl had no paranormal talent to strengthen her case, but who knew? Perhaps they would discover that she had a hidden ability like Mia's.

His mate had thought she had no talent but had ended up with one of the best. Enhancing the powers of others was invaluable, as had been proven during the Kra-ell rescue mission.

He couldn't have done what he had without her help.

Stepping outside into the cool night, Toven walked a few feet up the block before calling Kian.

"Toven," he answered right away. "Is everything okay?"

Obviously, he knew that Toven and Mia were not in the village and immediately assumed something had happened to them.

"Mia and I are fine. We are at a bar with Mia's friends, drinking margaritas."

"Ah." Kian sounded relieved. "That's my sister's favorite drink. Amanda and Syssi started their bonding over margaritas that Onidu made for them." He sighed. "It was a long time ago, when we were still living at the keep, and Amanda's penthouse was across from mine."

"Do you miss those days?"

"Only the incredible excitement of falling in love with Syssi, but then I fall in love with her every day anew."

It was odd to hear Kian express such romantic feelings. He must be in a good mood, which could be helpful now. He might not say no right away.

"I know how you feel. I look at Mia every morning when I wake up and thank the Fates for bringing her into my life. There isn't anything I wouldn't do for her, which brings me to the reason for my call. Mia's friend Frankie got fired from her job. Do you remember who I am talking about?"

"Yes, of course. Frankie and Margo are Mia's best friends, and you wanted to hire them as beta testers for the Perfect Match adventures."

"I'm impressed with your ability to hold information in your head. As you know, the machines in the village are almost ready, but by the time they are, we will be sailing to Mexico. To cut a long story short, Mia wants to invite her friends on the cruise."

"That's—"

"Hold on before you shoot the idea down. The cruise is only ten days long, so I can erase their memories at the end of it without causing them damage. Frankie getting fired two weeks before the cruise might be the Fates' doing. Perhaps they are trying to tell us something."

It was a feeble attempt, and Toven felt ridiculous for invoking the Fates for such a frivolous cause, but he wanted Mia to have her friends on the cruise, and Kian was a believer.

Kian laughed. "That's a stretch, but I get it. You want to do this for your mate."

"Very much so. I know that the case for Margo and Frankie being Dormants is weak, but they are nice girls, and it's worth a try."

Kian sighed. "Yeah, I hear you, and I also owe you and Mia for your help with the Kra-ell."

"Is it a yes, then?"

"Yes, conditional on you taking full responsibility for them, erasing their memories from the cruise, and creating new ones so they won't wonder why they can't remember anything."

"I've done that before." Toven chuckled. "Perhaps that was what got me writing in the first place. I was creating elaborate stories for my lovers to fill the missing time from the memories I had to erase."

"Good, then you know what to do. I don't expect either of them to find a truelove mate and start transitioning during the cruise, so this is not hypothetical. You will have to do it."

"I know." Toven started walking back to the bar. "There is one more complication. Margo is attending a bachelorette party in Cabo, and we might need to collect her from there. Is a stop at Cabo part of the itinerary?"

Frankie

"Did you start looking for a new job?" Mia asked Frankie after Tom left.

Frankie pushed the half-empty margarita glass away. "I've sent out resumes, but no one's gotten back to me yet."

"It has only been four days," Margo said. "Give it time."

"I don't have time. I have no savings to speak of, and my parents are barely making it as it is. They can't help me."

"You can move in with me," Margo offered.

"You live in a studio."

"So? Beggars and choosers and all that. You can sleep on the couch. You've slept on it before."

Crashing on her friend's sofa occasionally wasn't the same as giving up on having her own place. "I could also move back in with my parents and sleep in my old room. I'm twenty-seven, Margo. I should be independent by now."

"You are, honey." Margo reached for her hand. "You moved out of your parents' house when you went to college and never moved back. Many people our age can't do that these days. People are renting by the room or staying home long past the age they should."

Frankie let out a long-suffering sigh. "My apartment is crappy, but it's mine, and it's affordable. If I give it up, I'll never find anything I can afford and will have to room with other people."

Her place was in an iffy part of town and an old apartment building that desperately needed renovations. She'd furnished it with second-hand stuff and decorated it with pillows, throws, and other bargains from discount stores. It wasn't much, but it was cozy, it was hers, and it pained her to give it up.

Mia shook her head. "When Tom comes back, I will ask him to find you a job in one of the Perfect Match studios. You could be an adventure coordinator or a receptionist until something better opens up."

"Don't. That's probably what happened to my job at Hoffesommer and Partners. His niece or lover needed a job, so I got the boot. I don't want anyone fired to make room for me."

"No, of course not." Mia slumped in her wheelchair. "But maybe they are hiring, you know? A position might open that's right up your alley."

"Yeah, and pigs might fly. Sorry, Mia, but even when I'm drunk, I can't think magically."

"That's a shame." Mia slurped her margarita through a straw while looking at Frankie from under lowered lashes. "Magic happens. Just look at Tom and me. I couldn't have dreamt him up. A fairy godmother must have sprinkled me with magic dust."

As the subject of their conversation suddenly appeared behind Mia, Frankie blinked a couple of times. One moment, there was no one there, and then he just appeared as if out of thin air. Was she really that inebriated?

"Hello, ladies. Anything interesting happen in my absence?"

Mia looked up at him with adoring eyes. "Frankie is freaking out about losing her apartment because she has no savings. Can't you find her a job in one of the studios? It could be something temporary until we return from the cruise, and she can start on her beta tester's job."

Would strangling Mia make Frankie a terrible person?

How could she embarrass her like that? It was one thing for her besties to know how desperate her situation was and another thing entirely for a rich dude like Tom to know, someone who had never known what struggling to pay rent felt like.

She didn't want him to pity her and look down his nose at her like he did with most people. For some reason, Tom liked her and Margo and treated them as if they were special. It was probably because they were Mia's friends, and the dude would do anything to make his fiancée happy.

It was so damn enviable.

Tom frowned at her. "Why do you want to keep your apartment? Once the machines are up and running, you and Margo will move into the compound and live rent-free."

It would be rude to tell him she didn't trust his promises because he and Mia had been dangling that elusive job in front of her for months, but there was no way around it.

"I don't know if I can rely on that. Until now, I had a job, so I could wait patiently for your offer to materialize. But I can't afford to do that now. I need a new job yesterday."

"I understand." Tom smiled. "Here is what I suggest you do. Give your landlord notice that you are vacating the premises in two weeks. Pack up your things, and I will arrange for them to be stored until your new place in the compound is ready. In the meantime, you will get to know your future coworkers while enjoying a luxury cruise courtesy of your future employers."

Uttering a small gasp, Mia put a hand over her heart. "Did you speak with Kian?"

Tom nodded. "It took some convincing, but he agreed to host both of your friends." He turned to Margo. "I need the exact dates of the bachelorette party, so we will know when to pick you up from Cabo."

Margo's eyes turned as wide as saucers. "Are you serious? You will really have the ship dock at Cabo just so I can come along?"

He smiled. "The ships dock outside of Cabo, and passengers use water taxis to get on and off them. The cruise itinerary is flexible to some extent, but not much. If the dates don't work, I'll fly you to one of our other shore excursions."

As Margo jumped out of her chair, wrapped her arms around Tom, and kissed his cheek, Mia's expression turned almost feral.

Frankie hadn't known that her best friend had such a possessive streak. Tom was a catch, and Mia was right to guard her turf, but she had nothing to fear from Margo, and she knew that.

"Thank you," Margo squealed. "You are the best."

"That's enough," Mia hissed, and Frankie could have sworn that her friend's eyes started glowing.

"Sorry." Margo let go of Tom and smiled sheepishly. "It's just that no one has ever gone to so much trouble for me."

Frankie lifted her margarita and examined the remaining liquid for residual sediment.

Who could have drugged her while she was with her friends, and why?

She shook her head after briefly scanning the room and not seeing anyone shady. "I need to find out what kind of tequila they use in these margaritas. It must have been exceptionally potent."

Kian

After ending the call with Toven, Kian returned to the living room and sat next to Syssi on the couch.

Across from them, Amanda looked like she'd run her fingers through her hair too many times. The short strands stood up like little antennae, making her look like an anime character.

Still, despite her disheveled appearance, Kian knew that she was having the time of her life planning the ten cruise ceremonies. If their mother's favorite thing was presiding over weddings, Amanda's was planning them.

The truth was that Kian had gotten caught up in the excitement as well. It was a pleasant distraction from worrying about the Eternal King, the future of everyone Kian loved, and the fate of Earth and its entire population.

He still wasn't sure whether he wanted to warn Navuh as Annani had suggested. He very much doubted that their archenemy would decide to join them just because they had a mutual enemy much more powerful than either faction could defend against, and they needed to combine forces.

Perhaps once Aru got concrete instructions on how to proceed, there would be something to tell the clan's archenemy.

"Can we make the cruise a day longer?" Amanda asked.

"Why?"

"I'm trying to convince Sari and David to have their wedding ceremony on this cruise, too. It would be perfect if all three of us got married in the same week, but we don't have any dates left, and none of us want a shared ceremony. Unless I can convince one of the other couples to give up their date, I can't even nag Sari about it."

Kian cast her an apologetic look. "I hired the crew for those specific dates, and I know for a fact that they can't stay for another day. I was lucky to secure the dates on such short notice."

"I'm pretty sure that Kri and Michael will not mind waiting," Syssi said. "They are still so young, and the only reason Kri jumped on the idea was because all the other head Guardians are getting married on the cruise, and she didn't want to be the only one left out."

Amanda grimaced. "She's shopping for a wedding dress, so I know she's committed. She will give up her spot for Sari, but it wouldn't be fair. "

"Carol and Lokan would probably have liked to get married too." Syssi leaned her head on his shoulder. "They have so few opportunities to celebrate with the family."

Kian rubbed his hand over her exposed arm. "Perhaps some of the couples wouldn't mind a double wedding."

"Mey and Jin are close." Amanda tapped a finger on her lower lip. "Maybe they wouldn't mind a shared ceremony."

Syssi chuckled. "I think you will have more luck with Wonder and Callie."

"You might be right." Amanda sighed. "I'll make the calls tomorrow. The thing is, Sari is not at all eager to join Alena and me in seafaring nuptials. She wants to have her wedding in the castle with all her people. I told her it's silly since most of them are coming and will be there anyway, but I think it's a matter of pride with her. She is the all-important European regent, and it's beneath her to get married at the same time as her sisters."

Kian shook his head. "It's not about pride. I think her people would not like her to have her wedding on my turf so to speak. If she doesn't want to get married on the cruise, don't pressure her to do it. We have enough drama going on as it is."

He still hadn't told them about Mia's friends.

Amanda frowned. "You mean the three gods?"

He nodded. "I'm apprehensive about them meeting Mother."

Syssi turned to him. "Why? You had Edna probe them and Andrew verify their answers. Luckily, they weren't immune to our best methods of interrogation."

"True, and it gave me some peace of mind, but Aru refused to let Edna probe him, which worries me. He said that the secrets he keeps have nothing to do with us, but still. He might have told only a partial truth. Andrew's lie detection ability is not infallible."

Syssi seemed offended on her brother's behalf. "Andrew is never wrong. When he's not sure whether someone is telling the truth, he admits it."

"Yeah, well, he wasn't sure with all of Aru's answers. Some were evasive." Kian reached for one of the scones Okidu had made for dessert. "That's not all the drama either. I just got a call from Toven, and he implored me to allow Mia's friends to join us on the cruise. I agreed since they are potential Dormants and the cruise is short."

Amanda clapped her hands. "That's fabulous. There is no better way to spark romance than a cruise vacation. A couple of clan males will be very thankful."

"That was why I agreed. I also told Toven that he was in charge of erasing their memories after the cruise."

Syssi tilted her head. "But what if they find their truelove mates by then? What's the point of erasing their memories? You can just bring them straight to the village. Anyway, the plan was for them to start working as beta testers for the Perfect Match scenarios. Since Toven will be paying their salaries, that's a win-win all around." She smiled at him. "Isn't that your preferred way of doing business?"

"It is." He wrapped his arm around her shoulders and kissed her head. "And speaking of business, I should get back to it. I have a pile of work waiting on my desk."

Aru

Aru tried to slip out of bed without waking Gabi up, but she opened her eyes as soon as he pulled his arm off her.

"Where are you going?"

"I need to do something. I'll be back before you are ready to wake up."

She frowned. "What is it about?"

He leaned closer so his mouth was on her ear. "I need to contact my commander, and I don't want to do it from here."

Despite Kian's assurances that there was no surveillance equipment in the penthouse and despite the fact that Kian and his people most likely were not familiar with the language of the gods, Aru wanted to make the call outside, where he was sure no one was listening in on it.

"What happened? Did he contact you?"

Aru nodded. "I got pinged, and I have to respond within twenty-four hours, or they will assume that something has happened to us."

Nodding, she lifted her head and kissed his cheek. "Come back soon. And if you want to be my hero, bring me some pastries from the café downstairs. I'm craving sweet things."

"No problem." He kissed her forehead. "I'll get us coffee too."

Her smile was dazzling. "You are the best. I love you."

He chuckled. "You are easy to please, my love."

It had been almost a week since she'd completed the first stage of her transition, and during that time, Gabi's appetite had been ravenous in more ways than one. She couldn't get enough of him and his venom bites, for which he was thanking the Fates daily and often more than once. She was also eating quantities that exceeded what Negal and Dagor combined consumed in a day.

She'd been worried about gaining weight, but Julian had reassured her that a ravenous appetite was common for newly transitioned Dormants. Since Gabi had grown a little over an inch, she needed to replenish what her body had used to make her grow taller.

When dressed, Aru walked into the living room and was relieved that Negal and Dagor weren't up yet.

Their relationship had been strained lately, probably because the males resented him for their being stuck in

Los Angeles instead of searching for the missing Kra-ell pods.

He should remind them how much they had complained on the trek through Tibet.

Down in the lobby, he waved at the guards. "Getting coffee and sweet things for the lady," he said, knowing they were reporting to someone who was reporting to Kian.

Without meaning to, Gabi had given him the perfect excuse for his early morning outing.

As he stepped outside and walked around the corner of the building, Aru glanced over his shoulder to ensure no one was following him and then lifted his gaze to the sky, searching for a drone.

The irony of what he was doing wasn't lost on him.

He'd been peeved at Kian for bringing Edna and Andrew to test them because he didn't trust them, but he wasn't trusting Kian either.

Leaning against the wall, he pulled a cigarette box out of his pocket, took one of the cylinders, and put it in his mouth. He wasn't a smoker, but it was an excellent cover for spending several minutes outside, presumably doing nothing other than puffing on the stick.

His communicator was in his ear, which was covered by his chin-length hair. As he gave the verbal command for the connection to be made, he lit the cigarette and puffed out a plume of smoke.

The commander came online a few puffs later.

"Greetings, team leader Aru. Is everything well with you and your teammates?"

"It is, commander. Thank you for asking. Is everything well on board?"

"It is. Do you have anything to report?"

"Unfortunately, not yet." Aru hated lying to the male. It was one thing to omit information and another to lie outright. "We are still searching for the Kra-ell from the compound."

"Are you sure that they were not thrown overboard? The Kra-ell are not good swimmers, and you said the water was freezing in that area. They would have died, and their transmitters would have stopped broadcasting."

The scenario the commander suggested was plausible, and Aru should use it, but he just couldn't bring himself to do that.

"It occurred to me that someone might have used the threat of throwing the Kra-ell overboard to get them to talk, but I don't know what they hoped to learn. Humans would want to examine the aliens and wouldn't have disposed of them so quickly. They would have taken them to a research facility, and that's the lead we are following. Even if the abductors were Kra-ell, I can't believe they would have killed everyone unless they had a vendetta against them. It also occurred to me that they might have killed the original settlers and taken those born on Earth with them. In short, I feel compelled to continue the investigation."

He'd listed all the things he'd suspected before discovering that none of those scenarios was what had really happened. He had told the commander some of them before. Eventually, he would have to settle on one and ensure he had some supporting evidence he could show the commander.

"The high command seems to share your opinion because I have just gotten instructions to leave you and your team on Earth and not pick you up on our way back unless all the pods are found and all the Kra-ell are accounted for." The commander sounded apologetic. "Was there something you or one of your teammates did before this tour of duty to earn a punishment?"

Aru did his best to contain his joy and keep it from seeping into his voice. "Not that I know of, but you never know, right? Perhaps I said something offensive to someone."

The Supreme worked faster than Aru had expected.

"That is possible, and it is also a shame. I do not like losing you, Dagor, and Negal." There was a short silence, and Aru imagined the commander stifling a sigh. "We can drop more supplies for you when we pass by, but once we cross the barrier, you will lose communication with Anumati. The human satellite technology is in its infancy. You can't use it to communicate with home."

The commander was downplaying what humans had achieved in the last six hundred years on purpose, but it wouldn't work long-term.

"I know. I'm comforted by the knowledge that I will still have the ability to communicate with home for the next three hundred Earth years or so. Perhaps by then, we will be forgiven and allowed to return. Would you come back for us?"

"Of course, provided that the high command allows it and wakes me up from stasis."

"Naturally."

Dagor

Dagor had heard Aru leaving the penthouse, and he'd also known why. The commander had pinged all three of them last night, but Aru was responsible for responding. Dagor or Negal were to respond only if Aru was compromised.

Dagor had woken up, put the coffeemaker to work, and prepared a simple breakfast of eggs and toast for him, Negal, and Gabriella if she chose to join them.

Food on Earth tasted better than it did back home, probably because the ingredients were still mostly natural, but it wasn't reason enough to want to stay. He wasn't enthused about going home to Anumati either. Still, there were several colonies he was planning to check out after his tour of duty was over.

He'd heard that Peronia was beautiful and peaceful. It was an old and well-established colony with advanced technology and most of the comforts of Anumati, but it wasn't as stifling, and the class divide was less sharp.

Nenillia was another good choice. It wasn't as well developed, and it had several species of dangerous predators, but it was also rumored to be a hub of burgeoning technology, where commoners like him could get the kind of education that only nobility could afford on Anumati.

When the door opened, and Aru walked in with a tray of coffees and a bag of pastries, Dagor lifted his coffee mug in salute. "You shouldn't have. I've also made eggs and toast for breakfast."

"We can have both." Aru smiled, but his expression was tense, and Dagor wondered what news he'd heard from the commander. "Is Gabi up?"

"Not as far as I can tell. She hasn't emerged from your room yet."

The newly transitioned immortal required longer sleep than the three of them, and she usually wasn't up before eight in the morning.

"Good." Aru put the tray and the paper bag on the counter. "I need to talk to you and Negal."

Dagor's gut twisted. "Is everything okay back home?"

Negal put his fork down and wiped his mouth with a paper towel.

"Nothing bad happened to anyone we love, or at least nothing that the commander was aware of. This has to do with the three of us."

Negal let out a breath and went back to shoveling scrambled eggs into his mouth as if their fate was of no consequence to him.

"What about us?" Dagor prompted.

Aru winced. "We are not going home. Unless we find all the pods and all the Kra-ell are accounted for, they are not picking us up on the way back, but they will drop off more supplies."

For Dagor, this was worse than a death sentence or just as bad. There was no way to find all the pods and account for the Kra-ell. Some pods were undoubtedly submerged in deep water, and some might have been destroyed.

They were being abandoned on a forbidden planet. In three hundred years, they would no longer be able to communicate with home. They would be as good as dead to their families.

"Why?" Dagor stared at Aru. "What did you do?"

"Nothing, as far as I know."

That was a lie. The guilty look in Aru's eyes betrayed the truth he was trying to hide.

"Out with it. If I am to be buried on this godforsaken rock, I at least want to know why. It must have been something terrible to merit such extreme punishment."

"I don't think it's a punishment, and I don't think it's forever either. We are tasked with investigating what happened to the Kra-ell and searching for the survivors. Someone higher up must have realized that a hundred and fifteen years is not long enough to achieve these objectives. We might get picked up by the next patrol ship deployed for the sector." He smiled. "Or we can go home on a human-made ship. At the rate they are going, they might develop interstellar travel ability during the next seven hundred years."

Aru didn't seem upset, which was understandable since he'd found his truelove mate on Earth and couldn't take her home with him.

Dagor was happy for him and liked to think of himself as a progressive god, but he hoped that the mate the Fates chose for him was a goddess and not a hybrid. He really didn't want to get stuck on Earth for eternity.

He wasn't overly fond of humans, and their primitive technology left much to be desired. As little as he knew, he could teach the best of them a lot about programming and building hardware. He would have been an exceptional engineer if his family could have afforded the tuition. He could probably also learn a lot from them.

"I don't think they will." Dagor let out a sigh. "The best we can hope for are satellites that will allow us to communicate with home."

Aru turned to Negal, who had snatched the paper bag and was pulling out all the pastries and organizing them on a plate. "You don't seem to be upset."

"I'm not." Negal chose one of the pastries and put it next to what was left of his eggs. "I like the food here."

"What about your family?" Dagor asked. "Aren't you upset about not seeing your parents?"

Negal shrugged. "I'm not very close to them."

"A mate then? Aren't you disappointed that you will have to wait for another thousand years to have a chance to find her?"

The trooper shrugged again. "I'm not a young god like you two, and I've been all over the galaxy, but I haven't found my one and only yet. I don't think the Fates have one for me." He tore off a piece of the pastry, stuffed it in his mouth, and chewed quickly. "Maybe I'm not deserving enough to merit such a boon from the Fates."

Aru

The good news was that Negal didn't seem to mind their extended, or maybe even permanent, stay on Earth. The bad news was that Dagor seemed more upset about it than Aru had expected.

"You have suffered," Dagor said to Negal. "You were oppressed, and yet you remained a good person. Therefore, you deserve a boon from the Fates. Do not give up hope on ever finding your truelove mate."

Negal smiled. "That is true of most people, and yet only a few ever find their one and only. I think more is required to qualify, but no instruction manual details the feats of bravery or sacrifice needed."

"I think that's a myth," Aru said. "I found my truelove mate, and I haven't sacrificed more than the two of you or performed heroic acts."

Dagor groaned. "Maybe you've gotten Gabi as a reward for the suffering you will endure in your future."

Aru wasn't sure whether Dagor was being his usual sarcastic self or if he really believed in that. In either case, the words didn't sit well with him and brought a sense of foreboding.

Nevertheless, he was the leader of this team, and it was his job to inspire the others.

"We can do great things here." He touched Dagor's shoulder and gave it a light squeeze. "The news was a shock, and when you have had more time to think about it, you will realize it's not that bad." He let go of Dagor's shoulder and pulled one of the coffee cups from the tray. "Besides, if what you said is true, and I got Gabi as a reward for future suffering, and by that you meant being stuck on Earth, then you and Negal should get rewarded as well."

Dagor arched a brow. "Do you see any goddesses milling around here? Because I don't, and I do not wish to be tied to a hybrid female whom I can never bring home to my parents."

It was the perfect opening for revealing the secret Aru had been hiding from his men. Still, while he was thinking of a good way to broach the subject, Negal said, "I agree with Dagor. But since I'm not looking for a truelove mate or any kind of mate, I'm good." He let out a sigh. "Human females are so fragile, though. I hope we will get to meet sexy immortal ladies who will want to try out a god in bed." He waggled his brows. "How does the saying go? Once they sample a god, they'll never look back?"

Dagor chuckled. "That doesn't sound right, but I'm all for trying out those immortal females. It would be nice not to have to be so careful, for a change." He turned to Aru. "You said something about going on a vacation with some of the immortals?"

"They invited us to their clan's cruise, and many immortals will be on board." Aru leveled his eyes at his teammates. "I need your vow that you will never reveal what I will tell you next. Especially not to anyone on the patrol ship, because our communication channel with the commander is not secure. We must assume that everything said over that line is reported to the Eternal King's secret agents."

The men nodded, and Dagor put his hand over his heart. "A vow shouldn't have been needed. A promise would have been enough, but here it is. I vow not to reveal what you will tell us to anyone outside of Earth or on it. It will stay between the three of us."

As Negal repeated the same vow, Aru let out a breath. "Gods are living among the immortals. Turns out that Kian's mother is a goddess and wants to meet the three of us."

Aru had expected surprise, maybe some questions for which he would have no answers, but he hadn't anticipated that Negal and Dagor would exchange knowing looks.

"You knew?"

Dagor nodded. "We've seen the recording you deleted of Gilbert telling Gabi about the gods." When Aru opened his mouth to berate them, Dagor lifted his hand. "I only checked because I was afraid that you might have mistakenly deleted something important. I never expected you to hide things from us. We are a team, and you should have known you could trust us."

Son of a gun.

They had known for days and had kept it to themselves, waiting for him to tell them.

"Kian asked me to keep the information about the gods to myself, and I did. He didn't tell me that he was protecting his mother, but I should have guessed. He looks like a god."

"Why does she want to meet us?" Negal said. "And why didn't we find any clues about her when we searched?"

"I don't know." Aru put his hands in his pockets. "Kian didn't say. His mother must be curious to learn about people from her home world. I assume that she was born on Earth, and therefore had no tracker, so we didn't know she was alive. As to hints, the ancient texts we read were full of stories about gods, but then they disappeared, and the logical assumption was that they had perished, because we knew they couldn't have gone home."

"How many gods are there living with those immortals?" Negal asked.

"I don't know that either. But since Gilbert could have only been induced by a male god, there must be at least one male. Maybe Kian's mother and the male god are a couple."

Negal looked like he wanted to ask something else when the door of the master bedroom opened, and the sound of Gabi's light footsteps sounded in the hallway.

Aru had wanted to deliver the good news to her in private, but it was too late for that. Negal or Dagor might blurt out something and steal his thunder.

As soon as she walked into the living room he rushed to her, wrapped his arms around her, and lifted her to look into her blue eyes.

"I have something to tell you." He grinned at her sleepy face. "I'm staying on Earth. The commander informed me that we are not getting picked up when the patrol ship completes its rounds in this corner of the galaxy."

Gabi squealed, wrapped her legs around him, and kissed him hard. He started walking toward the bedroom with her when a throat clearing reminded him that his friends were there, and they were not done talking.

Turning around, he walked Gabi to the kitchen counter and sat her on a stool. "Dagor and Negal are staying too, and Dagor is unhappy about it. Negal doesn't care one way or the other."

Instead of joyously showering him with kisses, Gabi frowned. "I don't understand. Did you ask your commander to let you stay and stipulate that if you do, your teammates must also stay?"

"I didn't ask. I couldn't tell him about you, remember?"

"So, how come he's abandoning the three of you on Earth?"

"That's what I want to know," Dagor murmured.

"It's probably punishment," Negal said. "One of us must have said something offensive about the Eternal King and was overheard. It doesn't take much to get booted out into a hostile colony, or in this case, the forbidden planet."

Kian

As Kian escorted Annani onto the cruise ship, his eyes darted in every direction even though the Guardians were securing the area and Yamanu was shrouding it.

He'd instructed the team to return from China, not only because Yamanu and Mey were one of the couples who wished to be married on the cruise, but also because he could utilize Yamanu's unique talent to safeguard the excursion.

The truth was that there had been no reason for them to stay longer, and the only objective that they could claim to have achieved, if he could call it that, was improved relations between the Kra-ell and the clan members.

Peter and Kagra had become an item, but according to Syssi, who had heard it from Amanda, who had heard it from Mey, who had heard it from Yamanu, they were adamant about not making a big deal out of it. They claimed not to be fated to each other, and their fling was about having a good time and nothing more.

"Relax, my son." Annani adjusted the wide-brimmed hat that obscured most of her face and probably made it difficult for her to see. "You are overthinking it again. You will not have any fun if you let your paranoia flare."

"I'm aware of that, Mother. I will be less concerned once we are out on the water, but we have about eight more hours before we can set sail."

As soon as they were inside, she removed her protective sunglasses. "We could have waited until everyone was here, and then you would have had less to worry about, but you wanted me to be the first to board the ship so no one would witness my arrival. You cannot have it both ways, you know."

"You are not the first one to board. The Guardians, crew, and serving staff boarded yesterday, and Syssi's parents arrived early this morning. Besides, most of the immediate family is boarding along with you."

Annani looked over her shoulder at his sisters and smiled. "Indeed. Let us all go to my cabin and have a drink to celebrate." She turned to Syssi. "You probably want to say hello to your parents first."

"I spoke with my mother when they got here, and she said that they were going to sleep. I won't bother them until she calls me, and I know they are awake."

"Awesome." Amanda threaded her arm through Syssi's. "We can have margaritas. I just hope that the cabins are stocked with all the necessities."

"They are stocked," Kian said. "I put Wonder and Callie in charge of ordering supplies. As you know, Callie used to work in Brundar's club, so she knows a lot about cocktails." He also had an expert bartender, but that was a surprise they would discover later.

Pretending not to hear the remark about Brundar's club, his mother hid a smirk.

Only certain people in the clan knew about the Guardian's side hustle, and especially not what type of clientele the club catered to. Kian was absolutely sure that his mother knew all the details. She knew everything that was going on in her clan.

As they entered the elevator, Dalhu stood next to Kian with his hands resting on the handle of Evie's stroller. "Amanda told me that you hired the humans who came with the Kra-ell to be the serving staff."

"I did. Originally, I thought to hire an experienced serving crew and just thrall their memories after the cruise. Still, Eleanor convinced me to take the Kra-ell's former...employees." Kian didn't want to use the word slaves, but the truth was that they hadn't had much choice in what they did for a living and where they lived, so slaves was apt. "She said that they would be thrilled to visit Mexico, and since we managed to get proper paperwork for all of them, they can take turns with shore excursions. They are also very happy about the extra income."

Dalhu listened patiently to Kian's semi-apologetic explanation for his choice. When he was done, he clapped him on the back. "Yamanu said they have a great cook who runs an efficient kitchen. That's good enough for me."

Their group spilled out as the elevator doors opened, and Kian led them to Annani's presidential suite.

"This is beautiful," Alena said. "Is our cabin as nice as this one?"

"It's a little smaller but just as luxurious." Kian walked over to the bar and opened the cabinet. "I think Onidu has everything he needs to make margaritas."

The Odus were coming on a separate elevator with everyone's luggage, and given that Amanda didn't know the meaning of traveling light, it would take Onidu a couple of trips to bring up all of her suitcases.

When the ladies continued to check out the two bedrooms, Orion walked up to Kian. "Did you bring your cigars?" He looked longingly at the balcony doors. "I wouldn't mind a smoke, some good whiskey, and even better company."

"I don't have them on me, but I can pour us drinks." He glanced at Dalhu. "Can I tempt you with a shot?"

It was not even noon, but they were on vacation, and a shot of whiskey was an excellent way to start it off on the right foot.

Dalhu cast a look at his sleeping daughter and nodded. "As long as no one is smoking, I can take her out on the balcony."

A few moments later, the three were seated on lounge chairs outside.

"When is Kalugal arriving?" Dalhu asked.

"Soon. He and Jacki were supposed to leave with us, but he needed a little more time with his men. Some were unhappy about the village being locked down in our absence."

The Kra-ell weren't allowed to leave the village without supervision yet, so they didn't mind. Still, Kalugal's men were free to come and go as they pleased, and they didn't respond well to the news of being locked down for ten days.

"What is he going to do about it?" Orion asked.

"The usual." Kian took another sip of the whiskey. "Give them bonus pay to compensate them for the inconvenience. He already doubled their salaries for staying to guard the village and tripled it for the lockdown."

Dalhu shook his head. "I was surprised to hear that you were willing to leave the village to the Kra-ell and Kalugal's men to protect. I was sure you would leave at least half of the Guardians behind."

"It wouldn't have been fair." Kian wished he had his cigars with him because Dalhu's comment made him nervous. It hadn't been an easy decision, but he had taken all possible precautions. "William has every inch of the village under surveillance, and the lockdown ensures no one can enter. Besides, I invited the three gods to join us on the cruise so I can keep an eye on them here and not have to worry about them being a threat to the village."

Orion frowned. "Are you worried that they are a threat?"

"Not really, but you know me. I always prefer to err on the side of caution."

The balcony doors were flung open, and Amanda stepped out with a margarita glass in hand. "Here you are, darlings. The Odus brought up our luggage, so we should head to our cabins and unpack. Mother wants to see what ours look like, so you'd better get moving."

Frankie

"Thank you so much." Frankie watched the taxi driver unload her suitcase, carry-on, and makeup bag, ensuring he didn't forget anything inside the trunk.

Mia had told her that Tom had paid for the taxi, but she wanted to at least tip the driver. When he was done, she pulled out her wallet, but he lifted his hand to stop her.

"It's all been paid for, miss. Enjoy your vacation."

"Thank you."

Her suitcase was enormous and weighed a ton, but thankfully it had wheels. Not great ones, so Frankie still had trouble dragging it behind her, but at least she didn't need to lift it.

Hopefully there would be no stairs, or she would have to ask for help.

It was only ten days, but the thing was stuffed to bursting, and to close it, Aunt Rachel had to sit on it, contributing all of her two hundred and something pounds to the packing effort.

Most of it wasn't even Frankie's.

Her cousins Angelica and Bianca had collected evening dresses from her other female cousins, ensuring she had a new outfit for each of the ten weddings.

Some of the dresses were too big, others were too small, and most were too long on her petite frame, but several were nice, and only worn once or twice before. Still, Frankie didn't want to offend any of her cousins, so she packed all of them.

Then there were the shoes, a matching pair of heels for every dress, and those were all her own.

Frankie had a weakness for high-heeled, fancy-looking shoes, but since she'd gotten them all on sale, she had zero guilt about splurging on her one obsession.

Thankfully, the bikinis took up only a little space. She had two of her own and three more on loan from Angelica.

Frankie hadn't taken Tom up on his offer to store her things and had brought everything she wanted to keep to her parents' house.

Surprisingly, it was very little.

Moving was an excellent opportunity to get rid of old stuff, and she had donated at least half of her wardrobe and all the furniture, keeping only a few pictures, pillows, and throws.

Taking a deep breath, Frankie squared her shoulders and trudged toward the dock number indicated on her invitation, pulling the suitcase behind her.

It was easy to find a ship named the Silver Swan, and as she got closer, the two men standing at the entrance looked at her as if she was a lost tourist and there was no way she was getting onboard.

Did she look so out of place that they immediately knew that she was an outsider?

Nah, that was a stupid thought. The two probably worked for Perfect Match and knew all the employees. They simply didn't know who she was and that she would soon join their ranks.

Or so she hoped.

"Hi, I'm Frankie Canal." She pulled out her phone with the invitation. "Tom and Mia invited me."

One of the men said something very quietly into his earpiece while the other checked her invitation.

They were both very handsome and tall, making her feel tiny by comparison.

She was petite, only five feet two inches tall, but she was wearing four-inch shoes, and five feet six inches was a decent height for a woman.

"Welcome aboard, Ms. Canal. Can I see your passport?"

"Yes, of course." She fumbled in her purse until she found it. "Mia told me I would need one since we are going to Mexico." She handed him the document.

He flipped through it before handing it back to her. "Hold on to it. You will need it to go on shore excursions."

"Yes. I know." She looked at the darkened entrance. "Can I go in now?"

"Ms. Mia is on her way. She wants to welcome you on board and take you to your suite."

Her eyes widened. "A suite? Why am I getting a suite? Am I sharing it with someone?"

"I don't know." The guard said. "You will have to ask Mia."

"Sure." She put a hand on her hip and struck a pose. "Do you guys work for Perfect Match?"

The one on the left frowned. "No. Do you?"

"Frankie!" Mia drove her wheelchair at breakneck speed. "I told you to call me when you got here. I would have waited for you."

"I forgot." Frankie embraced her friend. "I guess I was too excited." She looked up. "Where is Tom?"

Usually he didn't leave Mia's side, which was sweet but, in Frankie's opinion, a little stifling. She didn't like her boyfriends to be so clingy.

"On his way." Mia turned her wheelchair around. "Come on, he'll meet us upstairs."

Frankie trotted behind her friend while pulling the suitcase behind her and wondering why Mia was in such a rush. She was also wondering why there was no one else around. "Where are all the guests?"

Mia turned to look at her over her shoulder. "The cruise organizers didn't want the usual mess of everyone boarding at once, so people were given different windows of arrival time. They are slowly trickling in and getting settled in their suites."

"About that." Frankie followed Mia into the elevator. "Who am I rooming with?"

"You have a suite of your own until Margo gets on board, and then you will share it with her."

"That's so fancy. I've never even been in a hotel suite or on a cruise. Now I'm getting both at the same time. I feel like a princess."

When the elevator door opened, Mia drove the wheelchair out into the wide corridor and kept going. "You are in suite number 217." She stopped before the double door, leaned over, and typed on the glass keyboard. "The code is your suite number, but you can change it if you want." She turned to look at Frankie. "Open the door."

"I'm almost afraid to." Frankie pushed the door open. "Wow, Mia. I even have a balcony."

Mia laughed. "What did you think, that we would put you below decks with the sheep and goats?"

Frankie frowned. "Are there animals on board?"

Mia waved a dismissive hand. "It was just an expression."

It wasn't one that Frankie had heard before.

"It's just that I'm not anyone important in the company." She walked in and parked the suitcase by the door. "I didn't expect to be treated like royalty. There is a kitchenette and a bar and everything." She turned around to look at Mia. "Can I live here? Because it's much nicer than any apartment I've ever rented."

"The village homes are just as nice if not nicer. I mean the compound. Some call it the village."

"It sounds better." Frankie sat on the super-comfy couch and didn't even try to stifle her delighted moan. "When you said compound, I imagined a dreary place with a big wall around it. Village makes it sound like a place full of greenery."

"It is." Mia smiled.

As a knock sounded on the door, Mia beat Frankie to it and opened up for Tom.

"Hi, sweetheart." He leaned down and kissed her on the lips.

Frankie rose to her feet and looked the other way, admiring the view from her balcony.

When the couple was done with their amorous greeting, she walked over to Tom and kissed his cheek.

"Thank you for inviting me and for everything else."

Dagor

"What kind of a name is the Silver Swan?" Dagor grumbled as he, his teammates, and Gabi walked up to the cruise ship, dragging their luggage behind them.

The ship was small compared to the others docked next to it, looking almost like a yacht next to the giant floating hotels that could accommodate thousands of guests.

"What's wrong with Silver Swan?" Gabi gave him a reproaching look. "I think it's a very nice name."

He shrugged. "I'm not a fan of ships."

"You're not a fan of anything," Negal said. "I don't think I've ever heard you get excited about anything other than a piece of tech to disassemble and reassemble."

"I find it interesting to take things apart and see how they work because I didn't get to do that on Anumati. Besides, you are one to preach. What do you get excited about besides a nice pair of legs?"

Negal shrugged. "To each his own. I have my hobbies, and you have yours."

The dock appeared nearly deserted, with Kian's redheaded guard waiting for them at the bottom of the gangway, while other Guardians were trying to blend in and look inconspicuous.

"Welcome to the Silver Swan." Anandur offered Gabi his hand. "It's her maiden voyage under the new name."

"Hi." Gabi put her small hand inside the guy's huge paw. "What was her name before?"

"It's a secret." Anandur winked. "Let's get you people inside. We are operating on a tight schedule."

Dagor looked behind him to see if there were any other passengers, but the four of them were the only ones. "Is Gabi's family already on board?"

"Yes, they are, and you can go see them later, but first, I need you to get settled in your suite."

Great, so they were sharing a suite again.

Hopefully, there was a lounge chair on the top deck and a bar, so he and Negal would have a place to escape and leave Aru and Gabi to their honeymooning.

When they entered the spacious elevator, Anandur pressed the button for deck number six.

"We figured that you would want to be together, so we put you in one suite, but if that's not convenient, we might be able to find accommodations for the bachelors on the lower decks."

"How good is the soundproofing on this ship?" Negal asked.

"Excellent. It belongs to the clan, and it's built for immortals."

As the door opened, Anandur walked out, and the four of them followed.

"Is everyone on board immortal?" Gabi asked.

"Not everyone." Anandur stopped next to a suite marked with the number 608. "The crew is human, including the captain and his officers, the servers, the cooks, and the maids. A few guests are human too, but there's only one who does not know about us." He typed in a code and opened the door. "We are going to thrall everyone who is not supposed to know about gods and immortals at the end of the cruise to forget any peculiarities they might notice, so you should feel free to be yourselves, but if you can limit using the terms gods and immortals to when you are in the company of people you know, that would be helpful. The fewer memories we need to suppress, the better."

Dagor looked around the suite and had to admit that he was impressed. It wasn't big, but it was very nicely decorated and had all the amenities, including a small kitchen and a bar stocked full of various liquor bottles.

"Do you want me to give you the tour?" Anandur asked.

"I think we can figure it out." Aru rubbed the back of his neck. "So, what's next? Is Kian going to come over and say hello? Are we meeting with everyone for dinner? We weren't given an itinerary."

"The welcome dinner is at seven-thirty in the evening, and it includes everyone. You can look up the itinerary on the cruise channel." He pointed at the large screen. "Right now, we are getting everyone on board and settled. If you are hungry, there is food in the refrigerator, or you can call room service." He pointed to the phone on the coffee table. "If you want to call Kian, you can use the clan phone you were given, but he's a little busy right now, so perhaps a text message would be better."

"Of course." Aru nodded.

"Okay then." Anandur flashed them a bright smile. "Get comfortable, nap, or sit on the balcony, and I'll see you all later."

After Anandur left, Gabi opened the door to one of the bedrooms and walked inside. "That's the master. We are taking this one."

Dagor looked at the other door and groaned. "We are sharing a room again."

"Let's just hope that there are two beds." Negal clapped him on the back and kept walking toward the other door.

"I'm not sharing a bed with you. I'd rather take Anandur up on his offer to find me a place below decks."

As nice as the suite was, privacy was priceless.

"We have two beds," Negal said from inside the room. "Come take a look."

"I'll take your word for it." Dagor had no intention of staying in the suite until dinner. "I'm going to explore."

Frankie

After Mia and Tom left, Frankie unpacked, hung her dresses in the closet, and watched television on the living room's big screen.

Sometime during the show, an announcement came on about a welcome dinner at seven-thirty that evening, but that was more than three hours from now, and although there were snacks in the fridge and plenty of drinks to tide her over until then, she was bored and a little hungry.

If Margo were with her, they would have been having drinks on the balcony, munching on the snacks, or better yet, looking for hot dudes to flirt with at the bar.

What was stopping her from doing it on her own?

"Absolutely nothing."

Well, flirting with strangers on her own without her bestie's backup wasn't something Frankie was comfortable with. Still, she could explore and mark potentials for when Margo joined them in Cabo.

She stopped to check her makeup at the entry mirror, smoothed a few flyaway strands, and dotted her wrists with fresh drops of perfume.

After closing the door, she used the camera on her phone to take a picture of the suite number so she wouldn't forget it and trotted down the corridor toward the elevators.

No noises were coming through the doors she was passing by. It would have been completely quiet if not for the soft ambient instrumental music playing on the loud-speakers.

Was everyone taking an afternoon nap, or had no one on her deck arrived yet?

Shaking her head, she called for the elevator. When it arrived and the doors started to open, Frankie plastered a smile on her face, expecting to see people inside, but it was just as empty as the corridor.

Had she stepped into *The Twilight Zone*?

Where was everybody?

Perhaps she should call Mia and ask her to come up to the upper deck and join her for a drink. Hopefully, the bar was open for business, and Frankie wasn't the only one seeking the company of other human beings.

Nah, Mia and Tom were probably resting, and if Mia came, Tom would too, and as much as Frankie liked the guy's generosity and what he was doing for Mia, she found him too stiff and standoffish even when he was trying to be friendly.

He was also too gorgeous to be human, and it was unnerving to look at him.

Who would have thought looking at an unnaturally beautiful guy would be disturbing? But it was.

Frankie's type was the guy next door, someone with a friendly smile who was good with his hands, mowed his lawn, and could build a swing set or a new deck.

In short, she wanted a man like her father, just a little better looking. Not that her dad hadn't been handsome when he was young, but he was on the shorter side, and she had a thing for tall guys. It was nature's way to ensure balance. A tall guy would counterbalance her short genes, so their kids would be average height.

Did it work that way, though?

She remembered learning about dominant and recessive genes in high school, but that had been long ago, and she had forgotten most of what she'd been taught.

Heck, where had the time gone?

It seemed like only yesterday she was starting college and had her whole life ahead of her. She'd blinked and was twenty-seven, still single, still struggling financially, and her family considered her an old spinster because all of her cousins had been married by the age of twenty-four.

She really needed a drink now.

Exiting the elevator on the top deck, Frankie walked over to the sliding glass doors that led to the outdoors, and as they swished open, she let out a relieved sigh.

She'd feared that, with her luck, the doors would be locked.

The ship was still docked, but most passengers had yet to arrive or were holed up in their cabins because no one was there.

Not ready to give up yet, Frankie headed to what looked like a bar, given the barstools and tables. It wasn't closed, but it didn't seem like anyone was tending it.

Still, she walked until she was at the counter and almost fainted when a robotic metal head popped up and smiled at her. "Good afternoon, mistress. It is my pleasure to serve you. What would you like?"

Her hand resting on her racing heart, she let out a breath. "You scared me. You shouldn't pop up like that and startle people."

She'd seen a robot serving cappuccinos in a coffee shop in Seattle, but there had been a big sign outside warning customers before they got inside that their barista would be a robot.

Also, the robot in the coffee shop looked like it had been modeled after something other than C-3PO from *Star Wars*, just with more arms.

The robot frowned, which looked very odd on his metallic face. "My apologies, mistress. I will do better in the future. What can I serve you?"

"A mojito, please."

"With pleasure. Would you like the passion fruit mojito, the mango, or the classic?"

"Classic, please."

"Coming right up."

The robot swiveled on its axis, and its long robotic arms reached for the required ingredients. All four of them.

Watching him prepare the drink with all the flair she would have expected from an experienced bartender was fascinating.

Was it a *him*, though?

The voice was male, and the face its creators had given it was male, too, but it had four arms, so 'they' might be more appropriate.

"Here you go, mistress." One of his four hands placed a napkin on the bar counter while another put the drink on top. "Would you like something to snack on with your drink?"

"Sure. What do you have?"

"We have peanuts, pretzels, and assorted nuts."

"Can I have all three? I'm a little hungry."

"Of course, mistress." He swiveled his robotic torso again, and three of his four arms filled small containers from the dispensers.

"Do you have a name?" Frankie blurted out.

The robot grinned. "I do. It's Bob."

She stifled the giggles that were about to escape her mouth.

Was that a joke?

"Nice to meet you, Bob. I'm Frankie. Can I ask you something?"

"You can ask me anything, mistress, but my ability to answer is limited by my programming."

"I understand. I'm curious if Bob is short for Robert or whether it has another meaning."

"I do not know, mistress. That is the name I was given by my creators."

Dagor

~~~~~~~~~~~~~~~~~~~~

Sprawled on a lounger with his back to the bar, Dagor stifled a chuckle. The exchange between the woman named Frankie and the robot named Bob was most amusing, but he didn't wish to startle her.

The poor woman had enough of a scare when Bob popped up from behind the bar, and her heartbeat was only now returning to normal.

She hadn't noticed him, which was how he preferred things to remain.

He hadn't come up here to socialize. He'd wanted to drink alone and ponder his uninspiring future. However, discovering Bob had perked him up a little, giving him food for thought.

The robot was much more advanced than anything he'd seen humans produce, and he suspected that it had been built by the immortals. Their technological know-how in cybertronics seemed superior, and although it was primitive compared to Anumati's, it was still more than he knew. He was very much interested in learning from them.

Since it looked like Dagor's dreams of saving up enough credits to attend one of Anumati's engineering schools were not going to materialize for the next millennium, or maybe ever, he should learn what he could from the immortals and perhaps even work with them to further develop their technology.

Besides, if he was honest with himself, his chances of passing the entry exams were slim, even if he could return as planned and have enough to pay for the tuition. The elite ensured commoners did not have access to the schools that prepared the best for higher education.

Supposedly, Anumati was a democracy, and no god was barred from achieving the highest station regardless of who their parents were. Still, in reality, the elite was an impenetrable clique of those with royal blood and old riches.

The best a commoner could hope for was one of the lower-tier schools that prepared workers for lower-tier positions.

"Oh, I didn't see you there." The woman startled him. "Do you mind if I sit here?"

The voice belonged to Bob's only customer, Frankie, but with the blazing sun behind her blinding Dagor, all he could see was a dark silhouette. Shielding his eyes with his hand and squinting, he tried to see more than the outline of her petite body, but the sun's glare made it nearly impossible.

Not that he cared what she looked like. He hadn't come up here to flirt, and she was encroaching on his private time.

"You can sit anywhere you want. This is not my ship."

There were at least thirty other loungers, and she could have chosen to sit anywhere else on the deck.

Why the hell did she have to sit next to him and disturb his peace?

Well, that was obvious.

Human females found his godly features appealing and weren't bashful about approaching him, Negal, and Aru. He could usually deter them with a scowl, but a squint was not a scowl, and it was hard to do anything else with the damn sunshine blinding him.

He should have brought his sunglasses, but he'd forgotten.

"Someone is grumpy," she murmured as she walked away.

Dagor felt like an ass, and when she sat down on the last lounger in the row, he sighed. "I'm sorry if I offended you. It wasn't my intention."

"I get it. You just want to be left alone." She lifted her drink in a salute, took a sip, and reclined while crossing her legs.

Maybe he'd been mistaken, and she hadn't planned on flirting with him after all. Even squinting, he still couldn't see her clearly, but he could tell that she had shapely legs and wore shoes with enormous square heels.

How could she even walk in those things?

Was she really that tiny?

Curiosity getting the better of him, he pushed to his feet and walked over to her.

Now that he had his back to the sun, he finally got to see the little pixie, and she was lovelier than he'd expected. She had a pert little nose, pouty lips painted with bright lipstick, and a compact figure that still had all the required feminine curves.

A discreet sniff confirmed what he'd suspected, though. She wasn't an immortal. She was human, and Anandur's instructions had been to avoid mentioning gods and immortals unless necessary.

"Hi," he said. "May I sit next to you?"

She pursed her lips. "I don't own this deck, so you can sit anywhere."

He chuckled. "Touché. I'm Doug." He crouched next to her and offered her his hand. "Doug Farkash." He introduced himself with the name on his fake identity, which was what he usually did with humans.

"Frankie." She looked at his hand as if it was going to bite her. "My hands are wet from the condensation on the glass, so I'll skip the handshaking."

"As you wish." He dropped his hand on his thigh.

He didn't mind that her hand was damp, but she seemed reluctant, and he wasn't going to insist. Instead, he pushed up and sat on the lounger next to her, cradling his drink and trying to come up with something clever to say.

"Is Farkash a Yugoslavian name?" she asked, saving him the trouble. "I've never heard that name before, but it sounds Eastern European."

"It's Hungarian."

"You don't sound Hungarian." She chuckled. "Not that I know what Hungarian sounds like. What I meant to say was that you sound American."

Dagor was thankful for the gods' ability to absorb languages effortlessly. Having a universal translator helped make the process even faster. Still, their innate ability allowed them to master the nuances of accents so they could sound like natives wherever they were.

"My grandparents were from Hungary." That was another lie that worked well. If she asked him about them, he would say they were dead.

As a long silence stretched between them, he tried to come up with another topic of conversation that did not involve his fake Hungarian roots.

Anandur had said something about the staff being comprised of humans, so maybe she was one of them and on a break. However, given her shoes, she probably worked in accounting or something else that did not require extensive standing or walking.

She also wasn't wearing a uniform, but since Dagor had yet to see any staff or guests, he didn't know whether the service crew even had uniforms. After all, it was a private cruise for clan members, so things might be more casual and relaxed, and no identifying attire was needed for the humans.

"Are you a staff member?" he asked.

Frankie

Doug's question cut through Frankie like a knife.

Was it that obvious that she didn't belong as a guest on this fancy cruise? Was everyone working for Perfect Match so loaded that their outfits were from Nordstrom, Saks, or some other fancy place?

That wasn't likely.

The most logical explanation was that Doug knew everyone who worked there, and since he didn't recognize her, he assumed she was a crew member.

With how gorgeous he was, his job was probably modeling for the creators of the male avatars. She wouldn't mind beta-testing an adventure with an avatar modeled on him, but in real life she would never go for a guy who was so much prettier than her.

"I don't work here." She waved a hand over the deck. "Tom promised me a job at the new Perfect Match testing lab as soon as the machines are ready, but there have been so many delays that I almost despaired of ever working there." She smiled. "I've been waiting for that position to open up for months, and I can't wait to start. It's so exciting."

Doug stared at her as if he had no clue what she was talking about.

Had she been mistaken about his part in the company? Everyone probably brought their significant others on the cruise, and Doug could be the trophy husband of one of the silent partners Tom had talked about. But hadn't he said that they were a married couple?

Not that it excluded him being a third partner.

Who knew?

A wealthy married couple could have a live-in lover boy to play with.

"Who is Tom?" Doug asked.

The guy must be as dumb as he was gorgeous. Even if he didn't work for Perfect Match, he should at least know who was hosting the cruise.

"He's one of the owners of the company. How come you don't know him?"

He still looked perplexed. "What company? Are you still talking about those virtual matchmaking studios?"

"Well, duh." She waved a hand. "This is a company cruise. All the guests are involved with the company in one way or another." As it occurred to her that he might not belong, she narrowed her eyes at him. "Are you a stowaway?"

That was not likely, given the tight security. Still, given his question, maybe he'd asked her if she was a staff member because he was a stowaway?

"I'm not a stowaway. I was invited."

"By whom?"

"Kian."

"Oh." Tom and Mia had mentioned asking someone named Kian if it was okay to invite her and Margo on the cruise. The guy must be Tom's silent partner or perhaps his assistant or manager. "How do you know Kian?"

Doug grimaced. "We are very remote cousins, and we have just discovered that we are related. We hope to get better acquainted during this cruise."

That explained why he knew nothing about Perfect Match, but she wondered why mentioning his distant cousin had made him grimace.

"That sounds lovely, and it was very nice of Kian to invite you. Why the face, though?"

He arched one dark brow. "What face?"

"The grumpy face." She waved a tiny hand with perfectly manicured nails over him. "Going on a cruise with newly discovered family should be exciting."

He shrugged. "I'm not the cheerful sort. In fact, my friends accuse me of always being a grouch."

Frankie didn't buy it. "Is there bad blood between you and your distant family?"

He shook his head. "I don't mind getting to know my relatives, but I'm unhappy about the cruise. I'm not a fan of deep water, and I also don't like sharing a cabin with my other two cousins, especially since one of them is newly engaged. He and his fiancée are in the honeymooning stage if you know what I mean."

Frankie laughed. "I do, and I envy you. It's awesome to be around people who are in love. Their happiness is infectious, and it brings good luck." She leaned over and pretended to whisper. "You might soon fall in love yourself."

"Fates, I hope not."

She frowned. "Why not? Being in love is the best thing in the world. We all live for the moment we find that one special person."

"I don't." He lifted his legs onto the lounger and reclined. "Love complicates things."

It wasn't a big surprise that a guy like him was not interested in a meaningful relationship. He could have anyone he wanted, so why choose to be stuck with just one person?

Frankie closed her lips around the straw and slurped the dregs of her mojito. "I wonder if Bob can serve drinks poolside." She turned to Doug. "Do you know if he is stationary or mobile?"

"I don't, but I can find out." He sat back up and extended his hand, reaching for her empty glass. "Do you want the same drink or something else?"

"Another mojito would be lovely, thank you."

"It's my pleasure." He dipped his head before pushing to his feet.

Frankie watched Doug walk over to the bar, admiring his tight backside.

The guy was a dream, but only looks-wise. He was emotionally stunted and vacillated between being borderline rude and overly polite.

Heck, she wasn't even sure that he liked girls.

Still, when she fantasized about Doug later tonight, she would pretend that he was into her and that they were having a fabulous time between the sheets in a Perfect Match adventure environment of her choosing. Better yet, she could create a new one just for the two of them.

Dagor

As Dagor walked over to the bar, there was a lightness to his step that he hadn't felt for the longest time.

Frankie was entertaining, and she was beautiful in a very human way.

He liked that she took great care with her appearance, and everything about her was polished to perfection, from her hair to her nails and everything she wore.

But what he liked most was that her blue eyes were full of life.

Yes, that was it. That was what he found most charming about her. She looked like someone who was upbeat by nature and didn't take things too seriously. She could be a perfect fling companion for this cruise and an antidote to boredom.

"What can I serve you, master?" Bob asked with a smile on his shiny metallic face.

"The lady you served earlier is wondering whether you can serve drinks poolside or are you confined to the bar."

"I am free to move around, master. Shall I bring you both new drinks?"

"Yes, please. Frankie wants another mojito, and I wouldn't mind another serving of the superb Japanese whiskey you suggested. Can I snatch a photo of the bottle? I would like to order some for myself."

"Of course, master." The robot reached for the bottle with his long arm and put it on the counter before Dagor.

"Tell me something, Bob," Dagor said while snapping a picture. "Do you have a record of everyone on board?"

"Naturally, master. I have the roster but don't have pictures attached to the names." He smiled again. "I am learning, though. Eventually, everyone will stop for a drink, and I will put their face next to their name on the roster."

"Who is your creator?"

The robot did an excellent job of mimicking a frown. "I have many creators. It takes more than one person to build a Bob."

"Are there more of you?"

"Not at the moment. I am a prototype. If I prove successful, more of me will be built." The robot froze momentarily as if listening to instructions and then smiled again.

"I shall bring the drinks to you and Mistress Frankie." He turned around.

Someone must be monitoring Bob's interactions with people, and whoever that was had realized that they should have better safeguarded what he could say and to whom.

When Dagor returned to Frankie's side, he was greeted with such a strong scent of female arousal that he was nearly knocked off his feet.

Had she been talking to a paramour while he was ordering drinks for them?

It was her right to do so, but it annoyed him for some reason. The reason was that he'd had plans for her, and if she was involved with someone, she wouldn't be open to spending the night with him.

"Bob will bring us the drinks." He sat back on the lounger.

Frankie uttered a throaty chuckle. "Since you walked over there, you could have brought the drinks already."

He arched a brow. "I thought that you were curious to see Bob serving drinks away from the bar, and the truth is that I'm curious, too."

As a whizzing sound announced Bob's approach, they both turned to look over their shoulders at the robot.

His torso was attached to a trapezoid base that moved on wheels, not legs. He held their drinks in two of his hands and bowls of snacks in the other two.

The body was crude for such a sophisticated artificial intelligence, and Dagor wondered whether it had been done on purpose. Humans were still wary of robots that looked and acted too much like them, and he couldn't blame them.

Even the gods realized that machines shouldn't be given humanoid features.

"Your drink, Mistress Frankie." Bob offered her the mojito. "And the whiskey for the master." He handed Dagor his. "I also brought more snacks." He smiled at Frankie. "In case the mistress is still peckish."

"Thank you." Frankie gave Bob a dazzling smile that went straight to Dagor's groin.

He'd been in trouble from the moment he had scented her arousal and tried not to respond because it hadn't been for him, but that smile was like throwing gasoline on a raging fire.

"Thank you, Bob. That will be all," Dagor said.

The robot bobbed his head in a way that was too similar to Kian's Odu, and then whizzed away.

"You were rude," Frankie said. "Bob was being nice."

"Bob is a machine, and he does what he is programmed to do. He's not a person, and he doesn't have feelings."

"Still, no reason to be rude." Frankie closed her lips around the straw, and Dagor felt his fangs starting to elongate.

"Excuse me for a moment." He put his drink down, pushed to his feet, and walked to the men's room.

Usually, he had better control over his reactions.

Back home, flashing fangs was considered bad manners, and on Earth, it was dangerous and required thralling whoever happened to see them. Being in control of such a reaction was second nature to Dagor, but Frankie had an odd effect on him, and he couldn't understand why.

She was pretty, but he had met prettier, and her compact body was curvy in all the right ways. Still, he had come from the planet of the gods, where every goddess was perfect in every way.

He was immune to physical beauty.

Frankie was entertaining in her directness, but again, that was no reason for him to react like a boy who had just discovered the wonders of sex.

After several long breaths and a splash of cold water on his face, Dagor felt composed enough to return to Frankie and discover what made her different from all the other females he had ever encountered.

Frankie

Something wasn't right about Doug. Why had he bolted like that? Because she'd told him that he was being rude?

Eh, whatever.

There was no reason to agonize over his peculiar reaction.

Frankie had already relegated the guy to the realm of dreams, where everything was possible. She could make him into Prince Charming or a bad boy mafioso with a heart of gold, depending on her mood.

It was a shame that real men couldn't be programmed to act according to her whims.

Closing her eyes, Frankie imagined a Bob who didn't look like the bartender aboard the Silver Swan, but like a real flesh and blood handsome guy, who could be whoever she wanted him to be and get out of her hair when she didn't want him around. No girl would ever want the real thing if there was a robot like that.

Well, except for procreation, but that could be managed with artificial insemination from donors.

Yeah, but children needed fathers, and she doubted a robot could be a good substitute. She couldn't imagine growing up without her dad's bear hugs, silly jokes, and the one-liners from movies that she and her brothers pretended to be sick of but secretly loved.

Frankie had a great family, and she would miss them when she moved into the secret compound of the eccentric owners of Perfect Match.

She would probably meet them on this cruise, and how exciting was that?

She had a strong feeling that her life would finally get on track, and if it meant that she couldn't see her family so often, she could deal with that.

As the saying went, nothing ventured, nothing gained. In other words, good things require giving up other good things or suffering through bad ones.

The universe demanded a balanced ledger.

"I'm back." The lounger next to her groaned as Doug lowered his big body onto it. "Sorry about earlier. I must have eaten something that didn't agree with me."

Oh, so that was why he'd been so grumpy. No one was in a good mood when they needed to pass gas, especially when trying to impress a girl.

Had he been trying to impress her, though?

If he had, he had a strange way of going about it.

"Do you feel better now?" she asked.

"Yes, much. Thank you for asking."

She chuckled. "I wondered why you were Mr. Grumpy one minute and Mr. Polite the next. Your tummy has been bothering you on and off."

Nodding, he leaned over to the side table and picked up his drink. "Now that I feel better, I remember you thought this cruise was for Perfect Match employees. What made you think that?"

She tilted her head. "It isn't?"

"Not as far as I know."

"So, who is it for?"

"I think it's mostly Kian's family and friends."

So, Kian was the name of the secret partner. He was the guy whom Tom had called to ask if he could bring her and Margo along, so it made sense.

"Yeah, well, he and his wife own half of Perfect Match Virtual Fantasy Studios, so it might be a combined event."

"I didn't know that." Doug finished his drink and put it on the side table. "I've seen the ads on television. Is the experience as good as they claim?"

"I've never done it myself, but I hear it's amazing." Frankie took a long slurp of her mojito and dove into telling Doug about Tom and Mia falling in love in a Perfect Match adventure. She omitted the part about Mia regrowing her legs because she wasn't supposed to tell anyone about it, but she told him about the Swiss heart clinic Tom had taken Mia to and the miracle treatment she'd received there. "That's why Tom bought half of Perfect Match. He wanted them to have access to it whenever they wanted."

"That sounds very romantic. I might have to try one of those adventures and see for myself."

"They are very costly." Frankie sighed. "That's why I wanted to become a beta tester for the adventures and help Mia develop new ones. There was no way I could afford them on what I was making as a glorified secretary."

He frowned. "I was not aware of a position titled glorified secretary. How is it different from a regular secretary?"

Was he teasing her?

He seemed perfectly serious, though. How was it possible that he had never heard that expression?

"An executive assistant is a glorified title for a secretary, and that was my job until two weeks ago. I'm supposed to start working for Perfect Match after the cruise. I assumed that all the employees were here, so I couldn't start right away, but that was silly of me. There is no way that all the studios worldwide are closed for ten days so every employee can be here. It must be just the company's top executives with a few key employees, and they are the only ones who can handle hiring new people."

Dagor

Interesting. So, the clan of immortals was involved with the Perfect Match Studios. Given the amount of advertising on network television and cable, it was a successful enterprise, and the clan was making a lot of money. The question was whether they used Anumatian technology to create the interface.

When Dagor had seen the ads, he'd dismissed Perfect Match as an overhyped multiplayer video game that was also trying to be a matchmaking service. But if the clan contributed advanced programming to the enterprise, it could be all that it promised to be.

On Anumati, entertainment of this kind was trendy, but no one expected to find their perfect match there. It was pure escapism and didn't require being hooked up to the contraptions he'd seen in those ads. It was as simple as crossing a threshold and stepping into the virtual world. Every patrol ship had several rooms that provided entertainment during the long intervals of travel between planets.

Stasis was practical for the extended period of time required for travel from Anumati to the sector the patrol ship was about to cover and for the return trip. However, it wasn't practical while they were actually performing the duty of checking on the different planets the gods had seeded in that sector.

"Doug? Is your stomach bothering you again?" Frankie looked at him with genuine worry in her expressive blue eyes.

"I'm sorry. I didn't realize that I had zoned out." He smiled to reassure her that he didn't have stomach issues. "I'm fine."

"What were you thinking about?" she asked.

"About Perfect Match and wanting to try out an adventure. Would you like to go on one with me?"

If she said no, he would know that there was someone else, but if she said maybe, a committed relationship was not a factor. He could initiate a hookup for tonight.

"I don't know." Her heartbeat accelerated. "We've just met, and as you know, those adventures are romantic. Also, I can't afford it unless we can beta test for the company. The sessions cost nearly four thousand dollars."

That was so expensive that most people couldn't afford it.

"Does it cost that much per person or per couple?"

"Per person. They might offer a discount to a couple wanting to join an adventure, but I'm not sure they do."

He could ask Aru for the funds. They'd come to Earth with a stash of pure diamonds that was worth enough to cover several centuries of living expenses for the three of them, and then Aru had also found a side hustle they could do while looking for the Kra-ell pods, and they'd made money on that. Still, they couldn't throw it around like they had an endless supply of it.

"It's probably too rich for my wallet too." He turned on his side and smiled at her. "If they let us beta test, what kind of adventure would you like to experience?"

"Space pirates," she answered without having to think about it. "Then the mer underwater adventure."

"Mer? Like mermaids?"

"Like mer people. I could go for a merman prince."

He frowned. "Aren't they supposed to have fish tails?"

"Yeah, so?"

"You said that the adventures are romantic in nature. How are they supposed to, you know...?"

She arched a brow. "Have sex?"

"Yeah."

"How do dolphins have sex? They are mammals, and all mammals have sex more or less the same way."

"I know that. But it's weird. Count me out for the mer adventure."

"How about the space pirates?" Frankie's breath hitched, and the scent of her arousal flared.

"I would love that one." He reached for her hand, and he smiled when she didn't pull it away. "Perhaps we could start planning it tonight. From what I understand, a lot of customization goes into those adventures."

She swallowed. "That's true. Mia spent hours filling out the questionnaire and drawing her avatar. She was very beautiful in her adventure. She's also beautiful in real life, but she had those cute pointy ears in the virtual world, and she jokes that they were the reason Tom fell in love with her."

"I'm sure her physical beauty was just a small part of the attraction." He leaned over and kissed the back of her hand softly. "It's what's inside that matters the most."

She chuckled throatily. "Says the guy who looks like a god."

Did Frankie know about gods and immortals?

That would make his life so much easier.

"I am a god, and all gods and goddesses are beautiful. That is why I can say with authority that physical beauty is not reason enough to fall in love with someone."

Frankie laughed. "You certainly have an ego, but I don't blame you. If I looked like you, I would have an enormous ego as well."

It seemed he'd been wrong, and Frankie didn't know about gods. Luckily, she'd thought that he'd been boasting or teasing.

He'd also failed to reassure her that he found her attractive, which could give her reason to refuse his invitation.

"I was just joking about the god thing, but I was serious about beauty not being reason enough for falling in love. I don't mind that you are gorgeous, though, and I'm still very interested, so how about it? Do we have a date for tonight?"

Frankie looked at him as if she was trying to gaze into his soul, and after a long moment, she nodded. "It's a cruise, and I'm supposed to have fun, so why not." She pulled out her phone. "Give me your number. I'll call you if I'm not too tired after dinner tonight. I don't know what they offer regarding entertainment, but maybe we can go dancing or something."

Was she being coy?

"I'm sure we can come up with ways to entertain ourselves with just the two of us for company." He gave her a pointed look.

Frankie chuckled. "Usually, I would ask your place or mine, but since you have roommates and I don't, I guess it will have to be my place." She looked at him from under lowered lashes. "We can listen to music, watch a movie, or talk."

Was she teasing him?

He could peek into her mind and get his answer, but what would be the fun in that? It would also be an invasion of privacy that he found abhorrent.

"How come you have a suite to yourself?"

"It's only until my bestie joins the cruise in Cabo."

"Your bestie? You mean your best friend?"

"Yeah. Margo, Mia, and I have been best friends since childhood. Margo is also going to be a beta tester for Perfect Match."

"I see." He leaned closer and tried to inhale her intoxicating scent as inconspicuously as possible. "Tell me more about the space pirates' adventure. What is it all about?"

Annani

"I'm nervous." Alena lowered herself onto the couch.

Her pregnant belly was quite evident by now, making sitting down and standing up a little more difficult.

"Why are you nervous?" Sari asked. "Are you worried about Carol and Lokan getting here tonight?"

Alena chuckled. "I completely forgot about that, and I'm not worried about them. I think they are being extra cautious, and that's a good thing. I'm nervous about the wedding."

"It's just a ceremony." Sari waved a dismissive hand. "It doesn't change anything between you and Orion. You are fated mates."

Annani gazed lovingly at her four daughters—the three she had birthed and the one she had acquired through her son's marriage. As soon as Sari arrived and settled in her suite, Annani invited all four for an afternoon tea. It was not often that she got to enjoy all of them at once.

While the ladies were having tea, Kian treated their mates to cigars on his and Syssi's balcony. Syssi's parents had Allegra, and Evie was in the hands of the clan's two young babysitters, Lisa and Cheryl, with Onidu on standby in case the girls needed help.

Alena rubbed her belly. "Orion and I are going first, which means our wedding will have the most blunders. It doesn't matter to me, but it does to Orion. I don't want him to be disappointed."

"He won't be." Syssi leaned over and patted her shoulder. "I'm more worried about whether you'll still fit into your wedding dress. Have you tried it on lately?"

Alena's wedding cruise had been postponed many times. In the meantime, the baby in her belly kept growing, so there was a good chance that the dress she had commissioned two months ago might not fit.

"It fits." Alena smiled. "I tried it this morning before packing it. It's so loose that I could get married the day my water breaks. I wasn't taking any chances."

"That's good to know." Amanda crossed her legs and put her hands on her knees. "I'm not nervous about my wedding, but poor Dalhu is. You know how he hates being the center of attention."

"He won't be." Syssi shifted her eyes to Annani. "All eyes will be on the Clan Mother, which brings the issue of tonight's welcome dinner to mind. How are you going to handle it?"

Annani frowned. "What do you mean?"

"You will need to shroud yourself from the human crew and staff."

"Kian has not said anything to that effect, and I do not see a reason to hide who I am while celebrating with my family. The crew and staff will get their memories altered at the end of the cruise."

Syssi nodded. "That's true, but perhaps we should let them gradually get accustomed to your presence. Otherwise, we will have broken dishes and spilled food everywhere."

Amanda snorted. "These humans lived with the Kra-ell, and in my opinion, the purebloods look much stranger than a glowing goddess. It won't be as shocking to them as you expect it to be."

Annani lifted her hand. "I am willing to suppress my glow when I enter the dining hall, and I can keep it down until the food is served. Once that is done, the doors can be closed, and the staff will be told not to come in. I will only release my glow when they are no longer present."

"The glow is not the only thing giving you away," Syssi said. "Your beauty and the way you dress are also pretty conspicuous."

"What do you suggest, Syssi, that I eat alone in my suite?"

"Of course not." Syssi recoiled. "But maybe we can dress you in something more contemporary and braid your hair. That will somewhat diminish the impact."

"I will do no such thing. This is my family, my clan, and I will present myself to them how they are accustomed. I will not make compromises to accommodate the humans."

"Eating in your suite this first evening is not a bad idea," Amanda said. "Did you forget about the three gods you want to meet? If they see you at dinner, you will lose the element of surprise. Your options are to meet them before dinner, which leaves you little time, or eat in your suite tonight and schedule the meeting for tomorrow.

Annani did not want to stay in her suite while her family gathered in the dining hall. It was a shame she would have to cut short her tea time with her daughters, though.

"I will call Kian immediately and tell him to get the gods here as soon as possible. You are welcome to stay and witness the meeting."

Sari and Amanda exchanged glances with Alena and Syssi, and then all four nodded.

"We will stay," Amanda said. "Although it might get crowded here with our mates and all the Guardians Kian will bring to protect you."

"We will manage." Annani pulled out her phone.

Kian

"Everyone who is supposed to be on board is here already." Anandur looked up from his tablet. "We can set sail."

"Inform the captain," Kian said.

"Will do, boss."

As Anandur walked back inside, Orion leaned against the railing and tapped the ash from his cigar into the water. "This is your first time on the ship, right?"

Kian nodded. "I was supposed to be on her maiden voyage, but then the Kra-ell needed rescuing, and her first passengers included a flock of sheep and goats." He grimaced. "I was afraid they would never be able to get rid of the smell, but thankfully, the restoration contractor brought her back to her pristine condition. We changed her name, though, so you can say that it's her maiden voyage as the Silver Swan."

"It was the Aurora before." Anandur closed the balcony door behind him to prevent the smoke from entering the cabin. "I liked that name—the goddess of the dawn. The Silver Swan has a negative connotation."

Kian wasn't aware of it. The only comment he'd gotten so far about the name was that it was also the name of a soy sauce. "What's the connotation?"

Anandur lifted one bushy red brow. "Don't you ever read comics? The Silver Swan is Wonder Woman's adversary. Wonder got upset when she saw the name, but I told her that you probably didn't know when you renamed the ship."

"Of course, I didn't. I also didn't know that the two of you read comics."

The only thing that bothered him was that Wonder had gotten upset for no reason. When the new name for the ship had popped into his mind, Kian hadn't questioned it.

Anandur opened his mouth to say something, and closed it as Kian's phone chimed with the ringtone he'd assigned to his mother.

Pulling the device from his pocket, he answered, "Hello, Mother. How is the tea going?"

"We are enjoying a very pleasant afternoon, but your very clever mate made a most relevant suggestion about my meeting with the three gods. I cannot wait until tomorrow to meet them because they will see me tonight at dinner, and I will lose the element of surprise. If I want to see their response, it must happen today."

"That's less than two hours from now."

"I am well aware of the time constraints, but since you did not want me to meet them before the cruise, it will have to happen right now. You can invite them to my suite. Your mate and sisters want to witness the gods' reactions to me, and they asked me to let them stay. I suggest that you and my sons-in-law join us as well." She chuckled, and as always, the sound made the skin on his arms rise with goosebumps. "I will hold court in my suite, and you all can be my courtiers. The Guardians will be my royal guard."

"I see that you have given it a lot of thought."

His mother laughed. "Two minutes were enough to imagine a grand setting. It comes naturally to me."

"Yes, I know."

"We should also invite Toven. Aru and his teammates will immediately recognize him for who he is, so it would be better for him to attend the meeting as well."

"If Toven suppresses his glow, he could be mistaken for an immortal. He and Orion look practically the same."

Next to him, Orion made a face. "I'm not as perfectly made as my father. The differences are subtle, but they are there, and they are noticeable."

He had a point, but Kian needed to find out if Aru would notice. He'd said that Kian looked more like a god than an immortal, and combined with everything else he'd said, it was clear that not all gods were as perfect as Annani or even Toven.

"You are right. Toven should be there, and therefore Mia. Where are we going to fit everyone in?"

"Amanda and Sari are shoving furniture into the other rooms, or rather directing my Odus where to take what. Their idea is to leave only one armchair in the living room and for everyone else to stand."

"Or kneel!" Amanda yelled. "I don't want anyone looming over our mother."

"We can put the armchair on top of the coffee table and drape it with the bed cover," Syssi suggested. "It will make it look like a real throne."

Kian shook his head. "I will leave the decorating details to you and your army. I need to call Aru."

"Yes, please do. I will await them at six o'clock sharp."

"Yes, Mother."

"Thank you." As she ended the call, Kian put the phone in his pocket and turned to his future brothers-in-law and the Guardians. "Well, you heard the Clan Mother. You will all meet the new gods sooner than you expected."

"I can't wait." David looked at his half-smoked cigar. "I should have saved this for after the meeting."

"I'm glad that we are heading out of the harbor." Anandur rubbed the back of his neck. "We have one more guest who doesn't know about gods and immortals yet, and when she finds out during dinner tonight, she won't be able to escape the ship."

"Who are you talking about?" Dalhu asked.

"Ms. Francesca Canal. Mia's best friend and a potential Dormant."

Dagor

"You look happy." Gabi regarded Dagor with a critical appraisal. "What did you find out on your exploration of the ship?"

Dagor couldn't wipe the smile off his face, but he didn't want to share Frankie with Gabi or with his friends. It was nice to have someone who was just his, even if it was for one night. He had gone on way too many double and triple dates with his teammates.

"I discovered a bar on the top deck, got a drink, and lounged in the sun."

Gabi looked skeptical. "That must have been a very good drink."

"It was. I even took a picture of the bottle to order it for us later, but the bartender was the most interesting part about the top deck bar. It's a very sophisticated robot—a far cry from an Odu, but superior to the simple robots they have on other cruise liners."

The truth was that he had yet to learn about robots serving drinks on other ships. He'd found out about them by searching the internet on his way back to the cabin.

Over on the couch, Negal chuckled. "Some males get excited over meeting an interesting female. Dagor gets excited about meeting an interesting piece of machinery."

"Bob is very exciting." Dagor sat next to Negal on the couch.

"Bob?" Gabi chuckled. "They named him Bob?"

Frankie had reacted similarly to the name, and Dagor wondered what was so funny about it. He'd met many humans named Bob.

"Why do you find the name amusing?" he asked.

Gabi laughed, and her cheeks reddened. "Bob, as a guy's name, is not funny. It's only amusing when it's given to a machine."

"You still didn't explain why."

Letting out a breath, Gabi lifted her eyes to the ceiling. "BOB is also an acronym for a battery-operated boyfriend."

Dagor's eyes widened. "I was not aware that humans had invented such sophisticated lifelike pleasure robots. Where can I get my hands on one?"

Gabi's shoulders started shaking, and a moment later, she was laughing so hard that Dagor and Negal couldn't help

167

but join her even though they didn't understand what was so funny about the question.

When Aru entered the living room and saw the three of them laughing, he arched a brow. "What did I miss?"

It took Gabi several steadying breaths before she was able to talk. "I explained to Dagor what BOB stood for, and he asked me where he could get his hands on one."

Both of Aru's brows shot up. "Why are you interested in a female self-pleasuring device?"

"Gabi said that BOB means a battery-operated boyfriend. If humans have developed advanced robots like that, I would like to reverse engineer one."

"I see." Aru ran a hand over his mouth, and a moment later, his shoulders also started shaking. "Perhaps you should show him," he told Gabi between one snort and the next.

"No way. He can find a picture on the internet."

That was a good suggestion, and Dagor implemented it right away, pulling out his phone and typing his query into the search engine.

"Oh." He frowned as he read the description. "It's a very crude device. I'm surprised that it's so popular among Earth ladies."

Gabi shrugged. "You are welcome to develop a fully functional Bob like your bartender, who could do more than serve drinks."

"Why bother with a BOB? You already have a neural link virtual reality service that can give you a fully immersive experience inside your mind—no robots required."

"Yeah, but who can afford that, and who has time to spend three hours in a studio whenever they get the itch? BOBs are inexpensive toys that are available whenever they are needed." By the end of her explanation, Gabi was as red as a beetroot. "I can't believe that you made me say that." She cast an accusing look at Aru, turned around, walked into their bedroom, and closed the door behind her.

"You've embarrassed your mate," Negal said. "You should apologize."

"It wasn't me." Aru lifted his hands in the air. "It was Dagor."

"What did I say?" Dagor crossed his arms over his chest. "I just wanted to know why she was laughing. How was I supposed to know that it was a sensitive subject?"

Women, whether human or formerly human, were touchy about anything that had to do with sex, yet they pursued it with quite the determination.

Aru's clan phone rang, thankfully ending the Bob episode.

He pulled it out of his pocket. "Hello, Kian. I've noticed that we set sail. I think the customary thing to say is *bon voyage*, right?"

"Yes," the immortals' leader said in his gruff voice. "But I'm not calling to wish you safe travels. My mother informed me that she wants to meet you today at six o'clock sharp. You and your teammates need to be ready five minutes earlier. I'll send someone to escort you to her suite."

Aru swallowed audibly. "How should I dress for the meeting?"

"You are going to a formal dinner straight from there, so dress formally. I hope you and your men have gotten tuxedoes. We are celebrating ten weddings on this cruise."

"We did. Should we bring Gabi with us?"

"Of course. The Clan Mother would love to meet her."

Frankie

"You lucky girl," Margo squealed in Frankie's ear. "You've been on that cruise ship for what, three hours? And you scored a gorgeous guy already? How did you do it?"

"Luck, I guess. But I feel kind of iffy about it." Frankie thought about opening the doors to her balcony and stepping outside, but she didn't want anyone to overhear her talking about Doug. Instead, she sat on the couch, kicked off her shoes, and tucked her feet under her. "You know about my minimum of three dates rule. I don't do first-date hookups. But this is a cruise, and he's out-of-this-world gorgeous, so I decided to break my own rule, and now I feel guilty and a little scared. I don't know anything about him besides that he is a guest of Tom's partners. Aside from what he'd seen on television, he didn't know anything about Perfect Match. How could he be a good friend of the owners and not know more details about their business?"

"Frankie," Margo interrupted her tirade. "Take a deep breath and think. You are on a ship full of people. If this guy is not to your liking, throw him out, and if he refuses to leave, holler, and someone will help you to get rid of him."

Frankie snorted. "That's what you think. So far, I've seen the guards who checked my paperwork, Mia, Tom, and Doug. I haven't seen anyone else, and unless this place has the best soundproofing ever, I'm the only one on this deck. I feel like I am in *The Twilight Zone*, with elevator music playing in the hallways to entertain the ghosts."

There was a moment of silence before Margo let out a breath. "That is odd. Maybe the ship has great sound-proofing. With how reclusive and paranoid Tom's part-ners are, I wouldn't be surprised if they'd ordered a custom-made interior built to the highest privacy standards."

"That could be." Frankie looked around the beautifully decorated living room of her suite. "The ship is really luxurious. I can't wait for you to join me so I won't be alone in this suite. It has two bedrooms, a living room with a kitchenette and a bar, and it's bigger than my apartment."

"That's lovely, but I'm worried now," Margo said. "If Doug is an ax murderer, no one will even hear you scream."

Frankie grimaced. "Thanks for that visual. Now I'm never calling him to come over." She chuckled. "I'll stay loyal to Bob."

She proceeded to tell Margo about the robotic bartender. As the two of them were having a good laugh about it, the doorbell rang.

"Hold on. Someone rang my doorbell." Frankie pushed her feet into her platform shoes and trotted to the door.

After what Margo had said about no one hearing her scream, Frankie wouldn't open up without checking who was on the other side. Thankfully there was a peephole, only it wasn't installed with short people in mind, and even in her four-inch platform heels, she had to stretch up on her toes. "I swear. This country discriminates against shorties. We need to start an equal rights movement. And unless the person on the other side is as short as I am, a ghost just rang my bell."

"Maybe it's Mia," Margo said.

"Could be, but after you scared me with talk about ax murderers, I'm afraid to open the door."

As a buzzer sounded, Frankie's heart leaped into her throat before she realized it was an intercom and pressed the button. "Yes?"

"It's Mia, and I'm getting old waiting for you to open the door."

The relief made Frankie weak at the knees.

"Sorry. Hold on." She unlocked the door and opened the way for Mia. "Blame Margo. After I told her about how quiet it is here, we figured that the ship had good sound-proofing, and if I invited a guy to my suite and he turned out to be a creep, no one would hear me scream."

"Hi, Margo," Mia said loudly as she drove her wheelchair into the room. "How is Cabo?"

"Terrible," Margo said in Frankie's ear.

"Let me activate the speaker so Mia can hear you." She pressed the icon and propped the phone on the table. "Go ahead. Tell us why Cabo is terrible."

"It's not Cabo. It's Lynda and all her weirdo friends. They are all like her. It's amazing how many Karens there are."

Frankie chuckled. "I assume you don't mean they are all actually named Karen."

"Three of her nine friends are called Karen, and the rest just act as if they are, and they are not even middle-aged."

"You know how the saying goes," Mia said. "Show me your friends, and I will tell you who you are, and since I have awesome friends, I must be awesome, too."

"You are." Frankie hugged her. "Margo, you are missing a group hug."

"I know. I can't wait for your ship to get here. I plan to make up a story about a fabulous guy I met who invited me to join him on a cruise. Even Lynda could not be mad about me leaving a day early."

"Speaking of great guys." Mia pinned Frankie with a mock hard stare. "Who's the guy you want to invite to your suite?"

Pretending innocence, Frankie arched a brow. "Who said anything about a guy? It could have been a hypothetical."

"Could have been but wasn't. So, who is he?"

"His name is Doug, and he's Kian's guest."

"Oh." Mia frowned. "I don't know anyone by that name. I wonder who he is."

"Of course, you don't know him. He doesn't work for Perfect Match, and he's a guest. I met him on the top deck when I went for a drink. Oh, did I tell you about the robotic bartender?"

Mia lifted her hand. "Hold that thought. My phone is buzzing." She pulled it out, read the message, and frowned. "I'll have to hear the rest of the story later. I need to accompany Tom to a meeting." She reached for Frankie and gave her a hug. "I'll see you at dinner. You can show me the guy you want to invite later tonight, and I'll tell you if it's a good idea."

Annani

C~~9

"I truly feel like a queen now." Annani took Kian's hand even though she did not need his help to climb her makeshift throne.

He chuckled. "Only now? I thought you always felt like a queen or an empress."

Annani laughed. "After all, royalty runs in my blood." She made herself comfortable on the armchair that was standing on top of a coffee table and covered with a brocade bedspread. "You knew that even before the Kra-ell and these gods shed more light on Anumati's politics. I am Ahn's daughter, destined to rule over the gods, and was groomed accordingly." She smiled sadly. "I expected to rule fairly and benevolently, with Khiann by my side to balance my impulsiveness with his rational and calcu-lating mind, but Fate had other plans for us. Our happily-ever-after was cut painfully short."

As she realized that her words had made everyone in the room uncomfortable, Annani squared her shoulders and gave them a bright smile. "Thank you all for preparing this room and building me a makeshift throne."

It was unnecessary, and Annani had agreed only because her daughters had insisted and seemed to have great fun preparing the room for the gods' visit. Annani would have preferred to leave the room as it was and accept the gods sitting on the couch, as she usually did when meeting with her clan members.

Her grandeur came from the inside—the power, the radiance, the regal bearing. She did not need external symbols of power.

Kian waited until she was done arranging the folds of her gown to her liking. "I would appreciate it if you did not mention your royal blood to your guests. They already know that you glow, so they know that you have some royal blood in you, but I don't want them to know that you are the Eternal King's heir. Not yet, anyway." He turned to the assembled company, which mainly consisted of his family and Guardians. "The same goes for you."

Annani regarded her son with a smile. "How am I supposed to become the heart of the resistance if they do not know I exist?"

"Did you change your mind about getting involved?" Kian put his foot on the coffee table and leaned his elbow on his knee. "I was very happy with your prior reluctance to become the resistance's alternative to the Eternal King. I think it was a wise decision. I want to keep your identity a secret for as long as possible. You know what will happen the moment your grandfather learns of your existence. It's not just your life on the line. It's the life of everyone on the planet."

"I know, my darling son." She leaned and cupped his cheek. "I have not decided anything yet. Let us play it by ear, shall we?"

Kian was about to respond when the doorbell rang twice, the signal he'd agreed on with Anandur, announcing that he had the guest gods with him.

Annani waved her hand, and Ogidu walked over to the door. Oshidu and Sari's and Alena's butlers stayed by her side. As a precaution, they had temporarily returned command of their Odus to Annani.

Ogidu opened the door and bowed. "Good evening, masters and mistress. The Clan Mother is awaiting your arrival. Please, come in." He moved aside and bowed again with his arm extended toward her.

"Thank you," she heard one of the gods say, and liked that he was polite toward the Odu.

As the three gods entered the room with a lovely young lady who she assumed was Gabriella, there was an intake of breath, and all four sets of eyes widened in unison. The gods dropped to their knees a split second later and lowered their foreheads to the floor. Following their example, Gabriella did the same, which was quite a feat with her tight evening dress.

"Your Majesty," the gods said in chorus.

Evidently the charade had worked, and her guests were impressed with her makeshift throne. A bit too impressed for the gods, though. Annani had expected the former human to react with awe to a glowing figure of otherworldly beauty. Still, gods should have been more reserved in their show of deference.

A simple bow would have sufficed.

"Please rise. It is permitted to gaze upon my face."

Their leader lifted his head but stayed on his knees, and a few heartbeats later, his companions did the same.

"Your Highness is a miracle," he whispered. "I had no idea." He dropped his forehead to the floor again, and his companions followed his example.

"Oh, enough of that." Annani rose to her feet and took Kian's offered hand to climb down from the coffee table. "Please, get up. I will not smite you with a blast of my power or any other means you fear."

"We do not bow out of fear." Aru lifted his head but kept his eyes downcast. "We revere the legitimate heir to the Eternal King's throne."

Kian

Kian's breath caught in his throat. How did they guess it so quickly? According to his mother, she had inherited much of her father's personality but not his looks. She claimed she looked a lot like her mother.

Motioning for him to stay where he was, Annani approached Aru and put a hand on his shoulder. "How did you know?"

Damn. Kian closed his eyes. She should have laughed it off, denied it, put doubt in their minds. Confirming their suspicions was the last thing she should have done.

The god tilted his head to look at her face and forced a polite smile. "Your Highness is the spitting image of her grandmother, the Eternal King's mate, and the only one whose descendants are considered legitimate heirs."

How could they know whether Annani was Ahn's daughter from his official wife or a concubine?

180

They were making assumptions, which happened to be accurate. Still, Kian hoped his mother realized she could lie about it if she decided not to get involved and use this as her exit card.

The only one who could attest to Annani's legitimacy was Toven.

Casting a quick look at the god, Kian offered a slight shake of his head. Toven nodded just as inconspicuously, indicating that he understood the wordless communication.

Annani smiled at Aru. "I might be the spitting image of my fraternal grandmother, but that does not necessarily make me a legitimate heir. I could be the daughter of a concubine or a paramour and not my father's official wife."

Annani was so petite that she was at eye level with Aru even though he was on his knees. The Odus and the Guardians were ready to jump in if needed, and so was Kian, but he had a feeling that his mother had things under control, and he was glad she had put doubt in the gods' minds.

Aru's face fell, and his two companions looked even more despondent.

The god took a deep breath. "No one needs to know that. I assume that there are no witnesses left to attest to Your Highness's legitimacy. No one can prove that Your Highness's parents were not officially married when Your Highness was conceived."

Annani laughed. "Please stop referring to me as Your Highness. The cumbersome third-person address is a tongue-twister. You can call me Annani, or Clan Mother if you prefer a formal address."

Aru swallowed. "As you wish, Clan Mother."

Annani motioned for Kian to stand by her side. "Let us put an end to this charade. I want to sit down and do not wish for everyone else to remain standing. Please tell the Odus to bring chairs for everyone and then serve refreshments."

"Yes, Mother." He helped her get back to her chair.

Not wanting the Odus to leave his mother's side even for a moment, he motioned for the Guardians to bring the chairs. As soon as Annani realized what he was doing, she leaned over toward her Odu. "Can you please lift this armchair off the coffee table and put it on the floor?"

As two Odus grabbed the chair on both sides and lowered it to the floor, Annani turned to look at Aru and his companions, who were still on their knees. She took her place again on the chair. "My daughters thought it would look grand to make me a makeshift throne, but I do not need one to feel important." She moved her knees to the side and leaned forward. "To tell you the truth, I have never owned a throne."

A muffled chuckle from behind the gods reminded everyone that they had forgotten Annani's fourth guest.

"Gabriella." Annani waved her hand. "Please rise and approach me."

"Yes, Clan Mother." Gabi pushed to her feet and walked over to Annani's armchair. "I don't know what I'm supposed to say, so I'll go with what I know. It's an honor to meet the mother of this clan of immortals who have done so many wonderful things for humanity."

Annani smiled brightly. "Who told you about that?"

"My brothers and their mates. They visited me and Aru several times, full of stories about how your clan lifted humans from the Dark Ages and taught them what they should strive for as a society. But I don't think they know who you really are, or maybe they do and are not allowed to tell me because I'm with Aru." She cast him a sidelong glance. "Why are you still kneeling?"

"It's improper for me to tower over her Highness."

That got another laugh out of Annani. "That is a really silly custom. Given my height, everyone around me would have to walk on their knees not to tower over me. Please rise and take a seat."

"You are most gracious, Clan Mother." Instead of rising, Aru lowered his head nearly to the floor again.

Watching these gods acting so deferential to his mother eased the knot of stress in Kian's stomach. He hadn't expected any trouble from them, and his precautions were out of an abundance of caution. Still, it was difficult for him to relax when his mother put herself out there.

Regardless, it seemed that the only threat these gods represented was showing Annani too much deference and reverence and inflating her ego to dangerous proportions.

"Don't worry about towering over my mother." Kian chuckled. "If she can look down her nose at me even though I'm nearly a foot and a half taller than her, she can do the same to you."

The Guardians were still bringing chairs, but there were already enough seats for the gods and Gabi to take, and all the ladies were seated.

Looking as if he was chewing on lemons, Aru nodded and pushed up, but he didn't straighten to his full height. Instead, he backed into a chair so he wouldn't have to stand or turn his back on Annani.

Dagor

Dagor pushed to his feet with trembling knees. Discovering that an heir survived was a shock he was still reeling from, but it wasn't the only one he'd experienced upon entering her Highness's chambers.

Four Odus guarded the goddess, two on each side, and none of them was Kian's butler.

How many Odus did the clan have, and did they know how incredibly valuable these cyborgs were?

These Odus had been built before the manufacturing process moved to the solid-state model that was impervious to reverse engineering. The Odus had been only one of the reasons for the change. The big conglomerates did not want their technology stolen by small operators in the colonies, where it was more difficult to ensure compliance with Anumati's laws.

The Odus guarding the heir were relics, but some of their components were no doubt solid state as well. Still, the rest might lend itself to reverse engineering.

Dagor would have loved to take a look, but the truth was that without formal qualifications in engineering, he didn't know enough to do so safely.

Once everyone was seated and the Odus had served drinks and other refreshments, the heir reclined in her armchair and regarded Aru with a kind look. "Tell me about my grandmother and in what way I resemble her."

"With pleasure." Aru put his water bottle on the floor beside his chair. "I wish I had a picture to show you. You have her face, down to the most minute details, but her hair isn't red, and she's much taller."

Kian's wife lifted a hand to her chest. "Is her hair silvery?" she asked.

"It is." Aru darted his gaze around until it landed on the tall brunette Dagor had taken notice of before. She also bore some resemblance to the heir. "The Eternal Queen is about your height, and you also have some of her features. You must be her Highness's daughter."

Turning her head toward the brunette, the goddess smiled fondly. "This is my daughter, Amanda. The charming blond lady is my daughter Alena, and the auburn-haired one is my daughter Sari. She is the regent of the clan's European branch."

As the heir continued introducing her family, her son's eyes shot daggers at her, and Dagor could not blame him.

The goddess was too friendly and too trusting. If she ever set foot on Anumati, she would be eaten alive by its political sharks, which would save the king the trouble of having her murdered.

It would take many years of training before she was a suitable candidate for the throne who could swim with the sharks on Anumati, but then the resistance was in no rush.

The problem would be getting someone knowledgeable in Anumati's complicated web of politics to Earth to train the inexperienced heir.

There was an heir to the throne, though, and that was the best news the resistance could have hoped for.

Aru would have to relay it somehow to the resistance's leaders without arousing the suspicion of those listening to the patrol ship's communications.

"Dagor." The heir turned to him. "Tell me about yourself and why you joined the resistance."

He'd zoned out momentarily and must have missed part of what had been said. Darting a look at Aru, he got a nod from his leader.

"I was unhappy with the way the elite perpetuated its status. We are supposed to be a democracy, and every citizen of Anumati is supposed to have equal opportunity. Still, nothing could be further from the truth. The elite families, those with royal blood in them, are the only ones who can afford the lucrative learning institutions that prepare students for the entry exams to higher education in certain fields. I wanted to study engineering, but even if I could pass the exams, which is practically impossible without having access to prior tests, I could not have afforded the tuition. This is a broken system, and it has to go, but the king will not do anything about it because he needs the support of those elite families to stay in power."

The heir regarded him with compassion and understanding in her eyes. "My uncle Ekin was a great engineer, but without the proper tools and materials, he could not build the mechanical wonders he must have known about and was forbidden to share. I did not know about Anumati until we rescued the Kra-ell, and Jade told us where we came from. The exiled gods did not tell their children they came from somewhere else in the universe. Growing up, I believed that gods had always existed on Earth, just like humans had. When I got older and met my beloved betrothed, he told me what his father had told him in secret, but even my Khiann did not know much." She smiled sadly. "I hope the three of you know your history well and can educate me about my home planet."

Aru

Aru couldn't stop staring at the miracle before him. An heir to the Eternal King. The resemblance to her grandmother was uncanny, with the most significant difference being their hair color.

It suddenly dawned on him that Kian's wife knew somehow that the Eternal Queen had silver hair, and the only way she could have known that was via a vision. It wasn't the loss of color that humans experienced as they aged, but instead was her family's trademark. Some even called them the silver-haired nobles.

But since there was no way Syssi could have seen a picture of the queen, she must have seen her in a vision, and that worried him, although a lot less than it had before. The secret of his telepathic communication with his sister would not stay a secret for long. Soon, he would have to tell her Highness Princess Annani that he could communicate with Anumati, and relay messages between her and her grandmother through his sister and the Supreme.

"There is one more thing that I forgot to mention." The princess looked at her son. "I don't see any reason to hide it." She smiled at the one called Toven and motioned for him to come forward. "My cousin, Toven, is the son of my favorite and only uncle, and he's a full-blooded god, not the immortal he was pretending to be."

As the god started glowing, Aru and his companions bowed their heads to the noble.

"Did I fool you?" Toven asked with a smile.

"Yes," Aru admitted. "I suspected Kian of being a god, but he is only a demigod, so I assumed that Your Highness was also a descendant."

Aru was trying to decide whether he should call Toven 'Your Highness.' Toven's father had also been the Eternal King's son, but not from the Queen. He was the son of a concubine, and therefore not in line to the throne, and the same was true of Toven.

"Please, call me Toven. I cringe at being addressed as Your Highness."

"Very well." Aru inclined his head. "It is a pleasure to meet you, Toven, son of Ekin."

Next to Princess Annani, Kian groaned. "Kalugal will never forgive us for not including him in this meeting."

"I've heard that name before," Aru said. "How is he related to you?"

The princess looked as if she wanted to say something, but a glare from her son stopped her.

"Kalugal is the grandson of my brother," Toven said. "Who is no longer with us. Thankfully."

"Oh, that's right." Aru nodded. "Now I remember. He's Navuh's son who crossed over to join forces with the clan."

"That's right," Kian said. "Except for the fact that Kalugal fled his father's control many decades before he joined us. He did so to escape tyranny and potentially a threat to his life."

"Why did he fear for his life from his own father?" Aru asked. "Was he also an heir with aspirations to the throne?"

"Kalugal was never interested in taking over from his father, but he wasn't as easy to control as some of his other brothers, and therefore Navuh considered him a threat."

Aru sensed that Kian was telling him a slightly altered version of the real story, mainly because the princess averted her gaze and pretended to be preoccupied with the folds of her silk gown.

She was not a good liar and would need extensive coaching to overcome that shortcoming. It was also possible that she was uncomfortable hiding things from him and was doing so only because of her son.

Aru could use that to his advantage to determine what Kian was adamant about keeping from him. The princess wanted to learn about Anumati, which could provide an excellent excuse for him to spend time with her without Kian hovering over her and censoring what she could and couldn't say.

It wasn't right for the son to censor his mother even if he was her most trusted advisor. Still, these immortals needed to learn the proper etiquette for royalty.

For now, though, Aru should focus on other issues, and the one that concerned him the most was Syssi's visions.

"Forgive me for changing the topic of conversation, but I have to ask." He looked at Syssi. "Did you see the queen in a vision? Is that how you knew that she had silver hair?"

Syssi nodded. "I had a vision of a goddess so luminous that I couldn't discern her features. I could only tell that she was tall and slim and had long, silver hair. She also wore a silver gown, if that's helpful."

"That sounds like our Queen. I've never had the privilege of meeting her in person or even seeing her from afar, but we've all seen her portrait as well as her televised addresses to the citizens of Anumati, and footage of her attending charity events."

"Is she a nice person?" Syssi asked.

He chuckled. "No one can survive Anumati's politics for as long as our Queen has done and be nice. Behind her gentle façade, she is as dangerous as the king."

Luckily, she was on the rebellion's side, or they would have no chance of ever succeeding, but that was a secret he couldn't reveal yet. In fact, he'd thought he would never have to reveal it. One day, when the resistance won, the queen would admit her part in toppling her husband's rule.

Or not.

Aru wasn't privy to her plans. He was just one more pawn in her very long game.

Frankie

⤜⤠⤐

The evening dress Frankie had gotten from her cousin Claudia was sapphire blue. The bodice clung tightly to her form, emphasizing her curves. Claudia was a little skinnier and a little taller, so it was a bit too tight and a bit too long, but other than that, it was great.

The neckline was a delicate scoop, showing her collarbone but covering her breasts and drawing attention to her exposed shoulders, which were one of her better features. The ballet lessons she had taken as a kid in the community center had yet to make her a great ballerina. Still, they had done wonders for her posture and deportment.

From the hips down, the skirt flared and was longer in the back than in the front. The dress made a statement and was not demure despite the conservative neckline and modest hemline.

The matching necklace and earrings were also Claudia's, and she'd boasted of getting both items for under thirty bucks in a discount store that Frankie had been planning to check out after the cruise. Since she didn't need to pay rent and had even gotten her deposit back, she had cash to buy a few new pieces of fake jewelry.

Would anyone notice that it wasn't real?

Eh, who cared. She looked good. Frankie smiled at her reflection in the mirror. "Doug is going to like."

As her doorbell rang, she walked over to the intercom. She pressed the button to activate the camera mounted above her door, which she'd discovered after Mia's previous visit.

It was her bestie again, but this time, she had her fiancé with her, and they both looked like a million bucks even when looking at them on the small screen.

Frankie opened the door. "You two look fancy."

"So do you." Mia smiled. "This dress is gorgeous. Where did you get it?"

"From one of my many cousins." She glanced at the time displayed on the screen. "It's still a bit early to head to the dining hall. Do you want to come in for a drink?"

"Sure." Tom rubbed the back of his neck. "We need to tell you a few things before we head out."

Tom looked uncomfortable, and Mia looked excited.

Was she pregnant? Was that what they needed to tell her?

"Then come in." Frankie walked over to the bar. "What will it be?"

"Water for me," Mia said. "I'm only allowing myself one drink daily, and I'm saving that for the welcome dinner."

The pregnancy hypothesis was growing stronger.

"I'll have some of that whiskey." Tom pointed at one of the bottles. "We don't have much time, so I'll try to make it short, which makes it very difficult."

Maybe Mia wasn't pregnant after all.

"I've got this." Her friend drove her chair to the bar. "Do you remember the Perfect Match adventure Tom and I shared?"

"Yeah. What about it?"

"What if some of it was real?"

Frankie snorted. "Of course, some of it was real. You two fell in love."

"I'm not talking about that. Can you believe that gods and immortals and people with all kinds of paranormal talents exist in the real world—our world?"

Frankie handed Mia a glass of water and Tom his whiskey. "I believe that aliens are real, and I also believe that they visit from time to time. As for people with paranormal talents, not so much." She grimaced. "My aunt Susanna claims to get messages from beyond, but so far she hasn't learned anything useful, so I doubt she does. She doesn't charge for it, so she's not a crook, but most of the others you see on television are fakes who do party tricks for money. What are you trying to say?"

Her friend took a deep breath. "I'm immortal. I wasn't before, but I always had the genes in me. They just needed someone to activate them, and Tom did that. That's how my heart was miraculously healed, and I started re-growing my amputated legs. It wasn't thanks to the fancy Swiss clinic or the experimental treatments I told you about." She smiled sheepishly. "I'm sorry about lying to you, but I'm sure you can understand why I couldn't tell you the truth."

Frankie gaped at her friend, waiting for Mia to tell her that it was an idea for a story she was writing. She'd wanted to see Frankie's reaction so she could describe it better. Or it was a stupid prank someone had put her up to.

Mia was too nice to pull something like that.

A long moment passed, and no one laughed or shouted 'Smile, you're on candid camera' or something to that effect. Frankie shifted her eyes to Tom. "Are you immortal?"

He made a face that was a mix between a grimace and a wince. "Yes, but I'm more than that." He flicked his fingers, and his skin started glowing. "I'm a member of a species of people who call themselves gods, and the reason I'm telling you all this now is to prepare you for what and who you are about to see during the welcome dinner. I don't want you to get alarmed when you see a beautiful, glowing goddess give the welcome speech."

Frankie looked down at the gin and tonic she'd made for herself. It couldn't be drugged because she hadn't drunk from it yet. She looked up, but Tom's skin was still luminous. Every part that wasn't covered by clothing was emitting a soft glow.

"It gets better," Mia said. "We think that you are also a dormant carrier of godly genes and can be turned immortal, and the same goes for Margo." She grinned. "We can be besties forever, for real."

Frankie felt dizzy. "I knew that I was in *The Twilight Zone*."

Toven

As Frankie started to fall, Toven zipped around the counter and caught her before she could hit the floor. "Is your friend prone to fainting?"

"Not that I know of. Maybe she's wearing a compression garment under that dress. It looks awfully tight."

He frowned. "I didn't know ladies still wore corsets. That silly fashion used to be a major reason for fainting." Carrying Frankie to the couch, he laid her down gently.

"Compression garments are not as bad as the corsets of yesteryear, and they shouldn't restrict breathing, but Frankie is not used to them. She probably put one on only because of the dress."

"What do we do now?" Toven looked at the woman and listened to her breathing and heartbeat. Both sounded fine, but he wasn't a doctor. "Do we call Bridget?"

"Let's give Frankie a moment." Mia parked her chair parallel to the couch and leaned over to brush her fingers over her friend's cheek. "Frankie, sweetheart. Can you look at me?"

The girl's false lashes fluttered, and then she opened her eyes. "What happened?" She lifted a hand to her forehead.

"You fainted. Is something wrong with you that you are not telling me about?"

Frankie pursed her lips. "I've never fainted before. But then I've never had my friend tell me crazy stories about gods and immortals and scare the bejesus out of me."

"Why were you scared?" Mia frowned. "Do you find me or Tom frightening?"

Frankie glanced at him and promptly closed her eyes. "Can I go back to sleep and wake up again, and you'll tell me that none of this is true?"

He'd forgotten to suppress his glow, and his skin was still luminous.

Mia sighed. "You don't have to fall asleep for Tom to make you forget this conversation ever happened. But there is a reason we dumped all of this on you now instead of doing it gradually."

Frankie opened her eyes and turned her head toward Mia. "And the reason is?"

Mia took Toven's hand. "Tom is not the only glowing god attending the welcome dinner tonight, and we didn't want you to freak out when you saw the Clan Mother enter the dining hall in all of her luminous glory. Besides, most people on this cruise are immortal and are here to celebrate several weddings. They don't want to have to be mindful of the one human who doesn't know about them and hide who they are."

"They don't all glow, though, right? Otherwise, you would be glowing too."

That was an astute observation, which Toven hoped meant that Frankie was over her initial shock.

As the girl licked her lips, Mia turned to him. "Can you bring a bottle of water for Frankie?"

Toven was glad to have something to do instead of standing beside the couch with his hands in his pockets.

"So, your boyfriend is a god?" Frankie whispered, unaware of his exceptional hearing.

"He is, and he can hear you, no matter how quietly you whisper. That's one of the perks of being a god or an immortal. Enhanced hearing, eyesight, physical strength, speed, stamina, and most importantly, the ability to heal almost anything, including re-growing amputated limbs."

Toven uncapped one of the bottles of water he'd brought and handed it to Frankie. He gave the other to Mia. "By the way, most people on board call me Toven. I go by Tom and Toven, so you can keep calling me Tom."

"Okay." Frankie lowered her feet to the floor and sat up. "I must have drunk a bit too much today."

"How much did you have?" Mia asked.

"Actually, not that much. Earlier, I had two mojitos at the bar, and I made myself one gin and tonic before you came and another one after, but I didn't even take a sip from it yet."

Mia leaned closer to her friend. "Are you wearing Spanx?"

"No." Frankie glowered at Mia. "That's not why I fainted, and if Tom, aka Toven, can hear your whispers, why do you bother?"

"Habit, I guess." Mia smoothed her hand over her short hair. "I was human most of my life and an immortal for about half a year. It takes time to get used to all the peculiarities of that world."

Mia hadn't complained to him about it. Still, he could imagine that the transition was about more than the physical changes and was more challenging than Mia made it seem.

"You will have to save the rest of your questions for later," he said. "We should get moving if we don't want to be late for dinner."

Frankie looked panicked. "Will I be the only human there?"

"No." Mia smiled. "All the serving staff are human, and several clan members are either too young to transition or can't for other reasons." When Frankie still looked like a deer caught in the headlights, Mia put a hand on her knee. "Gods, immortals, and humans are all people. The same things make them happy or sad, make them laugh or cry. As long as you remember that, you'll be fine."

As Frankie shifted her gaze to Toven, he nodded. "I put my pants on one leg at a time like everyone else. You've known me a long time yet never noticed that I was different."

A snort escaped Frankie's mouth. "Oh, I noticed, but it never occurred to me that you didn't just look like a god and talk like a king, but that you were indeed a god, and probably at some point in the past also a king."

Kian

After the gods left with Gabi, Toven departed with Mia, and the Guardians returned to their stations; the Odus restored Annani's living room to its previous condition.

Before dinner, there wasn't much time left to reflect on the meeting, but Kian wanted to hear her impression of the three gods.

Usually, his mother was a better judge of character than he was.

"So, what do you think?" He sat on the armchair facing the couch where his mother sat down with Amanda on one side and Sari on the other.

Syssi joined him in the large armchair, sitting in his lap and leaning against his chest.

"To see them drop to their knees and hear them call me Your Highness was startling." Annani's lips lifted in a sly smile. "It was quite refreshing to garner such reverence. Perhaps you all should start calling me Your Majesty."

"I'm serious, Mother. You wanted to see their unguarded response, which was a success. They couldn't have faked their reaction."

Syssi adjusted her position in his lap to accommodate the floor-length gown she was wearing. "We should get Tim to draw a portrait of the queen from their descriptions. I'm curious to see her face without the glow masking her features."

"That's not a bad idea," Amanda said. "We should have a portrait of the Eternal King as well." She smiled at Kian. "We can hang it in the room dedicated to Navuh and his adopted sons. One more evildoer to add to the wall of adversaries bent on our destruction."

"I agree." Kian smoothed his hand over Syssi's bare arm, feeling the goosebumps rise at his touch. "Tim should definitely draw their portraits so we know what they look like." He smiled. "Given the guy's uncanny talent, there is a slight chance that Tim is a Dormant, but given the antipathy most feel toward him, there's certainly no affinity."

"You should give him a chance," his mother said. "I remember him as an entertaining individual. Perhaps he has a personality disorder, and Vanessa can help him become friendlier."

"His friendliness or lack thereof is not the problem." Kian kept running his hand up and down Syssi's arm.

"But I don't want to waste time talking about him. I want your impression of the gods before it can fade."

His mother nodded. "I did not sense deceit from any of them. Aru is more than he claims to be, though. Once he was over the initial shock of seeing me and recognizing me for who I was, I caught a calculating look in his eyes. He was planning something."

"Of course, he was," Alena said. "He realized that he found the one person in the galaxy pivotal to the resistance's success, and he needed to find a way to communicate that to the leaders without the information of your existence falling into the wrong hands."

Aru claimed to have a way to communicate secretly with someone in the resistance, and after he and his teammates had been released from the obligation to return to the patrol ship when it passed over Earth on its way to Anumati, Kian no longer doubted that.

The god must have contacted someone and told them about wishing to stay on Earth to be with his fated mate. Given that his request had been granted almost immediately, Aru must be very well connected.

"Aru is scared of me," Syssi said. "It was the second time that mentioning my visions elicited a fearful reaction from him. He is afraid I'll see something that he's hiding."

Amanda waved a hand. "Then find out what it is."

Syssi shifted to look at her. "You know that's not how it works. I ask for one thing and get another that may or may not be related to what I asked for."

Amanda didn't look impressed with Syssi's self-depre-cating comment. "So, sometimes it works, and other times it doesn't. You wanted to find David's missing parents, and you did." Amanda lifted one finger. "You wanted to find out whether the new signals were coming from a friend or foe, and you saw the gods." Amanda lifted two fingers. "And when you asked about the gods again, you saw the queen. We still don't know what your last vision was about, but we will find out soon, just as we discovered the identity of the first goddess you saw."

Syssi let out a breath. "So, what are you saying, that I should court more visions?"

His mother and sisters all nodded.

"Oh wow, talk about pressure." Syssi chuckled nervously. "I can't do that every day. It takes too much out of me."

"Do only what you are comfortable with," Alena said. "But do it as often as you can without letting yourself get exhausted. Aside from being incredibly fertile for an immortal, I don't have any paranormal talents. However, I believe the more you practice inducing visions, the easier they will come, and they will also be clearer."

Then, there was Allegra's contribution that Kian didn't know how to feel about. Their daughter was asleep in her crib and had still managed to enhance Syssi's vision. What would happen when she was older and could do more?

Dagor

D agor ran a comb through his hair, put it in his tuxedo breast pocket, and straightened the lapels.

It was his first time wearing a formal outfit. It was very different from the latest fashion in formal wear on Anumati and much more stifling.

"You look dashing." Negal walked past him, opened the door, and exited their cabin. "Coming?"

"Aren't we waiting for Aru and Gabi?"

Negal cast a glance at the closed door to their room. "Nah. Let's go."

They had stopped by their cabin at Gabi's request to freshen up, and she knew they didn't have much time.

Now that Dagor knew who would deliver the welcoming speech, he was adamant about being there on time. One didn't offend nobility and get away with it without repercussions. The princess might seem kind, but he didn't want to put it to the test.

"I'll remind them to hurry up." Dagor walked over and knocked.

The soundproofing was excellent, so he couldn't hear what was happening inside the room, but his knock would be heard.

The door opened a crack. "Gabi needs another minute. You and Negal go ahead, and we will catch up."

"Don't be late. We don't want to offend the princess."

"We will be there on time." Aru closed the door.

"They are going to be late," Dagor murmured as he walked out the front door of their cabin. "You know what the consequences of such blatant disrespect would be on Anumati. I just hope that Princess Annani is more merciful."

Negal shrugged. "The heir seems much less strict than her grandmother."

Dagor nodded. "Do you think that Aru knew and didn't tell us?"

"Aru was just as stunned as we were. Kian does not look like his mother, so none of us could have known. The son must have taken after his father."

Dagor lifted a brow. "His human father? I doubt he was that handsome."

"He might not have been as good-looking as his son, but the godly genetics improved what was there." Negal pressed the button for the elevator.

The heir's children were nearly as beautiful as gods and goddesses, but not entirely, and the other immortals in the room were even less so. The more human blood they had, the less perfect they were.

The princess was incredibly fertile for a goddess, but perhaps the humanity of her partners had something to do with that. One thing was for sure, though. Her grandmother would not be happy when she found out about her hybrid great-grandchildren.

As the elevator doors opened, the cabin wasn't empty, and Dagor smiled at the group of immortals who were regarding him and Negal with puzzled expressions.

"Hi," he said with a smile. "I'm Dagor, and this is Negal."

"You are the new gods," one of the females said. "Nice to meet you. My name is Evelin, and this is Leah."

The introductions continued until the elevator doors opened on the dining hall's deck. Still, Dagor doubted he would remember any of their names.

He'd been too busy examining their faces and comparing their imperfections to the flawless faces of gods.

Why was he bothering, though?

Everyone on Anumati was physically perfect, but some were just more stunning than others, especially those with royal blood who were luminescent. Still, beauty and physical perfection weren't important to him. He was more interested in character and brains, another reason he was part of the resistance.

As they entered the dining hall, Dagor scanned the place for the human girl he had met earlier on the top deck, but she wasn't there, and he wondered whether she had lied about being a guest and not a staff member. Why would the immortals invite a human girl to their clan's celebrations?

Ten weddings were planned for the upcoming ten days, with the first two being of the heir's daughters. Alena, the oldest, was pregnant and marrying her mate, a demigod like her. Amanda, the Clan Mother's youngest child, was getting married the following day to a hulking immortal who wasn't nearly as good-looking as the others in the room had been, but he looked formidable.

"Welcome." A young human smiled at them. "What are your names?"

"I'm Negal, and this is Dagor."

"Excellent." She tapped on her tablet. "You are seated at table three."

"Thank you, miss." Negal dipped his head.

"The girl was human," Dagor said. "You don't need to bow to her."

"It's a habit." Negal scanned the tables. "I always dip my head to a lady."

Dagor chuckled. "You forget that I've been spending every moment of the day with you while we were mingling with humans. You didn't bow to any of them."

"It was easy to remember not to do that when humans were the only people we interacted with. Here, it's more challenging and better to err on the side of politeness. Don't you think?"

"The immortal females don't expect you to bow to them either. You only need to bow to the heir and the god named Toven."

Dagor spotted table number three and was glad no one else was sitting there. But given that there were six chairs and only four in their party, they would be sharing the table with two other immortals.

"Who do you think is going to sit with us?" Negal asked.

"If we are lucky, no one." Dagor turned to look at the entrance to the dining hall, where the human girl was still standing with her tablet and welcoming the guests.

People were trickling in slowly, but Aru and Gabi were still a no-show, and there were only a few minutes left before the doors closed, provided that these immortals were punctual.

Given how no one was in a rush, though, it didn't seem like they expected the head of their clan to start the festivities right on time.

Glancing at the doorway, Dagor's eyes nearly popped out of their sockets.

Toven, his wheelchair-bound immortal mate, and Frankie arrived together. They were waiting for the girl to tell them their table number.

What was Frankie doing with the royal?

Perhaps she was a personal servant to the mate?

That wasn't likely, given how she was dressed. The blue dress was a show-stopper, especially the way it accentuated Frankie's every curve.

She looked stunning. *For a human*, Dagor reminded himself.

He planned on spending an enjoyable night or two with her, but he wasn't stupid enough to get attached to a human.

Frankie

⚬⚬

F rankie walked in a daze, keeping her hand on Mia's wheelchair for balance.

Her best friend was mated to a god. Mated, not married, which was supposedly stronger than marriage, but some of these immortals were getting officially married on this cruise for the fun of it.

Mia had told her a few more things on the way to the dining hall. Still, Frankie's ability to process the bizarre was apparently limited, and she didn't want to faint again.

Her life so far clearly hadn't been eventful enough because she'd never heard anything that had caused her to faint before.

Well, that wasn't entirely true. When Mia's heart had given out, and the doctors had to amputate her legs, Frankie had felt like shattering into pieces, but somehow, she hadn't.

The helplessness had been overwhelming, but at least she could be there for her friend and try to support her as best she could.

She could have been more resilient back then. Perhaps her ability to absorb things had been better.

"You are seated at table seven," the girl with the tablet said. "Enjoy your evening."

Mia lifted her eyes to her. "Are you okay?"

"Yeah, I'm fine. I'll just hang on to your chair if you don't mind."

Mia nodded. "I'll go slow."

It was funny that the one with the healthy legs was relying on the one in the wheelchair to lead her. The good news was that Mia wouldn't need the chair for much longer. Her feet would take another month or two to form, and she would start walking again.

Talk about miracles.

As they made their way to the table, Frankie felt as if everyone was watching her and wondering what the lone human was doing in their midst.

Wait, was Doug an immortal?

Of course, he was. He probably was one of the immortals from Scotland, which was why Mia didn't know him. He'd told her he was from Hungary, but that might have been a lie.

Why Hungary, though?

It was such a random country to choose.

"Good evening." A beautiful brunette she remembered meeting at Mia's old house smiled at her. "Do you remember me? I'm Geraldine. My daughter Cassandra and I met with you several months ago." She smiled sheepishly. "But we are not Toven's cousins. I'm Toven's daughter, and Cassandra is his granddaughter." She turned to the handsome man sitting next to her. "This is my mate, Shai."

"Nice to meet you again." Frankie sat in the chair Toven had pulled out for her.

She wanted to shake her head but stifled the impulse, plastering an amiable smile on her face instead.

A god had pulled out a chair for her. His daughter looked like his sister or cousin, and her daughter looked older than her mother.

It would take time to get used to the idea of immortals and gods. She had to remind herself of what Mia and Toven had told her. They were just people; the same things made them happy or sad.

Well, they weren't really gods, right? They were just aliens who lived forever and did what?

Mia hadn't had enough time to tell her. Still, she and Toven had promised to continue their introduction to the alternative world after the welcome dinner.

"Cassandra is sitting over there with my other daughter, Darlene," Geraldine continued with the introductions.

"Darlene is mated to Eric, who is Gilbert and Gabi's brother, and they are sitting at the next table over. It's difficult to plan seating arrangements when everyone is related in one way or another." She continued prattling until a hush fell over the rest of the crowd, and everyone turned toward the entrance.

A procession entered, with a tiny glowing figure in the center and four couples escorting her.

The goddess was just as magnificent as Toven and Mia had described, with her luminescence and ethereal beauty clearly otherworldly. The Clan Mother was supposedly ancient, but she looked so deceptively young that it was freaky.

Frankie's eyes were still glued to the goddess when six butlers entered behind the procession. They were dressed in full butler regalia, and two of them were pushing strollers with babies inside of them.

The curious thing was that the butlers looked like sextuplets, nearly identical, but upon closer inspection, she could see the slight differences between them.

The goddess continued to a small podium erected toward the far end of the room, but in the center so everyone could see her, and no one had to stare at her back.

For a moment, Frankie wondered whether the goddess was hiding wings, but unless they were the magical type that disappeared when not in use, neither Tom nor the Clan Mother could fly.

Toven, she reminded herself. He used Tom when dealing with humans.

"Good evening." The goddess lifted her luminous bare arms. "I am overjoyed to have you all here with me. The last time we were all gathered was for Kian and Syssi's wedding, but not everyone was present. We also had a big show of people for Nathalie and Andrew's wedding in the castle, but this time, we will celebrate ten weddings in ten days with nearly all of the clan. The first wedding will be Alena and Orion's, followed by Amanda and Dalhu's." She turned to look at the table where the couples who had escorted her to the dining hall were seated. "We have all been waiting for these two to get married, and they are finally ready."

As everyone clapped and cheered, the goddess smiled fondly at her people. "You've all been given the itinerary of the ten weddings and other events we've organized for this first-ever clan cruise. The itinerary can also be found on the clan's bulletin board, which you can find on your cabin's television or your phones and other devices."

Frankie glanced at the fancy folded page beside her plate, which she'd assumed was the menu. She would look at it later. Right now, she didn't dare to look away from the goddess.

"While we are all gathered here tonight," the Clan Mother continued, "I would like to take this opportunity to introduce to you our distinguished guests." She turned toward one of the tables. "Please come forward and introduce yourselves."

As three guests rose to their feet and approached the podium, they bowed low to the goddess.

"It is my pleasure to introduce three gods from our home planet to you." She motioned for them to turn around and face the crowd.

Frankie's heart flipped in her chest. Was that Doug?

He looked so different in a tux, and he didn't glow like the Clan Mother or Toven, but the goddess had introduced him as a god.

"He said he was a god," she murmured. "I thought he was teasing." As the same dizzy feeling from before washed over her again, she tried to fight it, but it was no use, and as darkness consumed her, she felt herself falling.

Dagor

~~~~~~~~~

Something was wrong with Frankie. Dagor saw her sliding from her chair, and Toven catching her before she could hit the floor.

Turning around, Dagor hastily bowed to the goddess. "My apologies, Your Highness, but I need to check on that human."

"Go." She dismissed him with a nod toward Frankie.

He sprinted to the god holding Frankie in his arms.

"What happened to her?"

"You," Toven's mate accused. "You call yourself Doug, am I right?"

He nodded.

"She has just discovered that you are a god."

Dagor extended his arms. "I'll take her back to her suite and explain."

Toven shook his head. "What is your connection to Frankie?"

"None," his mate said. "He met her earlier at the bar, and they shared a few drinks. We should take her back to her cabin."

Toven looked conflicted. "You need to eat, Mia. Bridget was very clear about the importance of you getting enough nutrition."

"You didn't eat either," Mia said. "And neither did Frankie, which is probably why she keeps fainting. We can ask for food to be sent to her suite."

Dagor was ready to pry Frankie out of Toven's arms, but as he became aware of the power radiating behind him, he turned around and quickly bowed. "I apologize, Clan Mother. I offered to take Frankie to her cabin, but Toven doesn't trust me with her."

The heir looked at Frankie with concern in her eyes. "What is wrong with the girl?"

"Let me take a look at her." A redheaded female with an authoritative voice approached them.

"Thank you, Bridget," Toven said.

He hadn't addressed her as 'doctor,' and she wasn't wearing a doctor's coat, but it was evident that she was a physician.

Bridget checked Frankie's pulse and lifted her eyelids one at a time. "She might be hypoglycemic."

"What does that mean?" Dagor asked.

"Low blood sugar." The doctor turned to Toven's mate. "Do you know if she suffers from the condition?"

Dagor still did not know what low blood sugar meant. His knowledge of human physiology was less than elementary.

"Not as far as I know," Mia said.

"What's happening?" Frankie murmured.

Dagor released a relieved breath. She was talking, so she wasn't dying.

"You fainted again." Toven smiled at her reassuringly. "We are taking you back to your cabin, and we will have food delivered. The doctor thinks you have low blood sugar."

"I said that I suspect it," the doctor said. "Further tests are needed. Tomorrow morning, I want to see her at the clinic." She turned back to Frankie. "Please call me when you are ready."

"I will."

"Can I at least come with you?" Dagor pleaded.

Toven's mate looked at him with compassion in her eyes. "Of course. I'll have food delivered for you as well."

"Thank you." He bowed to her.

She might be just an immortal, but she was mated to a royal, so perhaps she deserved the same courtesy as the other royals.

When the four of them reached Frankie's cabin, Dagor noted the number. Once Toven and Mia left for the night, he would return to ensure that Frankie was okay.

Humans were so fragile, and she was alone in the suite. She needed someone to take care of her.

As Toven laid Frankie down on the couch, his mate parked her wheelchair, blocking her from Dagor's view.

"Frankie, sweetheart, you should take off this dress. It might be the culprit behind your fainting spells."

"Yeah, that's a good idea. But it's such a damn shame. I wanted Doug to see me in it. I mean Dagor."

"I did." He walked over and crouched next to the wheelchair. "You look spectacular, but then you looked just as good this morning."

A bright smile illuminated her unnaturally pale face. "You weren't kidding when you said you were a god."

"I'm afraid not." He smiled apologetically. "Once you get to know me better, you'll realize I don't have much of a sense of humor."

"That's okay. I have enough for the both of us."

Frankie's eyelids fluttered closed, but given that her lips were still curved in a small smile, he assumed she hadn't fainted again.

As Toven's mate moved her chair, giving Dagor more room next to the couch, he scooted closer to Frankie and took her hand. "Have you eaten anything other than the bar snacks today?"

She shook her head. "I was too nervous."

"That's understandable. You were about to dine with gods and immortals. I don't know why Toven invited you into their world. Still, it must be overwhelming for you to suddenly discover that humans are not the only intelligent species on this planet." He cast an accusing look at Toven. "Why did you invite her to the cruise without preparing her?"

"We planned to do it as soon as the ship sailed, but we got delayed, and we had to rush it."

"I didn't know," Frankie murmured. "I mean, I didn't know about any of it when I talked to you earlier. Mia and Toven came to my cabin just before dinner and told me the highlights so I wouldn't freak out when I saw a glowing goddess, but I freaked out anyway. I fainted when they told me and then again when I saw you."

So, Mia was right, and he had been the reason Frankie had fainted.

"I'm so sorry. I didn't mean to scare you."

Frankie

"You didn't scare me." Frankie lifted her hand and cupped Dagor's cheek.

He was warm to the touch, and other than the perfect symmetry of his face, the bright blue shade of his eyes, and the absolute smoothness of his skin, he didn't look alien.

He could have been a human with excellent genetics or some corrective plastic surgery, colored contact lenses, and an excellent skin routine.

But what moved her most of all was the concern in his eyes.

They had spent no more than an hour chatting at the Lido bar, and the attraction was there in force, but there was a difference between wanting to bed a woman and caring about her, and for some reason, Dagor seemed to care.

"You fainted." He leaned into her hand for a moment.

"It was just too much to process, and this dress is too tight."

"Do you need me to help you get to the bedroom so you can change?"

She chuckled. "Are you that desperate to see me naked?"

"Yes, but I promise not to look."

"People," Mia said, "did you forget that you are not alone?"

Frankie smiled. "Yes, I did, but can you blame me? Did you see Dagor's eyes? They are hypnotic."

Frankie had a reputation for being overly direct, though she usually wasn't as open with men she'd just met. But Dagor was a god, and hc could most likely read her mind, so what was the point of trying to play coy?

"He does have beautiful eyes," Mia agreed.

"Thank you." Dagor's lips turned up in a satisfied smirk. "I must find your eyes just as hypnotic because I, too, forgot that we are not alone." He put one arm behind her back and the other under her knees and lifted her. "I'm just taking you to the bedroom and bringing you a change of clothes. Then I will leave, and Mia can take my place."

"I'm fine," she protested weakly.

The truth was that being held in his arms and pressed against his chest was a treat. It was also a tiny taste of what she could expect later, provided that she didn't faint again and that Mia and Toven would trust Dagor with her.

"You are not." He glanced between the two doors. "Which one is your room?"

"The one on the left." She wrapped her arms around his neck.

As he carried her to her room, she was glad she had made her bed and hung up all the dresses she had tried on before choosing the blue one.

Perhaps she had done it subconsciously to match the color of his eyes?

When Dagor deposited her on the bed, Frankie immediately missed the warmth of his embrace and chided herself for getting carried away in her infatuation with the guy.

He was a god, and she was a human who might or might not have some godly genes. The most she could hope for was a shipboard romance, and she needed to be careful and guard her heart while giving in to the attraction. She also needed to remember what Mia and Toven had said about gods and immortals not being all that different from humans. They felt the same emotions and responded to the same stimuli.

She would treat Dagor the same way she would any hunky guy she wanted to hook up with.

Dagor opened the closet and peered at the selection of clothes. "I see mostly evening dresses. Where are your comfortable clothes?"

"Open the second drawer. I have some casual things there. You can pull out any combination you like."

It was cruel to give a guy loose instructions like that, but she was curious to see what Dagor would choose. Would he bring the entire drawer contents to her, or would he pick something?

She was betting on the second option.

Surprising her, he spent a few minutes lifting items and putting them back before deciding on an outfit. When he turned around, holding a pair of biker shorts and a breezy T-shirt with a colorful print on the front, she approved of his selection.

"Not bad." She smiled at him when he handed her the items. "Do you have a sister?"

Dagor shook his head. "I'm an only child. Most gods are lucky to have one, and very few get two. The Clan Mother was blessed by the Fates to have four children. Or maybe her human partners contributed to her fertility."

The Clan Mother was the glowing goddess, and her children were probably among the couples who had escorted her into the dining hall, but that was the extent of Frankie's knowledge.

She was dying to grill him for more details about his world and what it meant to be a god, but right now, she needed to get out of the too-tight dress so she could breathe normally.

"I have many more questions, but I should change clothes before I faint again. It happens every time I learn something new that gets my pulse racing.

The look in his eyes changed, becoming predatory. "I still intend to see you naked tonight. I might as well help you with your dress."

"Nope." She smiled. "You'll have to wait. Besides, I haven't made up my mind about inviting you tonight, so don't get cocky assuming that being a god means you've got it in the bag."

"I never assume anything, Frankie. You are the boss, and what you say goes." He smiled to reassure her. "I'll tell Mia that you are ready for her."

"Thank you."

Gilbert

As Gilbert and Karen entered the elevator, it was already packed and they were the last ones to fit in, or so he thought, until Ingrid and Atzil squeezed in just as the doors closed.

"We made it." Ingrid laughed and high-fived Atzil.

"Barely," Gilbert grumbled. "I hope we don't exceed the weight limit."

As the elevator lurched, he let out a relieved breath and prayed that they wouldn't get stuck.

"Come join us for drinks in our suite," Karen said to Ingrid. "The little ones are sleeping over at Kaia's tonight, so we have the suite all to ourselves."

"We would love to." Ingrid looked up at Atzil. "You're not tired, are you?"

"Nope." He unbuttoned his tuxedo jacket and let out a breath. "But first, I must get out of this monkey suit." He shrugged his massive shoulders. "I can barely move in this thing."

"Of course." Karen nodded. "I would like to put on something more comfortable as well." She cast Gilbert a sidelong glance. "Although I have to admit that you look very dashing in your tux, and I will be sorry to see you take it off."

Usually, Gilbert would have loved the suggestive undertones in her voice and demeanor, but knowing what she was plotting, he was seething.

It was true that they had talked about it, deciding that it was the only way to go, but Gilbert wasn't ready. He needed more time to get used to the idea, even if it only involved Ingrid and Atzil getting it on in the other bedroom and Atzil rushing over to bite Karen when his fangs and venom were ready for action.

When they got to their cabin, Gilbert glared at Karen. "You shouldn't have invited them without checking with me first. I'm not ready to proceed with the plan yet."

"We don't have to do anything tonight." She stepped out of her high heels and bent down to retrieve them. "I invited them for drinks, and that's all we are obliged to do." She continued to their bedroom.

Gilbert followed. "Eric said that I would need to be chained to the bed to prevent me from attacking Atzil."

Unzipping her dress, she cast him an amused glance. "Even in your new immortal body, you are no match for the cook. Did you see the muscles on the guy?" She stepped out of the dress and draped it over the bed.

For a moment, he just looked at her, desire stealing the words out of his mouth. Even after all the years they had been together, he still had difficulty keeping his hands off her.

Now was not the time, though. "That's not the point. I know he can beat me up, but neither of us should get hurt in the process, and for that to happen, I should be restrained. Besides, what if you start transitioning immediately? I don't think the clinic on board the ship has the equipment to monitor you. Also, do you really want to miss all those weddings?"

Knowing Karen, the last part was the one that would convince her.

"As I said, I only invited them for drinks." She reached for a loose summer dress and pulled it out of the closet. "It's not easy for me either, but I think the more time we spend with Ingrid and Atzil, the more comfortable we will become with them, and it will get easier." She pulled the dress on.

Letting out a breath, Gilbert shrugged off the tux jacket. "Yeah, you're right." He took out a hanger and draped the jacket over it. "I just don't know if Atzil is the right guy. It would have been nice if you could be induced by a god."

She cast him an incredulous look. "We are not asking Toven. There is no way he will agree, and even if he did, I would die of mortification."

"I wasn't thinking of asking Toven."

"Then who?"

"Aru."

Karen laughed. "You are kidding, right? He is mated to your sister."

Gilbert ran a hand through his hair, which was becoming thicker by the day. "I know it's a little weird to make love to you in our room while Gabi and Aru are doing the same in another, but I wouldn't feel as weirded out by Aru biting you because I know he has absolutely no interest in you."

Karen grimaced. "Thanks for making me feel like an old hag."

Reaching for her, he pulled her into his arms. "You are the most desirable woman in the world to me, but Aru only has eyes for Gabi. Atzil and Ingrid are not bonded mates, so he can feel lust toward you, and I know that he does."

Her eyes widened. "Did you smell it? He could have been having lustful thoughts about Ingrid."

"Perhaps. But I know how a man looks at a desirable woman, and that was how he looked at you."

"Well, that's good, right? Otherwise, he might not want to bite me. Which Aru might have a problem with, since he's bonded to Gabi, or at least we assume that he is. He might be repulsed by me."

That hadn't occurred to Gilbert. What if Aru wasn't able to do it? Or just plain wouldn't want to?

What if Gabi couldn't tolerate the idea of her mate biting another woman, even if it was Karen?

"We can ask, or rather I can ask. I know that it would be too embarrassing for you."

Karen shook her head. "Don't. You'll just get Gabi upset, and Aru will think that you are weird. In fact, both of them will think that you are creepy, but Gabi knows you and loves you, and she will forgive you, while Aru might not want to have anything to do with you."

"My request won't be received well, but if they agree, there are two significant advantages to Aru doing the deed. He's a god, so his venom is more potent than any immortal's, especially a diluted immortal like Atzil. He could also thrall us both to think that he is not there and that I am the one biting you. That would make all the difference."

Karen pursed her lips. "You make a good argument, but I won't jeopardize our relationship with Gabi and Aru just to make things easier for us."

"I agree. The best way to test the waters is to tell them our plan with Atzil and Ingrid and wait for them to volunteer."

She sighed. "If you have your heart set on a god inducing me, you can talk to the other two gods who are not mated. Just try to be tactful and broach the subject delicately."

Gilbert pretended to scowl. "When am I not tactful and delicate?"

Karen laughed. "You're funny."

Dagor

When Dagor returned to the living room, a couple of humans were busy setting up the dining table. They had brought a cart loaded with fragrant dishes and were transferring trays to the table.

"I think Frankie can manage on her own, but just in case she faints again..."

He didn't get to finish the sentence when Mia swiveled her chair and drove into the room he'd just left, leaving him alone with the royal and the humans.

Surprisingly, the servers smiled at Toven as if they knew him, and he smiled back and addressed them by name.

When the humans had removed the last trays from the cart and put them on the table, Toven thanked them, and then they were truly alone.

"Take a seat." Toven motioned at the table. "The ladies will join us as soon as they are ready."

"Are the humans working on this ship from the immortals' village?"

"No. Save for a few exceptions, Kian doesn't allow humans in there." Toven filled his glass with water and offered the pitcher to Dagor. "I'm surprised that you don't recognize them. They are from the Kra-ell compound, which you spied on for five years. When we liberated the Kra-ell, we also freed the humans, and they chose where they wanted to settle from several options that we gave them."

"Yes, I'm aware of that. I just didn't make the connection. The truth is that we should have paid more attention to the humans in the compound. Our job was to monitor the Kra-ell and find the rest of the pods, meaning we were gone for months at a time. The monitoring we did was sporadic."

"Did you find any more pods?" Toven asked.

Shaking his head, Dagor sighed. "To borrow a human expression, it's like searching for a needle in a haystack. We followed rumors of strange materials and places that emitted unexplained radiation. Aru came up with a great cover story for us that made it less suspicious for us to ask strange questions and also supplemented our funds. We searched for flea-market finds and hunted for artifacts. We made good money on the things we found and sold, but we had no luck with the pods." He took a sip from his glass of water. "By the way, we were told that the humans from the compound were settled in a resort that belongs to the clan and that they were given house-keeping jobs."

"That's right. The resort is actually owned by one of Jade's former tribe members, but the clan got a share of it in exchange for investing in the property. I'm told that it was in dire need of renovations."

Dagor cast him a stern look. "So basically, the clan still treats the humans as serfs, just as the Kra-ell did."

"Not at all." Toven didn't seem perturbed by Dagor's accusation. "They were more than happy to return to the ship that brought them to freedom and repay their rescuers with the best service they could muster. Obviously, they were also offered bonus pay." He smiled. "Kian is a great believer in win-win solutions. This is just one example of his philosophy."

The puzzle pieces started to fall into place in Dagor's mind. Toven's familiarity with the human occupants of the compound meant that he had been there, helping to free them. The only reason the immortals would have dragged a god along for such a dangerous mission was because he could do what they couldn't—override Gor's compulsion.

"You must be a powerful compeller." He looked at the god. "You were there when the Kra-ell were liberated, and you helped free these humans."

Toven acknowledged his statement with a nod. "I am a pretty strong compeller, but it wasn't an easy task to free the Kra-ell, especially the purebloods. The humans were a piece of cake."

"The Kra-ell are impervious to thralling and shrouding, and compulsion is the only mental power that affects them. Usually, the strongest female of the tribe has power over her subjects. Gor was a perversion."

"So, his original name was Gor? He wasn't very creative picking his fake name."

Dagor chuckled. "It's easier to remember when the sound is familiar. I chose Doug, Aru chose Uriel, and Negal chose Ned."

"And I chose Tom."

As the door to the bedroom opened and the ladies came out, Dagor rose to his feet and pulled out a chair for Frankie while Toven removed one of the chairs to make room for Mia's wheelchair.

"How are you feeling?" Dagor asked as she smiled up at him.

"I feel great." She sat down. "I'm sure the fainting spells won't come back."

"I hope not." He lifted her chair and pushed it closer to the table.

Frankie laughed. "My dad used to do that to me all the time. He would pick up my chair with me in it and push it closer to the table."

"Is he still around?" Dagor asked with trepidation.

"Oh, yes. He's very much around."

Dagor let out a breath. "Human lives are so fleeting."

Frankie's smile melted away. "They are."

Mia cleared her throat and smiled brightly. "We should eat before everything gets cold."

Frankie

All throughout dinner, Frankie kept stealing glances at Dagor, and each time, he looked even more gorgeous to her. Especially when he smiled. He was also brilliant, asking Toven about the technology behind Perfect Match and whether it had been developed by humans or by the immortals.

Thankfully, Toven wasn't much of a tech guy, so his answers were easy to understand.

"I would love to try out an adventure, but I don't think Aru will authorize the expense. We need to be frugal with our resources."

"Can Dagor be a beta tester like me?" Frankie asked. "That way, he can get to experience it for free."

Toven shook his head. "Regrettably, our three distinguished guests cannot enter the secret compound."

Frankie arched a brow. "And I can?"

"You can be thralled or compelled to forget where you've been," Toven explained. "They cannot. The mind tricks that work on humans don't work on them."

"I see." Frankie cut off a piece of cake and put it in her mouth.

It wasn't a big deal that Dagor couldn't come with her to the compound. She'd already decided that their fling would be confined to the cruise. Once that was over, they would part ways.

"Don't look so crestfallen," Mia said. "I'm sure you will be allowed to leave the compound to visit your family, and you could meet Dagor in the city."

Toven shook his head. "Dagor and his companions are searching for the missing Kra-ell pods. They will probably return to the search right after the cruise."

Dagor nodded. "We were waiting for Gabi to get strong enough to travel. She is no longer under the doctor's supervision, so nothing is holding us back now."

Why did his words hurt?

Hadn't she already concluded that she would have fun with Dagor during the cruise and no more?

"What was wrong with Gabi?" Frankie asked.

Maybe the gods emitted some sort of radiation that was harmful to humans?

"She transitioned into immortality," Mia said. "Aru induced her transition the same way Toven induced mine."

"Not exactly the same way," Toven said. "Aru didn't even know what a Dormant was and that they could be induced. I knew, but I didn't realize that Dormants were still to be found so many generations later. It had never occurred to me."

Frankie shot Dagor a glance before returning her gaze to Mia. "You said before that I might be a Dormant. What makes you think that?"

Mia looked uncomfortable. "The affinity. The theory is that immortals and Dormants feel affinity toward one another. It's like recognizing like." She smiled at Toven. "Apparently, gods feel it too, and it transcends physical proximity. Toven and I fell in love inside a Perfect Match simulation."

"Is it really that good?" Dagor asked Toven.

The god nodded. "It's uncanny. I forgot who I was for those three hours or three days inside the virtual world. In there, I wasn't a god; I was just an enhanced human like many others, and I served a god." He shook his head. "This was before I owned half of Perfect Match, and I feared my identity would be discovered inside the simulation. So, I designed the adventure to include gods in case I said or did something while in the virtual world to reveal my identity. The end result, though, was more than I had expected. The story had an almost prophetic feel to it. I tried to hunt down the programmer that helped me create it, but he turned out to be a phantom."

"What do you mean?" Frankie said. "As the company's owner, you can access all its employees. How hard could it be to find out who it was?"

"He called himself Brian, and there were several Brians working at Perfect Match headquarters at the time. I spoke to each one, and they all sounded different from the Brian I spoke to. I had a phone number and an email for him, but those belonged to a lady named Gina, who had no idea who had been using her email and phone extension."

"Those were the Fates," Mia said. "There is no other explanation. One of them pretended to be a programmer named Brian."

Frankie was lost. "What do you mean the Fates? Who are they? And how did we end up talking about a guy named Brian? I want to know what makes me a Dormant aside from some elusive thing like affinity. I'm an easygoing, likable girl. Many people feel affinity toward me."

"There was also Lisa. Remember her?"

"Yeah, Geraldine's niece."

"Lisa is not really her niece. Anyway, she claims to be able to sniff out Dormants. So once Toven mentioned how much he liked you and Margo, we thought it might be affinity, and we brought Lisa to do her thing. She thought that both you and Margo were Dormants. That's why Toven offered you the jobs as beta testers.

The idea was that you would come to the village, I mean the compound, and find nice immortal males to bond with who would induce your transition."

Frankie felt dizziness assail her again and lifted her hand to stop Mia from saying anything more. "I need a moment."

Dagor

Dagor didn't like the comment about other immortal males inducing Frankie, and it annoyed him that he was bothered by it. Even if Frankie was a Dormant who could turn immortal like Aru's mate, Dagor didn't want to be saddled with a hybrid he could never take home with him. He had no intention of spending his immortal life on Earth.

"I need a moment." Frankie's quivering voice got his attention.

"What's wrong?" He leaned to look at her ashen face.

"It's all too much. I can't process it all at once. I need time to think."

"Do you want us to leave and let you rest?" Mia asked.

Yes, please leave. Dagor wanted to be left alone with Frankie.

"Not yet. So, let's say that I am a Dormant. How do I become immortal, and what does it take?"

Mia frowned. "You just said it was too much, and you couldn't take it all in at once. Perhaps we should continue with the Immortals 101 course tomorrow after you've had a good night's sleep."

Frankie nodded and then turned to Dagor. "Can you stay a little longer? I'm afraid I will faint and no one will be here to revive me, and I don't want Mia and Toven to lose sleep because of me."

"We can stay," Mia said.

"No, I'll stay." Dagor took Frankie's hand. "I can spend the night on the couch in the living room. Just leave the bedroom door open so I can hear your breathing."

She gave him a dazzling smile. "We can both be on the couch or in bed and watch television until we fall asleep."

The faint scent of her arousal indicated that watching television was not what she had in mind.

"Sounds like a plan to me." He lifted her hand to his lips and kissed her knuckles.

Toven rose to his feet and pinned Dagor with a hard look. "Can I have a moment with you outside?"

Long years of deferring to royals had Dagor incline his head. "Of course."

Cursing his automatic response internally, he pushed to his feet and followed Toven outside the suite.

Frankie rolled her eyes. "Are you going to give him the big brother speech of treating your little sister with respect?"

"Something like that." Toven's smile looked strained.

"I'll wait for you here," Mia said. "I'll help Frankie clear the table."

"Don't touch anything. I'll do it when I return," Dagor shot behind him as he followed Toven.

"Bossy, bossy," Frankie murmured as she got to her feet. "Clearing dishes will not make me faint. It's your outlandish stories that make me dizzy."

Dagor was about to reply, but Toven's hand on his shoulder sent a clear message that the god had no patience for waiting.

Once they were out in the hallway, Toven let go of his shoulder. "So here is a crash course about Dormants. The transition gets triggered by venom and semen, meaning sex. We don't know what exactly happens, but it seems that the chemicals in our venom and semen are the catalysts. If you have sex with Frankie tonight, use a condom to prevent inducing her transition. She's just learned about our world, and she's not ready, neither mentally nor physically. The doctor can tell us more about the physical aspects tomorrow after she runs some tests. Is everything clear so far?"

"I think so, except for where to get condoms. I never use them." He wanted to add that the god probably didn't use them either, but it was none of his business.

Toven smiled. "They have them in the clinic. You can dash there, and I'll tell Frankie that you need to get something from your room. We will not leave her side until your return."

"Thank you." Dagor bowed his head.

"No need to do that." Toven clapped him on the back. "We are not big on protocol here, and until you came along, we were convinced that all gods were luminous. We didn't know that the glow signified nobility. I would like to keep things informal if you don't mind."

"As you wish." Dagor fought his instinct to dip his head again. "I'll be quick about it."

As it turned out, finding the clinic was more challenging than he'd thought. There were no signs indicating its location, and there was no one to ask since everyone was still in the dining hall.

When Dagor finally found it, he was surprised that the clinic wasn't deserted.

"How can I help you, Dagor?" a white-haired immortal asked with a curious gleam in his pale blue eyes.

"Who are you?"

"Forgive me." The guy inclined his head. "My name is Merlin, and I'm one of the clan's three physicians."

Oh well, at least the guy would know why Dagor needed what he came for. Since he couldn't contract or transmit sexually transmitted diseases, and he couldn't get anyone pregnant either because chances of that were so low that they were negligible, a god had no use for condoms unless he needed to avoid inducing a Dormant's transition.

"I was told that I could find condoms in the clinic."

The doctor frowned. "What for?"

Apparently, he didn't know. Perhaps Frankie, being a potential Dormant, was only known to some.

"I was told that using a physical barrier was the only way to prevent a Dormant from transitioning before she was ready."

"Ah." Merlin's eyes widened. "Now, that makes perfect sense." He opened a drawer and pulled out two boxes of condoms. "Have you ever used them before?"

Dagor shook his head.

"Perhaps you need to practice first on a banana." Seeing Dagor's mortified expression, Merlin chuckled. "Just kidding. There are instructions inside. Read them before you attempt it or let the lady do it. She might have more experience than you in rolling one on."

Dagor preferred to think about something other than how Frankie might have acquired that skill.

The thought was odd, and her having other partners shouldn't bother him. She wasn't his, and he didn't plan on her ever becoming his, so why the human-style possessiveness?

"Thank you." He tried to flatten the boxes to fit in his tuxedo pockets.

"Hold on." The doctor pushed to his feet, walked over to one of the cabinets, and opened it. "I have a little gift for you and your lady." He pulled out a gift bag and handed it to him. "The boxes should fit in there."

Peering into the bag, Dagor saw a small box of a famous chocolate brand. "Does chocolate have a therapeutic effect on immortals?"

"In a way, it does." Merlin chuckled. "I'm the clan's fertility specialist. The elixirs I produce don't taste good, so I give them out along with the chocolates to help the medicine go down." He ended with a wink. "One of the biggest problems with patient care is ensuring compliance. If the couples I treat don't drink the potions because they taste bad, then how will they conceive?"

"Do your potions really work?" Dagor pulled out the chocolate box, stuffed the two condom boxes inside the bag, and then put the chocolates on top.

The doctor shrugged. "So far, I've had only one success, and time will tell if that was a fluke. I hope it wasn't."

Frankie

❦

"Where is Doug? I mean, Dagor?" Frankie asked as Toven returned without him.

What had the god told Dagor to scare him off?

"Don't worry," Toven said. "He's coming back. He just needed to get something from his cabin."

"Like what?"

Toven shrugged. "He didn't say. Maybe he wanted to change out of his evening attire and get a toothbrush."

That made sense, and Frankie's momentary panic eased. "Yeah, that makes sense. Although there are new toothbrushes in the bathroom. Heck, there are even face lotions and makeup remover towelettes. Whoever equipped these cabins thought of everything."

Mia nodded. "No expense has been spared." She turned to Toven. "You probably want to take off the tux as well. I'll stay with Frankie until Dagor returns."

The god frowned. "I'm perfectly comfortable in the tuxedo. I'll wait with you."

Of course, he was.

The guy looked like a tux model and seemed perfectly at ease in it, most likely because it had been custom-tailored for him.

Mia rolled her eyes. "Whether gods, immortals, or humans, males have a problem getting hints. I want to talk to Frankie alone."

"About what?" Frankie chuckled. "I don't need the birds and the bees talk."

"Oh, you definitely need the immortals and gods style birds and bees talk."

Toven nodded in agreement. "I doubt that Dagor knows how to explain it properly. I'll leave you ladies alone to have the talk." He smiled. "Good night, Frankie. And good luck. I hope you feel better."

As the god closed the door behind him, Frankie frowned. "What did he mean by good luck? Are gods difficult to seduce or do they have trouble getting or keeping it up?"

Mia laughed. "If anything, they have the opposite problem. Not that it's an issue. Multiple orgasms are the norm and no morning-after soreness. You are in for the best sex of your life, but there are a few things you need to know, and I suggest that you lie down on the couch first."

"Why?"

"You fainted twice today already after getting too worked up in your head, and what I'm going to tell you might have a similar effect."

"I'm fine. It's not going to happen again."

"If it does, and you fall, I can't catch you." Mia glanced at the door. "You'd better hurry up and lie down before Dagor returns, or you will have to learn about the birds and the bees from him."

With a sigh, Frankie stretched out on the couch. "Would that be such a bad idea? Letting him teach me would be like being a virgin all over again, just without the pain. Could be fun."

Mia shrugged. "It's up to you. If you are more comfortable with Dagor explaining things to you, I have no problem. Still, I just think that hearing it from me would be less traumatic and therefore less likely to induce panic and fainting."

She had a point, and since the word traumatic had been included, Frankie was starting to panic already. Did these aliens have different anatomy than human males?

Mia had mentioned multiple orgasms and no soreness in the morning, so whatever it was couldn't be too bad.

"Okay, tell me." She crossed her arms over her chest with her hands resting on her throat.

"What are you doing?" Mia tilted her head. "You're freaking me out with this coffin pose."

"Sorry." Frankie lowered her hands to rest on her tummy. "Please enlighten me, oh goddess of love and lust."

Mia snorted. "I wish. Anyway, let's start with the anatomy."

Frankie winced. "I was afraid of that."

"Male gods and immortals have elongating fangs and venom glands. Their fangs respond to two triggers: one is aggression, and the other is arousal, and the two do not mix. They get aggressive only when they have the urge to fight, and it's always toward other males."

"What if they are sexually interested in other males? The signals could get mixed."

"I don't think so, but I don't know that for sure. I'll have to ask Toven." Mia narrowed her eyes at her. "So far, you are taking it surprisingly well. What's the deal with that?"

"You know how much I like reading vampire romances. The thought of losing copious quantities of blood scares me, but the fangs on their own do not."

Mia's suspicious expression morphed into a smile. "That's what you think. Wait until you see Dagor's fully elongated fangs. They are really scary, but the good news is that gods and immortals don't use them to drink blood. They are for injecting venom, which does wondrous things. It's a euphoric, an aphrodisiac, and a healing tonic all in one. You're going to orgasm like you never have before, then you're going to soar over the clouds and see strange and wonderful things, and when you wake up, you'll feel like a new woman, energized, vibrant, and ready for another round."

Frankie turned to look at her friend and grinned. "Why did you think telling me that would make me faint again? That sounds amazing."

"It is out of this world, literally, but after you reacted so strongly to what we told you before and to seeing the goddess and discovering that your new friend was a god, I was sure the mention of fangs would induce another fainting spell."

"Yeah, well. I fell down the rabbit hole, and it was scary, but now that I'm already in Wonderland, I'm ready to explore all it has to offer."

Dagor

Dagor stopped by his room to grab a quick shower, brush his teeth, and put on a pair of jeans and a T-shirt.

When he emerged from his room with the gift bag Merlin had given him, he found his companions sitting in the living room, Aru and Negal still in their tuxedos and Gabi in her evening gown.

"Is the girl okay?" Gabi asked.

"For now, she is. I will spend the night in her cabin to keep an eye on her, and tomorrow, the doctor will see her."

"How do you know her?" Aru asked.

He didn't have time to explain. "I met her on the Lido deck; we shared a drink and got friendly. Now, if you'll excuse me, a royal is waiting for me to show up and release him from his post of keeping an eye on his mate's best friend."

Dagor didn't wait for a response as he walked to the door and opened it. "Have a good night. I'll see you tomorrow at breakfast."

"Have fun," Gabi called after him.

He intended to, but he needed to figure out what fun he would pursue.

Something was wrong with Frankie, so perhaps watching television in bed would be all they could do. It was a shame because she looked so sexy in the comfy outfit he'd chosen for her.

There was also the issue of his fangs. Did she even know about that?

Surely her best friend had shared the details with her, but if not, he would have to do it, and he wasn't sure how. He had thralled all the other human females he'd been with to not notice his fangs or glowing eyes. After they had woken up from their stupor, he'd reinforced the thralling with fake memories.

There was no need to do that with Frankie, and since he planned on enjoying her company more than once, he shouldn't thrall her.

On the other hand, he might save her a fright, which was an essential consideration given her propensity to faint when overwhelmed.

When he got to her cabin, Dagor rang the doorbell and waited for the door to open while wondering if she'd discovered that she could open it with the remote. Until he'd told Gabi about it, she hadn't known that she could see who was on the other side of the door on the television screen and not just on the small one next to the door.

As the buzzing sound ensued, signaling that the lock was disengaged, but no one opened the door, he figured Frankie had found out about the first but not the second.

He pushed the door open and walked inside. "Hello." He smiled at both ladies. "My apologies for taking so long. I stopped by my room to shower and change."

"Toven told us." Frankie eyed the little bag with curiosity. "What did you get?"

"A surprise." He turned to Mia. "Did your mate leave already?"

"He did." She reached with her hand and put it on his arm. "Goodnight, Dagor. Take good care of my friend."

"I will."

After Mia left, there was a long silence, with him and Frankie appraising each other. She was spread out on the couch, and he didn't know whether to sit next to her or on the armchair.

"Come sit with me." She scooted back and patted the spot she'd vacated. "And show me what's in the bag. I love surprises."

Dagor pulled out the box of chocolates. "I hope you like them."

"I love them." She took the small box from his hands. "Thank you." Instead of opening it, she glanced at the paper bag that still looked full. "What else is in there?"

"Hope." He smiled sheepishly. "Maybe not for tonight, though."

When her eyes widened, and he sniffed a faint scent of arousal, he knew that she'd guessed the contents of the bag.

"Where did you get them and why? You're a god. Mia said that you can't catch or transmit diseases, and I'm on the pill."

It appeared as if Mia hadn't told her friend everything yet. "Did Mia tell you how Dormants are activated?"

She shook her head. "I asked, but I didn't get an answer. Mia said that we should leave it for tomorrow, and after you and Toven left, we talked about other stuff, and I forgot to ask her about it again."

Damn.

It was up to him to tell her. "Do you at least know about us having fangs?"

"Yes. Mia told me about that. But I wanted to ask whether the females had fangs too and never got to."

"They do, but they are minimal and don't elongate."

She frowned. "Mia's teeth are still the same as before she met Toven."

Dagor smiled apologetically. "I really can't comment on it because I know next to nothing about what happens during transition. Gabi gained half an inch in height, but she didn't grow fangs."

Frankie's eyes sparkled with interest. "I would love to gain some inches. I'm not saying I want to transition, but if I do, it would be nice to get a little taller."

He took her hand and brought it to his lap. "You are perfect the way you are."

"And you are a flatterer," she said with a chiding tone, but her eyes shone with satisfaction at his compliment. "Now tell me about your fangs."

"I've always thought of my fangs as a defensive weapon or as a way to bring pleasure to my paramours, but I've never thought they could be used in the way the clan does. I've only learned recently about the existence of immortals and dormant carriers of godly genes that can be activated with venom." He felt uncomfortable bringing up the second part of the equation.

He would ease into that.

Frankie

T hat was a lot of new information, but Frankie
wasn't getting dizzy, and her mind was focused
and sharp.

Perhaps because she was lying down this time?

Dagor was so cute when he used old-fashioned terms like
paramour instead of lover or sex partner. It was a nice
change from the guys she dated, who cussed left and
right.

The truth was that she used the f-bomb quite often, but
mostly quietly, so her boss wouldn't hear her.

Her ex-boss.

Her new boss, or who she hoped would be her new boss,
was such a perfect gentleman that she was sure the f-
bomb wouldn't pass her lips even once while working for
him.

It was all about the company one kept, as her mom kept saying. Luckily, she approved of Margo and Mia, or Frankie wouldn't have heard the end of it.

"What are you thinking about?" Dagor's thumb drew circles on the back of her hand.

She smiled at his gorgeous face. "That I'm doing okay and not fainting from brain overload. So, from what I understand, to induce a Dormant, an immortal or a god needs to bite her or him and inject them with his venom?"

"That's what I was led to understand. But there is more." With a sigh, he pulled a box of condoms from the gift bag. "It has to happen during unprotected sex, so if we get intimate, but you don't want to transition just yet, we need to use these."

The face he made was like they were the vilest things in the world.

But they were a necessity.

Still, it was kind of awkward to talk about sex when they hadn't even kissed yet. Well, Dagor had kissed her knuckles, but that didn't count.

"They are not so bad." She closed her eyes for a moment. "But perhaps it's a little premature to talk about condoms when you haven't kissed me yet. Besides, I have a three-date rule. I don't have sex with a guy until at least our third date."

Dagor's smile was predatory. "But it is our third date."

She laughed. "By what count?"

"The first one was this morning on the Lido deck."

"That doesn't count as a date."

"I beg to differ. We shared a drink, talked, and made plans for another date."

"What about the second one?"

"We've met in the dining hall, and when you fainted, I followed you here. Then I left and came back with a gift, and that counts as a third date."

"That's a very convoluted count, but I'll accept it because this is a cruise vacation, so regular rules don't apply."

If he would only stop talking and kiss her already, things would progress smoothly from there, but Dagor seemed hesitant to start anything. Should she take the initiative and kiss him?

He was obviously interested.

But maybe he wasn't sure?

He was a god, and she was a human, and maybe he was still undecided about wanting to slum it.

Nah. She could see the desire in his eyes but also the conflict.

She had two options. She could lift to her knees and straddle him, or she could pull him on top of her. Given her fainting spells, the second option seemed better.

Tugging on his hand, she signaled her intent and hoped he would follow because she doubted that she could actually pull him on top of her if he didn't cooperate.

He leaned over but remained seated, and as his eyes began glowing, Frankie tensed.

"Are your fangs elongating?"

He nodded.

"Would you be able to kiss me without hurting me?"

When he nodded again, she realized he didn't want to open his mouth.

"Show me. I want to see."

He shook his head.

"I promise that I will not freak out. I watched all five *Twilight* movies five times, and I had a big crush on Edward."

"Who's Edward?"

"Got you." She pointed at his mouth. "I saw your fangs, and I didn't panic."

Shaking his head, Dagor smiled, showing her his fully extended fangs, which were indeed monstrous.

How was he even able to close his mouth?

"Is that as big as they get?" She reached with a finger.

He caught it so fast that she didn't see him move. "Careful, they are sharp, and no, this is not their full length."

He sounded a little slurred, but it was sexy.

Heck, everything about the guy was sexy.

"You move as fast as Edward."

"You still haven't told me who this Edward fellow is."

It was easy to forget that Dagor wasn't really from Hungary, or from Earth for that matter, and that he hadn't seen *Twilight* or read the books.

She liked that he was jealous, though.

"Edward is a fictional character who is a vampire, but not an evil one. He is one of the good guys, and he protects humans."

When Dagor stared at her with confusion in his incredibly blue eyes, she frowned. "You know what a vampire is, right? As in a bloodsucker?"

His eyes brightened. "Like the Kra-ell."

"Who and what are the Kra-ell?"

Dagor

❦

"Never mind." Dagor waved a dismissive hand. "There are none on this ship. They don't like deep water."

Frankie gaped at him. "I still don't get it. Are they people who suck blood from other people and animals like vampires do, or are they some bat-like animal that lives on blood?"

"They are people from my home planet, and they mostly drink from animals. They are a different species."

"You mean different from the gods."

"Yes."

"Why do you call yourselves gods?"

He smiled. "Because we are the creators of all intelligent life in the galaxy, including Earth."

Her eyes widened. "Get out of here."

"Did I offend you? Is that why you want me to go?"

Frankie's lips twitched with a suppressed smile. "It's just an expression. I don't want you to leave."

He let out a breath. "That's a relief. I'm sorry about not getting some of your cultural references. I'm not much of a television or movie watcher, and I don't read fiction. My interests are more technical in nature."

She lifted her hand and cupped his cheek. "You would have been perfect for my other bestie, Margo. She loves smart nerds. But I call dibs, meaning you are mine because I saw you first."

"I'm good with that." He dipped his head and pressed a soft, experimental kiss to her lips.

Her eyelashes fluttered. "Really? You are okay with being mine?"

Not forever. For the length of the cruise, he was willing to be exclusive with Frankie, but she might not like his answer.

Still, he didn't want to mislead her.

"I'm yours until the end of the cruise. After that, my team is heading out to Tibet, and you are starting a new job at Perfect Match, so the best we will be able to do is talk on the phone or send each other messages." He smiled. "Long-distance relationships are difficult to maintain."

Frankie wrapped her arms around his neck. "We've just met, and I don't have any grand expectations from you. I just want to have some fun with a god." She frowned. "Damn, I won't be allowed to brag about it, right?"

"No."

"Oh well. I can still talk about you with Mia and Margo." She lifted her head so their lips were nearly touching. "And I'll cherish my memories privately."

There was a good chance that she wouldn't be allowed to keep even that, but he wasn't going to spoil the mood by mentioning it now. It could wait for later.

Much later.

"I am going to pick you up and carry you to your bed. Is that okay?"

Frankie nodded enthusiastically and then looked at the condoms. "Don't forget these. I don't want you to induce my transition."

He lifted her into his arms. "Ever?"

"I don't know." A shadow passed over her eyes. "To gain something, something else needs to be sacrificed. I'm unsure if I want to trade my family for immortality."

He carried her to the bedroom and put her down on the bed. "Your family is that important to you? You would give up immortality so as not to outlive them?"

"Yes. Perhaps I could have my cake and eat it too, which means that I will get to keep both, but I don't know the rules of the game yet, and I don't want to make any rush decisions, so for now, a condom is a must."

Dagor chuckled. "Condoms, as in plural. Didn't Mia tell you about the gods' stamina? Once is not enough for us." He dipped his head and nuzzled her breast through her shirt and bra. "We can go on and on, but since you are human, I will have to go easy on you."

It was so liberating to talk freely about who he was with a woman and not fear her reaction.

She arched into the touch. "Can you dim the light? I'm not bashful, but this much light is not romantic."

"Sure." He got off the bed.

"I thought you could do that with your mind. Isn't that what gods do?"

"No." He smiled as he did what she asked. "What we do is make you think that we dimmed the light. We have power over human and immortal minds. We don't have telekinetic abilities."

"Bummer." Frankie gripped the bottom of her shirt and pulled it over her head. "I thought that you could also teleport, but I guess the answer to that is 'no' as well?"

Dagor removed his shirt and tossed it over the back of a chair. "Sorry to disappoint you with my lack of talent in those areas, but I'm sure you won't be disappointed with my other talents." He prowled over her.

"You are such a show-off." Her eyes roved appreciatively over his muscled torso. "But hey, if you have it, flaunt it, right?" She wrapped her arms around his neck and pulled him down for a kiss.

Frankie

Frankie's bravado melted when Dagor lowered his body over hers and took over the kiss.

How did he manage to knead her lips so perfectly with those huge fangs in his mouth?

It was hard to concentrate and figure out anything while his hard body was pressed to hers, his powerful arms holding her to him and her skin tingling from the contact.

He was only kissing her, and it still felt like the most intense sex she'd ever had. Maybe it was the feel of the rigid rod still hidden inside his pants pressing against her thigh or the raw energy he was emitting, making her skin erupt in goosebumps.

Could he be dangerous to her?

What if that tingling electricity that made her so moist and needy was some radioactivity that could harm her?

The worry was like a distant humming in her mind, all too easy to ignore. Right now, she wanted to reach between their bodies and wrap her hand over that bulge, but without the barrier of his jeans in the way. She wanted them both to be naked, skin to skin.

As his lips moved to her neck and his hands smoothed over her sides, her hands roved over the rugged ridges of his back, and when he let her come up for air, she murmured against his lips, "Take off the rest of your clothes."

The smile he gave her somehow looked like a sexy smirk despite the fangs. The man was so gorgeous that even those sharp and scary things did not distract from his allure.

Not a man, she reminded herself, *a god*.

Sliding back, Dagor got to his feet and reached for the button of his jeans. "Are you curious, Frankie?" He popped the button.

"Very."

By now, she knew he could move with such incredible speed that she could barely see it. It was almost like teleporting. Now, he was going slowly so she could enjoy the show. Maybe he wanted to watch her reaction when he took his pants off, and she hoped he wasn't hiding anything weird behind the denim. Although, as hungry as she was for him, she was willing to forgive a lot of alienness as long as it wasn't something that would cause her pain.

She'd once dated a guy who had piercings on his shaft. Frankie had taken one look at that and shown him the door.

Who in their right mind did that?

Taunting her, Dagor turned around and gave her a spectacular view of his ass as he pushed the jeans down his thighs and then let them drop the rest of the way.

He either hadn't worn any underwear, or he'd pushed them down along with the pants.

Frankie held her breath as he stepped out of the pile on the floor and turned around.

A gasp escaped her throat as she saw his erection. There was nothing alien or strange about it, but it was massive.

"Wow. You're really big."

A frown creased his brow. "Is that a good thing or bad?"

She chuckled. "It's not about the size. It's about how you use it." It was a little about the size too, but there was no reason to make the god even more cocky.

His eyes blazing with inner light, he put one knee on the bed, then the other, and crawled toward her.

"You're overdressed, my darling."

Hooking his thumbs in the elastic of her biker shorts, he tugged them down her legs and tossed them on the floor.

Her panties got more gentle treatment, and when they were off, Dagor inhaled and closed his glowing eyes for a moment as if savoring a fragrant bouquet.

Mia had said that gods and immortals had enhanced senses, and he was probably smelling her arousal. It would have been embarrassing if not for the blissed-out expression on his face.

Putting his hands on her knees, he looked into her eyes and applied light pressure, indicating that he wanted her to spread her legs for him.

Frankie liked that he was asking permission and not assuming he had the right to pry her knees apart. Nevertheless, this level of intimacy with a guy whom she'd kissed for the first time only moments ago felt awkward.

Still, it was only fair. After all, he'd shown her his, so she needed to show him hers.

Not applying any counter-pressure, she allowed him to spread her legs, and the expression on his face turned from lustful to reverent.

A god was looking at her as if she was something special and didn't that make her feel like a goddess. A very aroused goddess who needed him to touch her before she went up in flames.

Just having him look at her like that brought her to the edge.

When he reached with his hand and gently brushed a finger over her wet folds, she bit on her lower lip to keep from pleading with him to put it inside of her, but when he brought that same finger to her entrance and just circled it, she couldn't hold it in any longer.

"Please," she half begged, half hissed.

A smirk lifting one side of his lips, he slid the finger inside of her. "You are so wet for me." He finally pressed his thumb where she needed it most.

The tension that had been building, first slowly and then speeding up exponentially, reached critical velocity, and Frankie had no choice but to let go.

When a breath whooshed out of her, she expected Dagor to get between her legs and feed her that enormous erection of his. Still, the guy had the self-control of a god, and instead of his shaft, she was treated to his tongue.

"Oh, my God, Dagor." She threaded her fingers in his hair.

"Yes, sweetheart?"

"Just keep doing what you're doing."

Dagor

After Dagor had wrung out every last drop of pleasure from Frankie, and she pushed on his head to make him stop, he crawled up on top of her and took her mouth in a kiss.

She was dazed, her arms wrapping weakly around him, but she hadn't fainted and hadn't freaked out. He'd given her plenty of opportunities to see his fangs and feel how sharp they were when he nicked her inner thighs and then licked the little hurts away.

Every time he had done that, her arousal had spiked higher.

"Mmm." She licked her lips once he let go of them. "I taste good on you. I wonder how you will taste on me."

He was already harder than an iron rod, and the image she painted in his mind made him harden even more. But having those luscious lips of hers wrapped around his shaft would have to wait. Right now, he needed to be inside of her more than anything. Even if the patrol ship had swooped by and offered to take him home, he wasn't sure he would have been able to stop.

"I need to be inside of you." He gripped his shaft and positioned it at her entrance.

"Wait." She put a hand on his chest. "Condom first."

He'd forgotten all about it.

With a groan, he rolled off her, reached for the box, tore it open, and pulled out a packet. "You'll have to put it on me. I've never done it before." He handed it to her.

"Oh, wow. How exciting." Frankie sat up, threw a knee over his thighs, and straddled them.

Tearing the packet open with her teeth, she took the small latex ring, which didn't look like it could encompass his girth, and placed it over the tip. "I hope it fits."

"So do I." He watched as she expertly pinched the top with the fingers of one hand while rolling it down with her other.

Surprisingly, it fit.

When she finished with a kiss to the tip, he nearly climaxed just from that. And when she lifted her bottom and positioned herself above him, he nicked his lower lip with his fangs.

"Is that okay?" She gripped his length and positioned it so the tip was at her entrance.

"It's perfect."

Holding up his sheathed erection, Frankie rubbed it in her juices but didn't push herself on it yet. "Some men don't like to be under a woman."

He smiled, which should have terrified her, but the sight of his fangs seemed to excite her. "You can be over me, under me, to one side or another, and upside down. I'll take you any way I can get you."

"Sexy devil." She leaned forward and brushed her lips over his.

"Don't you mean god?"

"Sometimes it's hard to tell the difference." She lowered herself, taking in just the tip.

Dagor saw stars. "Take me deeper."

"Patience, lover god. You're large, and I'm small. I need to do this slowly."

He nodded. "Take as long as you want, but just know that you are torturing me."

She smiled. "Your self-control is impressive. Any other guy would have surged up already."

Hope shone in his eyes. "Do you want me to?"

Frankie shook her head. "I'll let you know when you can take over." Her smile turned evil. "Let's see how long you can manage to hold back."

Silly woman. She didn't know that he would do anything to win a challenge.

Fisting the sheet to avoid gripping her thighs, he returned her evil smile with one of his own. "I won't move a muscle, but I can't guarantee that there will be no spontaneous eruption."

"You'd better not." Her hold on the base of his erection tightened. "You will wait until I tell you that you can come."

Dagor suppressed a laugh.

The tiny sprout was a closet dominatrix. Or maybe she was openly dominant?

He could definitely see her in the role, wearing a leather corset, thigh-high boots with enormous platform heels, and wielding a crop.

Dagor had never thought he would enjoy being dominated by a female during sex, but as long as it was just fun and games, he could play along.

"You're on, darling." He released the sheet and lifted his arms over his head. "Take me. I'm yours."

Frankie

Frankie had a god sprawled under her, and he was putting himself at her mercy.

Talk about a heady feeling.

She had no intention of tormenting him for long because it would be torturous for her as well. Still, she had no doubt that the moment things got more intense, he would flip them over, and the little game she was playing would be over.

Just watching him sprawled out under her was a treat.

Dagor was a self-proclaimed nerd, yet he had an impressive eight-pack and a drool-worthy chest.

In fact, Frankie was drooling already.

With his sizable shaft firmly lodged inside of her, she could let go of it and brace both hands on those defined pectorals for purchase.

Lifting a fraction of an inch, she came down, taking a little more in and feeling the stretch.

The guy, correction, the god, was bigger than any man she'd ever been with, and she also hadn't had anything bigger than BOB inside of her for nearly six months.

Compared to Dagor, though, BOB was a toy in more ways than one.

"You're evil," Dagor hissed.

"Says the guy with the razor-sharp fangs." She wiggled her bottom, getting him a little deeper, but not by much.

Realizing that she wasn't doing this just to torture him, Dagor lifted one of his arms and reached with his finger to gently massage her clit.

"Take as long as you need. Worst case scenario, I'll provide extra lubrication to ease in."

She lifted up almost to the very end and then pushed down, this time getting nearly half of him in.

"You have a condom on, so your lubrication won't help." Panting, she held herself still. "I don't think I've ever been with a guy who talked so casually about premature ejaculation."

As he laughed, his abdominal muscles rippled. "That's because it won't slow me down. I will be up and ready again immediately." The glow in his eyes got so intense that it was difficult to look at him. "Again and again for as many times as you want me."

"It must be nice to be a god." She lifted up and, gritting her teeth, pushed down, intending to get him all the way in but not quite managing it. "Damn. This is like being a virgin again."

This was supposed to be a sexy game. Still, her arms were trembling from the effort of keeping herself suspended above him. The stretched-out, slightly burning feeling of having him inside of her was just on the right side of painful.

His finger kept drawing lazy circles around her clit. "Do you want me to take over?"

"Only if you can be patient."

"I have all the time in the world." He wrapped his arms around her middle and rolled her under him. "This angle will be better for you."

He dipped his head and kissed her neck while pushing a hand under her bottom. Squeezing her butt cheeks together, he lifted her bottom a little. It should have made things more difficult, but to her surprise, the new angle was enough to allow for a smoother glide.

When he was fully seated inside of her, they both groaned, and then he kissed her again while gently rocking in and out of her.

The god was the most considerate lover she'd ever had, and the thought brought tears to her eyes because he wasn't hers to keep.

"Frankie," he breathed her name as if it was precious to him.

The gentle rocking continued for a while longer until he was gliding in and out of her with ease, and she wanted him to start going faster.

He must have sensed the change in her, and everything about him changed between one blink of an eye and the next.

Gone was the gentle lover, replaced by a lustful beast who grunted as he pulled nearly all the way out and slammed all the way in, hitting the end of her channel.

All she could do was wrap her arms and legs around him and hold on for dear life.

The sensation of him inside of her, on top of her, all around her, was incredible. Soon, she was coiling up, readying for another explosion. When it slammed into her, she heard herself saying things she had never spoken to any other guy out loud, the f-bomb combined with harder and faster.

Dagor hissed and clamped a hand over her head, tilting it sideways. As his erection kicked inside of her, announcing his release, he licked the tender spot between her neck and shoulder and struck.

She felt his fangs slicing into her flesh, but the pain she'd expected never came. It was more like pressure with a little sting, and then something cool entered her bloodstream, and she came again.

The string of orgasms that followed rocked through her and exhausted her to the point of blacking out. Then she was soaring above the clouds and looking at the most beautiful surreal alien landscapes. Only they weren't totally alien because she remembered someone describing them to her.

It was nearly impossible to string together two coherent thoughts while soaring, and she promised herself to think about that later after she floated back to Earth.

Aru

Aru waited for Gabi to be deeply asleep before contacting his sister. It wasn't that he feared his mate could see or sense what he was doing, but she was a distraction. He needed to concentrate to open the channel and deliver the news about the heir.

It was good that Aria had developed excellent memorization skills since becoming the Supreme's scribe, so she would be able to recount everything he would tell her word for word.

The problem was the oracle's relay to the queen.

The oracle was only sometimes entirely in this world, and often she confused reality with what she saw from all over the universe and sometimes from other universes.

Most oracles as powerful as she had gone mad at a young age, but Sofringhati, the most powerful oracle ever born, had outlasted the best by many thousands of years.

Perhaps it was her sense of humor that kept her sane or her long friendship with the queen. Still, it was a miracle that she was lucid enough to keep the best-guarded secret on Anumati and beyond. Without her, the resistance wouldn't have been possible.

The queen couldn't have done it all on her own.

When he sensed Gabi was deeply asleep, Aru opened the channel to his sister. *Are you available to talk?*

Yes, brother of mine. It is night-time over here, and I am in bed. What news do you bring?

How did you know that I have news?

She laughed. *We are twins, Aru. I can sense your excitement even when you try to appear calm.*

He needed to tell her about the heir, and a long preamble wouldn't do. Finding the princess was such an unexpected miracle that no amount of hinting could make Aria guess what news he was bringing. He had to take the risk and assume that no one could eavesdrop on their mental conversation and speak plainly.

I have incredible news. The queen's son had a daughter, and she lives. The only legitimate heir to Anumati's throne was born on Earth and lived on after the bombing, and she seems to be just the type of ruler we need.

How do you know she is the daughter of Ahn?

Annani is the spitting image of our queen. They have the same face, but Annani's hair is red, and she is about a foot shorter than her grandmother. She must have inherited her diminutive size and hair color from her mother.

The Eternal King was not a large male either. In fact, he was quite short, but no one dared to say that out loud or make fun of the fact that the king and queen never addressed the public together because she was half a head taller than he was.

Did she inherit any traits from her grandfather? Aria asked.

I do not know. I have only spent about an hour with her, and she did not disclose her abilities. Her power is palpable, though, so I do not doubt she inherited at least some of his strength. But that is where the resemblance ends. Annani is benevolent, leading her clan of immortals with wisdom and care. They call her Clan Mother, and they all love and respect her.

When Aria did not respond for a long moment, Aru asked, *are you there?*

Yes. Forgive me, brother. A thousand thoughts are going through my mind while I try to memorize what you have told me word for word. Did you find out how big the clan is?

He had expected that question and knew that his sister, the oracle, and the queen would all think that leading a small clan did not equate to leading the galaxy. *The clan is only several hundred people strong, but they have done a lot of good for humans throughout the millennia since the other gods were eliminated, and they did it while fighting their archen-emy, who has a stronger army of immortals and whose goals are opposite to theirs. Where Annani and her people want humans to become an enlightened global society that promotes equal opportunity for all and meets all the basic needs of Earth's citizens, their enemy wants humans to remain dumb, backward, and in-fighting so he can easily subjugate it.*

Over the past two weeks, Aru had conducted many conversations with Kian about the clan's history, what it had achieved, and its plans for the future. He had only recently learned that Kian was not the head of the clan but only the regent for his mother, leading the American arm of it. His sister Sari fulfilled a similar role in Europe.

I will do my best to relay everything you've told me to the Supreme. I hope she will understand the details when she sees the queen and tells her the good news.

Can't you go with her? Aru asked. *You are her scribe. It will not look suspicious.*

It will. Aria sighed. *The queen and the Supreme have been meeting for thousands of years in seclusion. It is always just the two of them with no witnesses. We cannot change the tradition without arousing suspicion.*

Dagor

❧

Dagor had stayed awake most of the night, listening to Frankie breathe, monitoring her heartbeat, and thinking about his future.

She had exceeded his expectations in every way. Even though he'd been more careful and reserved with her than with most of the human females he'd been with, it had been one of the best nights of his life, and it hadn't been only about the sex.

He'd had fun with Frankie, and he'd felt something for her that he hadn't felt in a very long time.

He wanted more with her.

When Dagor was a young god, barely of the age of consent, he'd fallen in love with a young goddess who'd lived nearby. They had been together for nearly a full Anumati year, and then she had left to serve on one of the colonies, and he'd been drafted to the service. For a while, they had kept in touch, but slowly they had drifted apart. There was no point in keeping the flame going when there was no chance for them to be together.

In time, the love he'd felt for her had dimmed until it faded completely. He'd been lucky that Lilat hadn't been his fated mate or the separation would have devastated them both.

Being fated mates could have added gravitas to their request to be stationed together. Still, it was difficult to prove the claim, and commoners like them were rarely accommodated, even in extreme cases.

Turning onto his side, Dagor gazed at Frankie's sleeping face.

She was a lighthearted girl, easy to smile and laugh, and generous with her body and her feelings. It was a shame that they wouldn't see each other after the cruise.

He was going to Tibet, and she was going to the immortals' village to start her dream job as a beta tester for the Perfect Match adventures.

Perhaps he could convince Aru not to leave immediately, so he could try out one of those adventures with Frankie. He was curious about the technology and how much of the gods' know-how had gone into it.

He would love to spend time in their headquarters and work with their programmers. He had never received an official education in the subject. Still, he'd taught himself much about Earth's tech from watching instructional videos.

Frankie's eyes suddenly popped open, and a smile spread over her face. "You stayed."

"Of course. I told you I would. I was watching over you."

"The entire night?"

He nodded. "Gods don't need as much sleep as humans. I can catch up on some shuteye later. How do you feel?"

"I feel great." She scooted closer and tucked herself into him. "I have my own guardian angel." She kissed the underside of his jaw. "So, what's the plan for today?"

"Breakfast." He put his hand on her stomach. "Your belly started rumbling about an hour ago. I was sure it would wake you up."

"I had wonderful dreams. I didn't want to wake up." She closed her eyes. "I'm having a hard time deciding between staying awake to be with you and going back to sleep so I can dream some more."

Smoothing a hand over her naked back, he reached her buttock and gave it a gentle squeeze. "We can get up, have a cup of coffee, grab something to eat, and get back in bed." He was already hardening, and since she was pressed against him, she was feeling it.

"Right." She chuckled. "I fell asleep after your first climax and deprived you of the chance to show me your impressive recuperating time."

"You didn't fall asleep. You blacked out."

Frankie paled. "Did I faint again?"

"No, that wasn't it. It's normal for the female to black out after a venom bite. The euphoric element of the venom sends you on a fun trip that you are not in a rush to end. Do you remember any of it?"

"I do." Her eyes lost focus as she looked inward. "It was out of this world, literally. I saw translucent beings that were made of energy. They smiled and waved at me while I was passing over them." Her eyes refocused on him. "Do you know who they are?"

He shook his head. "Everyone reports more or less the same experience, but I don't know whether they are common hallucinations induced by chemicals contained in the venom, or something more."

"What about your spiritual leaders? Don't they have something to say about it?"

She could only imagine what humans would have made out of that. Some would have blamed the devil and called it a grave sin, while others would have made it into a religious experience.

He smiled. "If I could get an audience with an oracle, and if one was willing to grant me an answer, I could ask that question, but oracles are rare, and getting an audience is nearly impossible. People wait many years until their name is drawn in the lottery."

Frankie

ᕫᕬᕬᕭ

Dagor's home world sounded fascinating, and Frankie wondered how much he would be willing to tell her about it. Still, right now, she was most interested in those translucent beings made of energy.

If the oracles had the answers, how come no one had asked them about it yet?

That didn't seem likely. Dagor was probably just avoiding answering her question to keep up the mystery.

Still, it was possible that the goddesses on Dagor's planet didn't see the same things human females saw when tripping on venom. They might not be as susceptible to the venom's effect.

It was difficult to think with Dagor's hands roving over her back in a very suggestive way, but Frankie commanded her libido to stand down. Her body had already been sated last night, and it could give her mind a chance to satisfy its curiosity.

"I have a few questions."

Dagor smiled. "Usually, human females are much more loopy when they wake up from a venom trip. You seem perfectly lucid and ready to fire away."

"What can I say?" She batted her eyelashes. "I'm special. Do goddesses react the same way to the venom?"

"Not as strongly, but yes. They do."

"Do they see the translucent energy people?"

He nodded. "Everyone sees them when they are tripping. Even males sometimes see them, but since they usually have short trips, they don't remember much from them."

"How do males get to trip? I mean the heterosexual ones." She looked at him from under lowered lashes. "Do you have bisexual and gay gods?"

He laughed. "People who live forever eventually try everything, but there are those who are predominantly one or the other."

"That makes sense. So, what about those who never engage with other males? How do they get to trip on venom and see people made of energy?"

"In fights, gods bite other gods, and that's how they experience a venom bite, but in a very different way than females do. The venom is more concentrated, and its effect is stronger and shorter, but since we are very civilized now and no longer try to kill each other, the fighting is limited to sports, which are not very popular."

"That's good. I wish it was the same for humans." As his finger brushed over the seam between her butt cheeks, Frankie squirmed. "Are you doing this to make me stop asking you questions?"

He smirked. "No, you can keep asking for as long as you can hold back. This is payback for keeping me on the edge last night."

That was fair, and it was also a game Frankie knew that she would win. He had no idea how stubborn she could be.

"Did you ever get to experience a venom trip?"

Dagor nodded. "Troopers train in hand-to-hand combat. To my great shame, I often lost and got bitten."

"Why shame?"

He shrugged. "You know how males are. Gods, immortals, and humans are all the same in that regard. We are prideful, and we want to best our opponents."

Since the gods created people in their image using their own genetic material, it made sense that there were many similarities.

She cupped his cheek. "It's not the strongest who wins, but the smartest and those who persevere. I'm sure that you won in all the mind and strategy games."

"I won many of those, but there were better gods than me. It's hard to be exceptional in a society of trillions."

She couldn't imagine so many people. Earth's population was about eight billion. One trillion was a hundred and twenty-five times that.

"How many trillions?"

"There are about three trillion gods on Anumati and one trillion Kra-ell."

Frankie let out a whistle. "That's five hundred times Earth's population."

"That's only Anumati. Together with the colonies and settlements around the universe, it's close to double that."

"Incredible. Now I understand why it takes so long to get answers from the oracles, especially if there aren't many of them."

"I think that only the Supreme can answer questions of that magnitude," Dagor said. "Still, even if she could, it doesn't mean she would. She might decide that this is not the kind of information mere gods should possess."

As Dagor's fingers dipped into her moist center, Frankie's eyes rolled back in her head. "You win. The rest of my questions can wait for later."

He chuckled. "You are supposed to call the doctor and tell her when you are ready to see her. Can that wait, too?"

"Definitely."

Aru

"Good morning," Gabi greeted Dagor with a knowing smile. "How is Frankie doing?"

Given that the two had entered the dining hall holding hands and smiling at each other like a couple in love, Gabi's assumption wasn't surprising. Dagor seemed to have no problem with everyone knowing that Frankie was his. He'd even kissed the girl's cheek, and as she tried to pull her hand out of his to go to her friend's table, he'd held on for a couple of seconds too long before letting go.

"I wasn't allowed inside the patient room, but Frankie told me that the doctor wasn't too concerned. For now, she should be more mindful of her eating habits, and if the symptoms persist, she should see her regular doctor and have some tests done."

"I'm glad the human is fine," Negal said. "You seem taken with her." There was a gleam in the troper's eyes.

The guy would never admit it, but he was a romantic.

"Frankie is fun to be with, but it's just a vacation fling, so you can wipe those smug expressions from your faces. I'm not in love with her, and I won't be. Once this cruise is over, we go our separate ways."

Aru put down his fork. "Frankie is rumored to be a Dormant, just like Gabi was. If you feel a connection to her, she might be the one for you, and if she turns immortal, you can have a future together."

The stubborn expression Dagor often displayed slammed over his features. "I'm happy for you and Gabi, but this is not a path I can follow. I don't want to spend the rest of my immortal life on this godforsaken planet. I want to go home one day, even if it's in a millennium, and I can't bring a hybrid mate."

It was a valid point, and trying to figure out a way around it was keeping Aru awake at night. Like Dagor, he also wanted to go home one day and introduce his mate to his parents and sister. Still, as long as hybrids were considered abominations on Anumati and its colonies, that wasn't an option.

"I don't know if that's a wise approach," Gabi said. "A thousand years is a long time to be alone."

"Who said anything about being alone? I can enjoy myself with various females like I have been doing for five years. It hasn't been a hardship."

Aru didn't respond because it was futile to argue with Dagor. Sooner or later, he would realize that his reaction to Frankie was different and that there was more to their meeting than a casual sea-voyage trip.

"I'm always fascinated by matters of the heart," Negal said. "The heart takes over from the mind and commandeers the driver's seat."

"Not in my case." Dagor snatched a piece of toast from the tray and started spreading butter over it, but he was pressing too hard, and the toast was crumbling. "Damn. Why don't they use tougher bread?" He dropped the pieces on his plate and took another slice.

Negal chuckled. "As I said, matters of the heart take priority. I'm so glad no female has ever gotten her hooks into my soul."

"That's a rude thing to say," Gabi admonished. "You make it sound like I did something bad to Aru."

Aru took her hand and brought it to his lips for a kiss. "You illuminated my life, my love. Before you, I lived under a cloud and didn't even realize that not enough sunshine was coming through."

"Oh, Aru." Gabi brought their conjoined hands to her lips and kissed his knuckles. "My heart overflows with love for you."

Dagor chuckled. "And that's why I will never allow it to happen to me. Love turns perfectly normal people into sappy puddles of sweetness."

"I don't know what that girl sees in you," Negal said in their native language. "You have the tact of a monkey.

Perhaps I should offer her a better alternative." Negal started to rise.

"Sit." Dagor clamped his hand on the trooper's shoulder. "For the duration of this cruise, Frankie is mine. So, back off."

People sitting at the neighboring tables were glancing their way. Aru wasn't sure how much of their language they understood. But even if they didn't understand a word of the gods' language, it wasn't difficult to interpret Dagor's response to Negal's suggestion to take Frankie off his hands. First of all, he'd said her name, and secondly, the barely contained rage in his tone had been impossible to miss.

"Relax." Negal clapped Dagor on the shoulder. "I was just trying to prove a point, and I did."

Frankie

~~~

"What did Bridget say?" Mia asked as soon as Frankie got to her table.

She had expected her friend to ask about the night she'd spent with Dagor, which was much more eventful than the short visit to the clan doctor. But maybe she didn't want to do that in front of Toven and the others sharing their table and was waiting to have that kind of talk with her in private or with Margo on the line.

It was only fair that Mia would demand the details. After all, Frankie and Margo had done the same to her. Still, now that the shoe was on the other foot, Frankie regretted hassling Mia to reveal intimate details.

It was okay to talk about dates and hookups, but it was different when the person was someone she'd grown to care about. She'd known Dagor for less than twenty-four hours, but the connection had been pretty immediate. Perhaps her mother hadn't been a silly romantic when she'd said that when the right person showed up, Frankie would know.

Was Dagor the one for her, though?

He didn't seem interested in a long-term relationship, and she'd told him that a cruise fling was all she was interested in, too. It wasn't fair to him to change her mind and start talking about forever.

Besides, they were basing their assumptions about possible dormancy on her likability, which was the least scientific method she could think of. Chances were that she was just a human. If so, a future with Dagor was impossible regardless of his aversion to long-term relationships.

Sitting on the chair Toven had gallantly pulled out for her, Frankie shrugged. "She said that it was probably because of excessive alcohol consumption without eating. It can prevent the liver from releasing glucose from its glycogen stores to the bloodstream, leading to hypoglycemia." She chuckled. "At least I've learned something thanks to my fainting spells. I didn't even know that the liver stores glycogen. Did we learn that in school?"

Mia shook her head. "I don't remember. You told me that you had bar snacks with your drinks, and before going to the bar, you also snacked in your room. Those weren't the healthiest choices, but you had something in your stomach. You shouldn't have fainted."

Frankie had forgotten entirely about the snacks and had told Bridget that she hadn't eaten. Well, according to her mother, a few pretzels and a small bag of mixed nuts didn't count as a meal, but Mia was right about her stomach not having been empty.

"Maybe it wasn't enough. Anyway, the doctor told me to eat regular meals and see if the problem returns. If it does, I'm to march myself into my regular doctor's office and ask for a fasting glucose blood test to start with and a bunch of other tests to determine the underlying cause."

"You should do that regardless of whether the fainting returns." Mia handed Frankie the tray with the assorted cold cuts. "Now eat and tell me about your night with Dagor. Did the two of you end up watching television?"

"Yes." Frankie batted her eyelashes. "Until the wee hours of the morning and then again before seeing the doctor."

Mia stifled a laugh. "The movies must have been exciting."

"Yes, the best."

Toven's lips twitched as he pretended to be absorbed in his oatmeal. Still, the other couple sitting at their table were grinning and not trying to hide their amusement.

"What are your plans for the rest of the day?" Mia asked. "I mean until the wedding or a little before to get ready." She narrowed her eyes on Frankie. "Just don't wear the dress you wore yesterday, and make sure to eat throughout the day and not wait to stuff yourself at the reception."

That was precisely what Frankie had intended to do. To keep her weight under control and still enjoy her social life, she often skipped meals before a dinner date or an event.

"I know, I know. I've learned my lesson. I told Dagor that I intend to laze by the pool and enjoy Bob the robot's drinks. It would be great if you and Toven could join us."

Mia grimaced. "It's going to be hot up there, and the sun glare will make it miserable for Toven. Your boyfriend will probably not enjoy it either."

"He's not my boyfriend." Frankie cast a sidelong glance to where Dagor was sitting with his teammates and Aru's mate. He didn't look happy, and it seemed like he was arguing with Negal.

Was it about her?

"You are right." Mia chuckled. "Dagor is not a boy. He's not even human. Maybe we can call him your god-friend?"

"Just a friend." Frankie cut a piece out of the omelet and put it in her mouth.

She wasn't a breakfast person, and the eggs made her nauseous. A piece of toast would have been better, with a little jam.

Except, she had a feeling that it wasn't the eggs that were making her stomach roil. It was the aggravated expression on Dagor's face. She much preferred to see him relaxed and flirty.

Did it have anything to do with her?

She swallowed with difficulty. What did she care about what made him angry? As long as he was nice while with her, she shouldn't worry about arguments he had with his friends, right?

God, she was such a damn people pleaser.

Well, her former bosses would strongly disagree with that statement. A contrary brat would be their more likely description of her.

That was because she was only eager to please those she cared about, and for some reason, she had added Dagor to that list. Given her enormous family, there were many people she cared about, but other than that she didn't have a lot of friends.

In fact, her only real friends were Margo and Mia, and they were more like sisters to her. The rest of the people she knew were acquaintances.

There were a couple of boyfriends that she'd cared about in the past, but getting into her bed didn't automatically mean getting into her heart, especially not in one day.

Kian

There was no assigned seating for breakfast, and as Kian scanned the dining hall, Kalugal waved him over, pointing to the two chairs at the table where he sat with Jacki, Amanda, and Dalhu. The rest of the family wasn't there, and he wondered whether they were late or had already eaten.

His mother was probably having breakfast in her cabin, and perhaps Alena and Orion had joined her. Although if that was the case, why hadn't she also invited him and Syssi?

"Good morning," Syssi greeted the two couples.

Kian repeated the greeting and pulled out a chair for Syssi. "Are Lokan and Carol still asleep?"

"I guess so," Kalugal said. "We waited for them until four in the morning. The speedboat they chartered to the ship was not as fast as its owner had claimed. Lokan was ready to go back and strangle the guy for lying to him."

The speedboat had been supposed to catch up to the Silver Swan two hours earlier, so Lokan had a good reason to be pissed.

"I don't know why they bothered in the first place." Amanda poured coffee into her mug. "Yamanu was shrouding the entire dock, and the Guardians took care of the port's surveillance cameras. Carol and Lokan could have just gotten on board without any trouble."

"I'm always in favor of more caution." Kian sat Allegra down in the highchair. "If they had a tail, it couldn't have followed them on the water without them seeing it."

Kalugal nodded. "I agree. If we didn't need Lokan to be our ears and eyes in the Brotherhood, I would have advised him to fake his own death a long time ago and cross over."

Lokan wasn't interested in joining the clan, though. He still dreamt about liberating the island from his father's yoke and rehabilitating its inhabitants.

The guy was a dreamer, and in this respect, he reminded Kian of Annani. His mother also believed in rehabilitating the monsters.

Kian was not as forgiving, perhaps because he'd been exposed to their evil-doing and hadn't shared the details with his mother to save her the heartache.

His philosophy was simple. Anyone who had raped and murdered didn't deserve to live and was beyond redemption. Then again, Dalhu had ordered Mark's murder, a defenseless civilian, and here he was, mated to Amanda, father to Evie, sitting at the table with the family.

Dalhu had been following orders, but sometimes Kian wondered how far his obedience would have gone. If Navuh had ordered him to rape and murder children, would he have done it?

Compulsion was a powerful force, but Kian had a feeling that Dalhu would have slit his own throat before obeying such orders.

Besides, even Navuh wasn't that evil.

"Kian." Kalugal waved a hand in front of his face. "Whatever you are thinking about right now, think about something else. The waves of aggression you're emitting are unhealthy for our children."

"You are right." Kian took a deep, centering breath and glanced at Allegra's worried little face. "It's okay, sweetie. Daddy is not angry."

Fates, one day the responsibility for all this crap would fall on her shoulders, and he wanted better for her. He wanted the utopian world his mother imagined, but he knew that it would never come.

Wishing it wouldn't make it so, nor would all the effort his mother and his clan had put into changing things for the better.

The best he could do was keep his people safe and hope his efforts would do.

"I'm not going to warn the Brotherhood about the Eternal King's threat." He reached for a piece of toast. "Navuh would not help us. If anything, he and his minions would try to sabotage our efforts."

Kalugal took Darius from Jacki and cradled the baby to his chest. "Regrettably, I have to agree. I just want to save my mother."

"People," Amanda said in an exasperated tone. "We are here to celebrate, and you are depressing everyone."

"Sorry about that." Kian cast her an apologetic look.

Kalugal, being Kalugal, plastered a smile on his face. "I haven't been introduced to the new gods yet, and I'm offended that Jacki and I weren't invited to the meeting with them yesterday."

"I can introduce you right now." Kian pushed away from the table.

The disturbing thoughts had ruined his appetite.

Kalugal handed the baby back to Jacki. "Do you want to come with me to meet them?"

His tone indicated he wasn't in favor, and Jacki must have picked up on it.

She shook her head. "Perhaps later."

As he and Kalugal headed toward the gods' table, Kian wondered whether Aru had contacted his leaders on Anumati. If what he suspected was accurate and the god could communicate telepathically with someone on his home planet, he could do that from anywhere and could have done it already.

Aru and his teammates had met Annani and figured out who she was. Now, the question was what he would do with the information. Kian needed to get Aru alone and ask him point blank how he communicated with his leaders.

Stressed couldn't begin to describe how Kian felt.

Perhaps that was why he had been inundated by thoughts of the past that he thought he had suppressed. The past never stayed in the past, and the cycle of horrors was always repeated. People just never learned.

As they got to the gods' table, Kalugal offered his hand to Gabi first.

"I'm Kalugal, Kian's much better-looking and more charming cousin. I'm also a council member."

"Hi." She gave him her hand and rose to her feet. "I'm Gabi. It's nice to meet you."

After hearing that Kalugal was a council member, the three gods rose to their feet as well.

"No need to stand." He smiled. "I just came to introduce myself."

He shook hands with the three gods, who remained standing, exchanging names and pleasantries.

"Please, join us." Aru brought over a chair from the next table for Kian, and Negal did the same for Kalugal.

"By the way, congratulations." Kalugal turned to Gabi. "On your transition as well as on finding your mate. You must have done a lot of good in your short life to deserve such a boon."

She shook her head. "I have no idea what I have done to deserve a god for a mate, but I'm thankful to the universe and the Fates for blessing me so."

"Indeed." Kalugal nodded.

"By the way," Kian said. "We are having an impromptu bachelor party for my future brother-in-law in my suite. Would you like to join us for whiskey and cigars?"

He might get an opportunity to take Aru aside and talk to him privately, away from the ears of his companions.

The god inclined his head. "We would be honored to attend."

Alena

"Carol!" Alena squealed as the tiny blonde sauntered into the cabin. "You are a sight for sore eyes." She opened her arms to welcome the clan's hero.

The petite blonde walked into the embrace with a grin on her face. "Why are your eyes sore? This is your wedding day. You should be merry."

"Your being here makes my day even merrier." Alena kissed her on both cheeks.

After extracting herself from Alena's arms, Carol turned to Annani and dipped her head. "Hello, Clan Mother. How have you been?"

As the question seemed to take Annani by surprise, Alena realized that people rarely asked her mother how she was feeling, which was a testament to how well she played her role.

"I am overjoyed to be here, helping Alena get ready for her wedding." Annani smiled at Carol.

Carol nodded and moved to hug Jacki and caress Darius's cheek. "Hello, little guy. I've missed you all so much." She walked over to the couch and sat next to Syssi. "And where is your little darling?"

"Allegra is with my parents. I won't get her back until the wedding tonight. She and my mother are bonding."

Carol smiled. "It may persuade your parents to finally retire and move into the village."

"I doubt it." Syssi sighed. "My mother is one stubborn lady."

Carol patted her knee before changing the subject. "I heard that I missed a big event last night."

"Yeah, well." Syssi put her half-empty margarita glass on the coffee table. "Everyone already knew about the gods, but only a few had seen them before last night. Then we had a bit of excitement when Mia's human friend fainted."

Carol frowned. "Since when is Kian allowing human friends to visit clan territory, which this ship technically is?"

"Frankie is a potential Dormant," Amanda said. "Toven likes her and Mia's other best friend a lot, and given that he's a recluse who doesn't like many people, we suspect that it's affinity at work. We also had Lisa sniff them both, and she thinks they are both Dormants."

"Lisa, David's little sister?" Carol looked doubtful. "She's still human, so even if she can identify Dormants, I find it hard to believe it's developed enough to work."

"True." Syssi sighed. "But Toven insisted on inviting Frankie and Margo on the cruise, and at the end of it, he will thrall away their memories of immortals and gods or compel them to silence, depending on whether they come to work for him in the village."

Carol shook her head. "I find all of the latest developments strange. We have a new group of aliens living among us, and Kian's entrusted the village's protection to them, and now humans are coming to work in the village. What happened to him?"

Alena sighed. "That's just the tip of the iceberg. I'm glad that we have the Kra-ell to reinforce our ranks, although, given the danger we are facing, they will not be all that helpful."

"Can you stop that?" Amanda got to her feet. "Stop talking about depressing things. You are getting married tonight, and we are here to help you get ready, not only with makeup and hair but also with mood."

"It's hard." Alena caressed her belly. "I can't help worrying."

Amanda grimaced. "And I can't even get you drunk because you're pregnant. That would have helped get you in a festive mood."

"Maybe Carol can entertain us with stories about China," Annani suggested.

"Lokan and I are enjoying China more than we expected. Lokan is in his element, talking to government officials and meddling, and I practically run the fashion business, which is very exciting."

As Carol kept telling them about the clothing industry and the difficulties of working with and around the Chinese regime, Alena leaned back against the couch cushions and closed her eyes.

"You look tired," her mother said. "Perhaps you should rest a little before the party."

"I can't." Alena opened her eyes. "I'm too excited to rest."

"Do you want me to sing you to sleep like I did when you were a little girl?"

Alena laughed. "I'm over two thousand years old. I don't remember ever being a young girl."

"I am much older, and I remember." Annani smoothed the folds of her gown. "I remember every lesson my mother taught me even though I did not want to follow her instructions. It took me long years to realize the wisdom of her lessons." She sighed. "I still miss her, and I miss my father. That never goes away." Her eyes misted with tears. "But most of all, I miss Khiann. Not a day goes by that I do not think of him."

Following her mother's words, a sad hush fell over the room, but it didn't last long.

"This is a time to celebrate." Amanda glared at their mother. "I don't know what has gotten into all of you.

No negative thoughts are allowed in here." She waved at Onidu. "I need another margarita."

"Yes, mistress. Another margarita is coming right up."

"Where is Evie?" Annani asked.

"Napping in her stroller. I put her in the bedroom with a baby monitor." Amanda tapped her ear. "If she wakes up, I'll hear her."

"I hope she wakes up soon," Carol said. "I want to see her."

"Careful," Syssi said. "Babies are known to be contagious."

Carol laughed. "I'm immune. There are no babies for me as long as Lokan is playing the double agent role. It's too dangerous."

As everyone nodded and another hush fell over the room, Amanda shook her head. "What did I say about bringing up depressing topics? Only happy thoughts are allowed in here."

Annani

The truth was that Annani was trying to appear cheerful for Alena's sake, but at times like this, she missed Khiann more than ever.

He should have been there with her, celebrating the weddings of his children, but the Fates had been cruel to her and robbed her of a life with him.

The children born to her had been fathered by humans, good, intelligent, courageous men whom she had picked carefully. They all resembled her Khiann in one way or another, so she could pretend that he had been their real father, and maybe in spirit he was.

The prophecy she had been given had said so, and it had promised her two more children.

Except, that would be a tough act to pull off, given how rarely she got intimate with humans lately. It was not like her to abstain, and it worried her that, as of late, she had no desire for the pleasures of the flesh.

Was she getting to the age when some gods were starting to lose their minds?

Was she depressed?

Having Vanessa assess her mental state was out of the question because Annani had an image to uphold. Her clan looked up to her, and she needed to appear strong at all times. Her only option was to seek out a human psychologist in the city and shroud herself while going to sessions.

It could be fun to get out of the village a couple times a week and spend an hour talking to someone who did not know who and what she was.

Annani chuckled to herself. The therapist would probably think that she suffered from delusions of grandeur and had a god complex.

The other problem was that she would have to tell Kian, and he would get worried. Oh well, she could always blame her melancholy on loneliness. Since losing Alena as her companion, Annani had been lonelier than ever.

"I have been thinking about the Fates lately," Syssi said, pulling Annani out of her somber thoughts. "Are there only three for the entire universe, or does each planet get its own trio? Maybe even each continent?"

Jacki chuckled. "I think there should be a trio of Fates for each zip code. Just think how much work they have to do."

"That's an interesting concept." Amanda tapped her margarita glass with the tip of her fingernail. "They may be known as the three Fates because they always work in teams of three. Kind of like the gods. Perhaps it's not a coincidence that Aru's team has three members."

Alena put her teacup down. "One thing is for sure. The Fates did not take over the bodies of these three gods to send us a message. Those three are just too male to house the energy of female entities."

The same thought had occurred to Annani, and checking her hunch that the Fates had guided the gods to the clan had been one of the reasons she had wanted to meet them in person. Regrettably, she had dismissed the idea for the same reason Alena had. There was nothing even remotely feminine in the way those gods conducted themselves. If the Fates had been involved, they had done it through other means. They had not taken over the gods' bodies.

"I think I met the Fates," Syssi said quietly. "My grand-mother, may her soul rest in peace, had three dear friends in the retirement home she lived in until she died. I used to visit her and read to them, and after she had passed, I continued to do so. They were always pushing my buttons for the fun of it, making me read racy stories to them just to see me blush. Still, when I met Kian and brought him with me to my reading session, they really went overboard, pushing me to overcome my shyness and show Kian that I was interested. Then, after Kian and I became a couple, the three of them suddenly decided to move to Florida, and I lost track of them. I think that's very suspicious."

With a groan, Alena pushed to her feet. "As fascinating as the subject of the Fates is, I should start getting ready. I will run a bath and soak in it until I feel relaxed." She turned to Amanda. "After that, I'm all yours to do with as you please."

"Can I cut your hair?" The dangerous gleam in Amanda's eyes did not bode well for Alena's hair.

She lifted the heavy rope of her long blond hair and pursed her lips. "I loved this hairdo I got when I was pretending to be a Slovakian supermodel, but it wasn't me. It also doesn't fit my simple wedding dress."

Carol lifted a finger. "A fairy princess style. That's what you should go for."

Alena smiled brightly. "That's what I'm aiming for."

Frankie

~~~

"I want to see Bob." Mia swiveled her chair around in an expert maneuver that had Frankie shaking her head. "Toven is with Orion and the rest of the guys, smoking cigars and drinking whiskey, but I was not invited to Alena's pre-wedding get-together."

Frankie arched a brow. "Were you hoping to be invited?"

Mia shrugged. "I think it's only her mother and sisters. Anyway, put on your bikini and let's go. Dagor is with Toven and the others, and based on past events, cigar smoking takes a long time. We have at least two hours."

That answered whether she should wait for him or go alone.

"My bikini is already on." She opened her robe to show Mia. "What do you think?"

Mia grinned. "That purple color looks amazing on you. When Dagor is done smoking and comes looking for you, he will have a hard time keeping his fangs from elongating once he sees you."

The reminder had Frankie's nipples pebble, and as she pulled the robe closed, she hoped that Mia hadn't noticed. "Thanks." She tied the belt around her waist. "What about you? Still too self-conscious about being seen in a swimming suit?"

They'd argued about this before, with Frankie trying to convince Mia that she looked hot despite her condition and should put a swimming suit on and enjoy the beach.

"I'm not going into the pool, so there is no point. I'm comfortable as I am."

It was on the tip of Frankie's tongue to point out that Mia's legs were nearly fully regenerated and that no one on the ship cared about her having no feet, but she swallowed the retort and nodded. "You're the boss."

As they left the cabin, Frankie was glad to discover that the hallway wasn't deserted, and other occupants were emerging from their cabins or returning to them. Several had their bathrobes on, so she assumed that they were on their way to the pool as well.

"I have a feeling that we are not going to be alone on the Lido deck today."

Mia nodded. "It's going to be crowded, but that never bothered you before, so why should it now?"

Frankie chuckled. "Yeah, but that was with normal people and not gods and immortals."

"You are dating a god." Mia drove her chair into the elevator. "So that shouldn't faze you."

As people made room for her, Frankie squeezed by and didn't respond.

Mia had made her comment before entering, so no one had heard her, but Frankie wondered how many knew about her and Dagor.

According to Mia, he had rushed to her side when she'd fainted and everyone had seen it, so there must be rumors, but she wasn't going to confirm it for them.

When the elevator stopped on the top deck, she waited until they were outside before leaning over to whisper in Mia's ear. "I don't want to make our relationship public. I don't know how many people know about it and if Dagor is okay with it."

Mia laughed. "After your entrance to the dining hall this morning, I doubt that there is anyone who doesn't know. He held your hand, looked at you lovingly, and kissed your cheek. Given that public display of affection, I don't think Dagor minds everyone knowing you are together. In fact, I think he was making a statement to deter others from approaching you."

Frankie swallowed. "I forgot about that."

After the night and morning they had spent together, holding hands and kissing had been natural, and it hadn't registered as anything unusual.

Maybe she'd still been loopy from his bite.

There was a lightness, a floaty feeling that she'd ascribed to the fabulous sex, but maybe there was more to it. She should have remembered to let go of his hand before entering the dining hall.

Who needed all the rumors?

Frankie lifted her head and scanned the people sitting around the pool. Several looked at her, some with smiles, some with frowns, and some with interest.

They probably wondered what a god saw in her, a mere human.

"Maybe it wasn't a good idea to come up here." She tied the belt tighter around her waist.

Mia regarded her with a raised brow. "Who are you and what have you done with the Frankie who is unafraid of anything?"

"I'm not afraid. It just feels weird to have everyone looking at me."

"Let's get a drink." Mia steered her chair toward the bar. "I want to see Bob."

There was a long line in front of the bar, and when people offered to let Mia go ahead of them, she refused.

As their turn finally came, Bob greeted her with a big smile on his shiny chrome face. "Mistress Frankie. It is so good to see you again. Would you like a mojito?"

"Yes, please." She turned to Mia. "What would you like?"

"A lemonade, please."

When Bob started on the drinks, Frankie leaned down to whisper in Mia's ear. "He remembered the drink I ordered yesterday. Isn't that fabulous? He must remember every drink he ever made and who ordered it. Bob is the perfect barman."

"Not quite," the guy standing behind them said. "Earlier, I tried to share my woes with him, and he just looked at me with round, unblinking eyes. A real barman would have offered advice." He smiled and extended his hand. "I'm Max."

"I'm Frankie." She shook what he offered. "I'm Mia's friend."

"I know." He waved his other hand around. "Everyone here does."

Given his tone, Max hadn't meant that everyone knew she was Mia's friend. He was referring to her relationship with Dagor.

Well, calling it a relationship was an exaggeration. It was a prolonged hookup.

Ten days, with only nine remaining.

"Oh, God." Frankie rubbed a hand over her face.

He chuckled. "Yeah, that too. Gossip is a big problem in a small community. You'll get used to that."

"Here are your drinks, mistresses," Bob announced cheerfully, handing a beverage to each of them with his long robotic arms.

"Thank you." Frankie brought the glass to her lips and took a small sip. "Just as perfect as the one you made me yesterday."

"I'm glad that you find my service satisfactory." Bob turned to Max. "What can I make for you, master?"

"Same as before," he said.

"Coming up." Bob swiveled his torso and reached for one of the bottles hanging from the bar's ceiling.

Max turned to Frankie. "Save a dance for me tonight?"

She felt her cheeks warm. "Normally, I'd say I would be delighted, but I don't know whether Dagor will be okay with me dancing with someone else."

Max's expression turned predatory. "Perhaps you can save me a dance for when you arrive at the village. The god is not welcome to follow you there, and when he leaves to search for the missing pods, I will be waiting for you."

Talk about direct.

This guy didn't mince words or beat around the bush, and usually she liked that, but right now, it just made her uncomfortable.

Which was stupid.

Max was handsome, charming, and confident, and if she weren't with Dagor, she would have flirted with him right back. But Dagor was leaving soon, and Max was a perfectly suitable replacement. Yet, she couldn't bring herself to even think about him in romantic terms, let alone show interest.

Kian

"Orion, buddy." Kalugal wrapped his arm around Orion's shoulders. "Let me give you the prescription for married bliss."

Kian felt that his cousin was inebriated, although he hadn't seen Kalugal drinking to excess. Four of the ten bottles of whiskey he'd brought for the occasion were empty. Still, given the number of partakers, that wasn't enough to get anyone drunk.

Anandur had brought two cases of Snake Venom, though, so perhaps Kalugal had gotten some of that before moving on to the superb whiskey.

"I'm all ears." Orion's smile was a tad too bright.

Maybe they had started drinking before coming to the bachelor party. That was the only way they could already be drunk.

"Never disagree with your wife," Kalugal lectured with a raised finger. "Say yes first, and then present counterarguments if you have any. It'd be better if you didn't, though. Most of the time, it's not worth the effort because she will get her way no matter what you say, and arguing about it will only rattle your nest."

Orion pretended to consider his words for a long moment. "I don't see how this is any different from what I'm doing now. Given that my mate is much older and wiser, it only makes sense for me to defer to her."

Toven lifted his glass. "My son is a smart male."

"What about you?" Dagor asked. "Your mate is a very young female. Do you defer to her judgment?"

Toven's expression turned serious. "On some subjects, yes. I'm ancient, but I still have a hard time understanding humans. Mia is better at this than I am."

Kian hoped others would join in the discussion so he could take Aru aside and ask him whether he had communicated his findings about Annani to his supervisors on Anumati, or wherever the resistance leadership was located.

"Relationships are complicated," David said, "but if there is mutual respect and open communication, even couples who don't see eye to eye on some things can have a successful relationship."

Catching Aru's eyes, Kian lifted his drink and motioned for the god to follow him to a corner of the balcony that wasn't occupied.

Aru said something to Negal and then followed Kian. "Don't you find the discussion interesting?" He leaned against the railing, cigar in one hand and a glass of whiskey in the other.

"I do, but since my cousin summarized married life so succinctly, I have nothing to add."

Aru's lips quirked on one corner. "I sincerely doubt that."

Kian leaned on the railing next to him and puffed on his cigar. "In many ways, females are smarter than us. The things males do better are not the qualities I'm proud of."

Aru nodded. "I know what you mean. I have been fortunate not to fight in real battles, only simulations, but even those consumed a piece of my soul. I don't like killing, even if it's computer-generated evildoers."

The answer made Kian's heart constrict with sympathy and foreboding. Aru was still young, but he was eternal, which meant that one day he would have to fight and kill to protect those he loved. The cycles of peace and war might be longer on Anumati, but from what Kian had learned from Jade, the gods had yet to evolve out of warfare.

It was an ugly world, and it was kill or be killed, or rather, kill or see your loved ones murdered.

Shaking his head, Kian took another puff of his cigar and then one more until he felt the tension abate. "Have you communicated to your leaders what you learned yesterday?"

Aru affected a frown, but it looked fake. "How? I haven't left the ship."

It was an evasive answer, but it wasn't an outright lie, which meant that Aru didn't enjoy lying or that lies didn't come easily to him. In either case, his response earned him merit points with Kian.

"Let's cut to the chase," Kian said. "I suspect that you can communicate telepathically with someone on Anumati, and that person has access to the resistance leadership. You don't need to leave the ship to do that."

Aru didn't confirm it, but the fear that passed through his eyes was as good as an admission. "What makes you think that?"

"Logic and conjecture. Two members of my clan, a mother and her daughter, can communicate telepathically as if they were conducting a phone conversation. They can do that regardless of distance, no matter how vast. It's a rare ability, and they are the only two I know of who possess it, but if mere immortals have it, then I'm sure some gods can do it as well."

"It's a rare ability among gods, too," Aru said. "Those who are found out are either eliminated by the Eternal King or made to work for him."

"I see." Kian took another puff. "You are afraid of admitting your ability because you are protecting the person on the other end, who I assume is a family member. I don't need to know who they are, only that they can access the resistance leadership." He pinned Aru with a hard look. "You've learned my most guarded secret. It's only fair that you share yours with me."

Swallowing, Aru nodded. "It has to stay between the two of us. No one else can find out."

Kian lifted a brow. "Not even the heir to the throne if she decides to join your cause?"

"For now, I need your word that it stays between us. If further down the line we need to include the princess, we will."

Aru

Aru had as much as admitted that Kian had guessed correctly, but he couldn't go the final step and tell him more.

"Let's assume that I can communicate with someone. I'm not saying I do, but if I could, what would you like to say to them?"

Kian let out a breath. "I don't know. I don't want my mother anywhere near the resistance, but it's not my call to make. She's still the head of the clan, and I answer to her. What I want to know is what their response was to the revelation that a legitimate heir to the throne lives on Earth."

Tension radiated from the immortal, and Aru could understand why. Kian was protecting his loved ones as best he could.

"I didn't get a response yet, but I assume it would be greeted with jubilation. The person that this information will be delivered to will protect it with their lives. You have nothing to fear from them."

"Is it the queen? Ahn's mother?"

Kian's guesses were too accurate for Aru's comfort.

"I can't confirm or deny because I'm not privy to that information."

Kian chuckled. "Should I call Andrew over and verify that statement?"

Damn. Aru had forgotten about the truth-reader.

He shook his head. "The same way you are protecting yours, I am protecting mine. I will not say more. I cannot."

"I understand." Kian took a puff of his cigar. "I'm anxious to hear their response, and I'm even more anxious about my mother's reaction to it. She's reckless, especially when she believes in a cause, and she believes in yours."

"And you don't?"

Kian shrugged. "I don't know enough to pass judgment. The Eternal King has kept the gods in line for hundreds of thousands of years. Who knows what would have happened with someone else at the helm? I've seen enough examples of rulers who were too decent for the good of their people, and in the end, the people suffered. I've also seen rulers who weren't good and restricted their people's freedoms. Still, once they were removed from power, the so-called liberators became much worse monsters. I don't think my mother can be ruthless enough for people to fear her, and therefore keep the peace. The most important thing for a ruler to realize is what kind of enemies they have and in what way those enemies will respond to them. As human history indicates, enemies raise their heads when they perceive weakness."

"The gods don't have enemies."

Kian smiled. "Right now, they don't because the Eternal King rules mercilessly over them. With a weaker ruler at the helm, factions might break away from the collective and form their own countries or planets or whatever. Wars could start over resources, over colonies, over ideologies, and the Fates know what else. Take us and the Brotherhood. We are the same people, and we both need to hide from the humans, but Navuh and his mercenary army want to annihilate us, and there is nothing we can do to change their minds about it. We can either hide, fight, or die. Those are our only three options. And since we can't fight a force so much larger than us, we must choose the first option."

"What about technology?" Aru asked. "Can't you get a leg up with that? From what I have observed, brute force is no longer the determining factor. Whoever controls the technology wins."

"Only to a certain degree." Kian finished the last dregs of the whiskey. "Besides, Navuh realized the same thing, and now his focus is to bring his forces to the twenty-first century, and soon we won't have even that advantage."

Aru didn't envy Kian his position. It seemed hopeless.

"Why does he want to eliminate your clan?"

"Different ideology. We want peace and prosperity for all; he wants to dominate and subjugate. It also serves his agenda to have a handy scapegoat to rally his troops." He gave Aru a sad smile. "That's actually the one speck of light in the dark. He might not want to do away with us completely because he would lose his scapegoat. Humans are not a good substitute for a hated enemy."

"The Kra-ell are," Aru said.

"He doesn't know about them. Not yet, anyway. I hope it stays that way."

Aru finished his drink and took another puff of his cigar. "You need the resistance to establish its headquarters here and to be on your side. That's why you are willing to help us."

Kian nodded. "It's one of the reasons. I'm much more afraid of the Eternal King than of Navuh's Brotherhood. Given what you've told me, though, it might take thousands of years before the resistance makes a move, and it might be too late for us."

"Then we need to impress upon the resistance leaders the urgency of the situation on Earth. The heir's survival could be at stake if they don't act more swiftly."

Dagor

Dagor watched Aru depart with Kian and huddle in the farthest corner of the balcony, wondering what it was all about.

He knew Aru was hiding something, but he no longer cared. What he wanted was to leave and go to Frankie.

What was she doing right now?

Should he call her or text her?

Nah, he'd better not. He was getting attached to a girl he'd met a little over twenty-four hours ago, and if he wasn't careful, he would end up like Aru or worse.

At least Gabi was an immortal who could live as long as Aru did. Frankie might be a Dormant, but she also might not, and if he fell in love with her, he would be setting himself up for a lot of heartache.

"To the groom!" Anandur raised his glass for the umpteenth time.

"To Orion!" All the guys cheered and emptied their glasses. Again.

The redhead grabbed another bottle of whiskey, uncapped it, and poured everyone a new shot. "One more time! To Orion!"

Was he trying to get everyone drunk before the wedding?

Orion seemed unsteady on his feet, and Dagor wasn't the only one who had noticed.

The god wrapped his arm around his son's shoulders and led him to a lounge chair. "I think you've had enough. You don't want to be drunk for your own wedding."

"*Pfft.*" Orion waved a dismissive hand. "I'll burn through it in minutes. I'll be fine."

Toven smiled indulgently at his son. "Can I get you a cup of coffee?"

Orion nodded. "That would be nice. Thank you, Father."

The god's expression changed, surprise flickering through his eyes for a moment, and a smile bloomed. "My pleasure." Toven opened the balcony doors and stepped inside the cabin.

Was the reaction about Orion thanking him or about him calling the god Father?

Dagor sat down on the lounger next to Orion. "How are you feeling?"

"Excellent." The immortal beamed. "How about you? Do you like being on Earth?"

"Not really."

Orion's smile turned into a frown. "Why not?"

"It's not home, and it's far from civilized. People are still killing each other because of religion and other nonsensical reasons, kidnapping and selling young defenseless women for sexual slavery, and the list goes on. Anumati has problems, but it's light years better than here."

"I can't argue with that, but I would like to point out that the Kra-ell we rescued don't have such a favorable opinion of your home planet."

Apparently, the immortal wasn't as drunk as he appeared.

"I don't have a good opinion of it either. I hate the politics, the class differences, the lack of privacy, and many other issues. Still, I'll take it over Earth's crap any day."

Orion sighed. "I guess utopia doesn't exist anywhere."

"Maybe it does." Dagor thought about the energy beings that Frankie had described. "Maybe there are other universes where all beings coexist in harmony. Perhaps it's the next step in evolution."

Orion nodded sagely. "Perhaps that's what's waiting for us beyond the veil."

"I wouldn't go that far." Dagor leaned over to find the ashtray someone had left at the foot of the lounger and tapped his cigar to dislodge a pillar of ash.

"Why not?"

"Because we don't know if anything exists beyond the veil. It might be just stories we tell ourselves to diminish the fear of death."

"Right," Orion agreed. "I believe in the Fates, though. They are innocuous enough. At least no one kills anyone in their name."

"True." Dagor puffed on his cigar. "That's one more reason why Anumati is superior to Earth."

"The Kra-ell believe in the Mother of All Life," Anandur said as he sat down on Orion's other side. "What are we talking about?"

"He doesn't like Earth." Orion pointed an accusing finger at Dagor. "Tell him why he's wrong."

"Everyone is entitled to their opinion." Anandur smiled at Dagor. "But since you are stuck here for the foreseeable future, you should learn to like it more."

"Wise words." Orion lifted his empty glass. "Mind refilling this for me?"

Anandur shook his head. "Your father is getting you coffee. Once you sober up, I will be happy to get you drunk again."

"That doesn't make any sense." Orion held the glass up. "Just one more."

As Dagor's phone pinged with an incoming message, he put his half-smoked cigar on the edge of the ashtray and pulled the device out of his pocket.

His heart skipped a beat when he saw it was from Frankie.

You didn't ask, so I'm asking instead. Will you be my date for the wedding tonight?

Smiling, Dagor typed his answer. *I will be honored to be your date. It's going to be our fourth. Is there anything special I should know about the fourth date?*

Frankie had told him about the three-dates rule, so maybe there was also a four-dates rule?

Hmm. Maybe. You will have to find out.

He chuckled. *Can I find out before the wedding? Where are you now?*

When his phone rang a moment later, he excused himself, pushed to his feet, and walked in the opposite direction of where Aru and Kian were. Thankfully, the balcony wrapped around the bow of the ship and offered plenty of space for the guests to spread out.

"Hi," he answered.

"Hi, yourself. How is the bachelor party going?"

Given the noise in the background, Frankie was up on the Lido deck, and the itch to go to her got even more urgent.

"The cigars are fine, the whiskey even finer, and the groom is drunk and demanding more booze."

"That's all? No strippers?"

He laughed. "Just a bunch of guys smoking cigars and drinking whiskey and beer. It's actually nice. I'm getting to know some of the immortals. How about you? From the sound of it, you are on the upper deck."

"Yeah, I'm here with Mia. She wanted to meet Bob."

Dagor relaxed. "Did she like him?"

"Of course. What's not to like? He remembered who I was and the drink I ordered yesterday, which was awesome, but then the guy who stood in line behind us said that Bob couldn't replace a real bartender because he couldn't offer life advice."

Dagor's good mood turned into irritation. Someone had flirted with Frankie, and perhaps he was still around.

"It depends on the programming. Who's the guy?"

"An immortal named Max. Why?"

"Tell him that you're taken."

Frankie chuckled. "He knows. You made quite the statement this morning at breakfast when you kissed my cheek in front of everyone. Was it intentional?"

"No. I just felt like kissing you, but now I'm glad I did. For the duration of this cruise, you are mine, and I want everyone to know that."

Frankie

F rankie stood before the mirror and examined the intricate coif Mia had arranged. "This is amazing. And to think that you did it by following YouTube instructions."

Behind her, Mia grinned. "Necessity is the mother of invention. As fabulous as this cruise is, there is no hair salon or spa. Perhaps I should drop a note about it in the suggestion box."

Frankie didn't know if there was a suggestion box or if Mia was talking hypothetically. "Who is doing the bride's hair?"

"Her sisters, I guess. They were holed up in her cabin the entire afternoon." Mia brushed a hand over her short hairdo. "I'm so glad you and Margo convinced me to cut my hair. I don't need to do anything to make it look great."

"True." Frankie turned to her friend. "But you still need to get dressed."

She'd done Mia's makeup and had offered to do something with her hair, but Mia was happy with it the way it was.

"Are you okay by yourself here?" Mia asked.

"I'm ready." Frankie turned in a circle. "Cinderella is awaiting her prince." Dagor was coming to her cabin and would escort her to the wedding.

Mia mock-frowned at her. "Don't let him convince you to have a quickie before the wedding. I will never forgive you if you ruin this updo."

"Yes, ma'am," Frankie saluted.

"You've been warned." Mia pointed a finger at her before turning her chair around. "See you at the wedding, Cindy, and please, don't lose your glass slipper."

"Not a chance."

The prince might not come looking for her with the glass slipper in hand. Besides, her lilac chunky heels were strapped to her ankles, and they were not coming off unless she unstrapped them.

They matched the lilac chiffon evening dress she'd gotten from one of her cousins. It had a deep V-neckline that showcased her collarbone, and just the very tops of her breasts, and the dainty straps allowed her shoulders to be on display. The bodice was adorned with intricate embroidery that attracted the light, adding a hint of shimmer to the subdued color. From the cinched waist, the chiffon cascaded in gentle layers, creating a floor-length skirt that swayed with every move she made.

If not for the five-inch platform heels, the dress would have been too long, but with the heels, it just barely cleared the floor.

"Not bad, Frankie," she told her reflection. "You clean up nicely."

When her phone rang, she rushed to retrieve it from the nightstand and almost tripped but managed to reach it without incident.

Expecting it to be Dagor, she was surprised to see Margo's face on the display.

When she accepted the call, there was a slight delay, reminding her of the security rerouting Mia had warned her about.

"Hi, Margo." She sat on the bed and cradled the phone to her ear. "How are you surviving Cabo?"

"Barely. I can't wait for your ship to get here so I can get out of this place. Not that there is anything wrong with Cabo, it's a lovely vacation spot. It's the company that I can't stand."

"You'd better learn to. Lynda is going to be your sister-in-law."

"I know. I can tolerate her in small doses. But let's talk about you. What happened with that guy you were planning on hooking up with?"

Frankie smiled. "He's picking me up to escort me to the wedding."

"That's not the answer I wanted. Details, Frankie. I want them now."

Even if there was no surveillance, Frankie wouldn't have been able to tell Margo anything about Dagor being a god, or that he had fangs, or that he had bitten her, or about the venom trip. Toven had made sure of that with his compulsion.

"The only thing I can say is that it was out of this world and that I want more."

"Oh my God, Frankie. Don't tell me that you are falling in love with him."

"I'm not. What makes you think that I am?"

"Your refusal to tell me details. It means that you care about him and want to keep seeing him."

"Well, yeah, but it's still just a shipboard romance. After that, he's going to Tibet."

"Why Tibet?"

"I don't know. Something about treasure hunting, flea market finds hunting, or something like that. Doug and his friends deal in antiques that they find all over the world."

"That's a damn shame. How long is he going to be gone?"

"I don't know." Frankie put a hand over her chest. "I don't plan on waiting around for him. I met another guy today." She wasn't interested in Max, but she could introduce him to Margo. "You'll like him. He has that boy-next-door charm with a little bad boy mixed in."

"Ooh, tell me more. Is he tall?"

"Yep." She was about to continue when her doorbell rang. "I'll tell you about him tomorrow. Doug is here to pick me up."

"Have fun tonight."

"Thank you. You too."

"I'll try." Margo sighed. "Snap a picture of him and send it to me."

"Whose? Doug's or Max's?"

"Both."

Laughing, Frankie ended the call, put her phone in her evening bag, and walked to open the door.

"Hello, handsome." She gave Dagor a thorough once-over.

Standing with his hand in his pocket and one eyebrow lifted, he made a great James Bond impression, only she didn't think that he'd seen any of the movies.

Dagor always had an air of quiet confidence about him, but draped in a finely tailored tuxedo, he exuded sophistication. The jacket hugged his broad shoulders while the trousers accentuated his lean physique. Polished black shoes completed the ensemble. Every detail, from his cufflinks to the subtle pocket square, spoke of a man who had put a lot of thought into his appearance, and she wondered whether he had done it for her.

He'd never looked more like a god than he did now.

The dark hair that was impeccably styled, the piercing blue eyes, the chiseled jawline with a hint of stubble added a touch of ruggedness to his otherwise polished appearance—it was enough to make a girl get dizzy and suffer another fainting spell.

However, it never came because Dagor reached for her waist and pulled her to him. "Wow, Frankie. You look stunning."

With the spell broken, Frankie lifted a hand to his chest. "Don't mess up my hair, or Mia will kill us both. She spent over an hour on this updo."

Dagor laughed. "I wouldn't dare." He let go of her waist and took her hand. "Come on, princess. Let's do this wedding."

Orion

As Orion stood at the foot of the podium with his groomsmen and his father by his side and his newfound family seated around the tables, his eyes were glued to the dining hall's closed doors.

Soon, his bride would be coming through there, and they would pledge their lives to each other. It wasn't as if they needed the ceremony for that, but it felt right to tell Alena how he felt about her in front of her entire family.

They were all there, looking at him with acceptance and fondness that made him feel like he belonged.

The feeling was priceless.

Letting out a breath, Orion tore his eyes away from the doors to appreciate the work that had gone into transforming the ship's dining room into a grand banquet hall for the wedding.

The tables were draped in white tablecloths, and a golden fabric runner bisected each. The chairs were also draped in white and adorned with golden sashes tied in the back in large bows. Tall golden candelabras with dozens of candles were placed on each table, and between them were arrangements of flowers, their fragrance wafting through the air and creating a pleasant blend of fresh scents.

Through the tall windows, the vast expanse of the ocean stretched in every direction, the gentle waves casting shimmering reflections of the moon in a cloudless sky.

It reminded Orion of the centuries he'd spent alone, thinking that he was the only immortal on Earth, a freak of nature who couldn't age or die from injuries that killed other men.

He'd been adrift in the ocean of life.

The Fates had guided him to the clan and to Alena, his one and only, the light of his life, the mother of his unborn child, his everything.

As a soft melody started playing, signaling the start of the ceremony, a hush fell over the gathering, and all eyes turned to the double doors of the hall.

Two Guardians dressed in fine tuxedos opened the doors, and in walked Alena's bridesmaids. Their dresses were different yet somehow coordinated, but Orion didn't pay them any attention.

His heart thundered in his chest as he waited for his bride to appear. There she was—his Alena, effortlessly striking in her simple loose gown and her pale blond hair flowing freely down her back in soft waves.

Orion smiled, his heart swelling with love and gratitude to the Fates for granting him this incredible boon.

His stunning bride hadn't let her sisters paint her face or style her hair in an elaborate coif. Other than the shimmering fabric of her dress and the jewelry she had donned, all gifted to her by him, she hadn't done anything special for her wedding. She looked the same as she did every day, and she was perfect.

Alena smiled back, but then her gaze shifted to the guests she was passing by. She smiled and nodded at her children and grandchildren and great-grandchildren, reminding him that she was the de facto Mother of the Clan.

And yet, she had chosen him, a young immortal only five centuries old. How had he gotten so lucky?

Why had the Fates chosen him for Alena?

Was he worthy of her?

His father's hand on his shoulder fortified Orion's confidence. He was, after all, a demigod, and so was she. Perhaps they were better matched than his momentary panic had him believe.

As she turned her eyes back to him, so full of love and adoration, the last vestiges of his doubt evaporated, and Orion squared his shoulders.

He might not be worthy of Alena now, but they had eternity before them, and he would dedicate his life to her. They might not have another dozen children together, and the clan she had created would always outnumber their new family, but that was okay. His goal was not to father a new clan.

All he wanted was to make her happy and raise the child she was carrying together. If the Fates granted them more children, he would be overjoyed. Still, he was perfectly satisfied with what he already had.

Alena

The rhythmic pulse of the ship was a backdrop to the anticipation that filled the air, or maybe just Alena's lungs. She hadn't expected to be so excited, so breathless.

The wedding had been postponed many times, and she would have been delighted with leaving things the way they were or just having a small ceremony in the village square.

After all, a clan wedding had no official significance. It was merely a celebration of her union with Orion. In her mind, weddings were needed only for arranged marriages because they provided a binding legal agreement between the parties. But she and Orion were truelove mates, which was as binding as it got.

Still, butterflies fluttered their wings in her stomach, or maybe it was the life growing in her womb.

"Breathe," Amanda whispered in Alena's left ear.

On her right, Syssi reached for her hand and gave it a gentle squeeze. "Just look straight at Orion when you enter the dining hall."

Nodding, she forced a breath into her lungs.

Why was she so anxious?

The excitement hadn't hit her until two days ago when it had become clear that it was happening and there would be no more delays.

It would have been less unnerving if she had followed Syssi's example and entered the room holding hands with her groom instead of doing it the more traditional way and having him wait for her.

It had been Amanda's suggestion to do it that way. Since Alena trusted her sister to plan the perfect ceremony for her, she hadn't argued. But maybe she should have been more involved with the plan instead of leaving everything to Amanda.

It might have made her less anxious.

As the first notes of the age-old melody she'd chosen for the occasion began to play, Alena took another deep breath, and her fingers feathered over the soft curve of her belly.

Once her bridesmaids took their stations next to the podium, Alena entered, fixing her gaze on her striking groom as Syssi had suggested.

Orion stood tall and regal, his dark hair smoothed back and his piercing blue eyes glowing with love for her. But it was his sensual smile, the one that had won her heart, that sent a wave of calm washing over her.

Whatever happened, he was there for her, and she would never be alone again.

With each step Alena took, memories of her long life flashed before her eyes — moments of joy, sorrow, love, and loss. Shifting her gaze to her guests, she searched for the faces of her children, and when she found them, it was a relief to see the approval and support in their eyes.

It meant a lot to her that they had all accepted Orion as her mate.

To the side, a lavish dessert table caught her eye. Towering wedding cakes, delicate pastries, and an array of sweets were displayed on ornate platters, and she wondered whether her grandson had made them.

No one else was such a talented chef, and it warmed her heart that Gerard had done that for her.

But the biggest thanks she owed to Amanda.

Her sister had truly outdone herself with this celebration. Between transforming the dining hall into an elegant event venue and coming up with a menu the human staff could pull off with the help of the Odus, she'd crafted a perfect celebration.

Turning back to the podium, Alena looked up at her mother and smiled.

The mischievous gleam in her mother's eyes was softened by the love that radiated from her almost as powerfully as her glow. Yet, Alena was suddenly worried about Annani's plans for the ceremony.

Her mother's unique and unpredictable style promised a unique and exciting experience. Still, since she never prepared and always made up her speeches on the spot, it was somewhat unnerving for Alena, who loved structure and didn't like surprises.

As she reached the podium, Alena took her place beside Orion. When he took her hand, the warmth radiating from it and the love shining in his eyes soothed the remainder of her frayed nerves.

She was ready, and together they turned to face Annani.

Annani

Annani regarded her eldest daughter with a mix of motherly pride, love, and a little bit of sadness.

Alena had been her companion for the first two thousand years of her life, but now that she had found her one true love, she needed to spend her days by his side.

That was how things should be, and every mother should wish that her daughter found love and safety in the arms of a worthy partner.

Orion was that and more, but he was taking Alena away, and as much as Annani tried not to resent him for it, a little bit of it still lingered. She might be a goddess, but that didn't make her a selfless angel.

Stifling a chuckle, Annani smiled benevolently at the couple and lifted her arms to signal that she was about to begin.

"Usually, I open the ceremony by addressing my children, grandchildren, great-grandchildren, and so on, but my community has grown to include my nephews, mates who are the descendants of other gods, three new gods, Kra-ell, who are not here for various reasons, and even a few humans. So, from now on, I will address you as ladies, gentlemen, gods, immortals, and young souls."

A few chuckles sounded among the guests, and Annani waited patiently for them to end.

"We gather here aboard the Silver Swan to witness a love that transcends time. I have presided over several ceremonies, each unique and a testament to the power of love, but today, I once again stand not just as the officiant but as a mother. The first wedding I ever officiated over was my son's and his lovely bride Syssi, and today, I'm marrying my daughter Alena and Orion, the son of my cousin Toven."

She paused, looked fondly at the couple before her, and then back at the hall filled to bursting with her people.

"In the vast tapestry that the Fates weave, every soul has a string—a path. For a few lucky ones, these paths intersect, creating unbreakable bonds that last an eternity. Intertwined, they continue their journey to write a shared destiny.

"Orion, with your youthful spirit and unwavering determination, you have brought light into my daughter's life. Your love brings her joy and hope for the future.

"Alena, my dear child, you have journeyed by my side through millennia, gathering wisdom and experience, but it is time for you to spread your wings and soar through the clouds with your chosen companion. In Orion, you have found your perfect match, a mate who complements your strengths and a shield against life's inevitable hardships.

"Love, in its truest form, is not just an emotion. It is a force, a power that binds, heals, and elevates. As you both stand here, ready to embark on this new chapter in your lives, remember that love is your anchor. In moments of doubt, let it guide you. In moments of joy, let it amplify your happiness.

"To the union of two souls, two legacies, and two eternities, I bestow my blessings. May your love be as boundless as the ocean on which we sail, as enduring as Earth herself, and as radiant as the stars lighting up the night's sky.

"I now pronounce you bound by love, united in soul, and partners in eternity. Let your journey together be filled with adventures, laughter, and endless joy."

As Annani ended her blessing, the ambient glow of the lights of the dining hall shimmered a bit brighter, casting a golden hue over the couple standing before her.

Turning to Orion, Alena took his hands in hers. "From the first moment we met, I felt a pull that drew me to you. I tried to resist it because I was afraid of losing myself to you, but you showed me that my fears were groundless and that together, we were much more than the sum of our parts. Today, as I stand before you, with eternity stretching out ahead of us, I vow to cherish the light you've brought into my life and to be the beacon for you in times of darkness, just as you have been for me. I vow to be your partner in every adventure and to celebrate every joyous moment together. I vow to respect and honor the differences between us, for it is in our differences that our strengths lie. I vow to stand by you, to uplift you when you're down, to laugh with you, and to offer my strength when yours needs bolstering. And above all, I vow to love you unconditionally and eternally with every beat of my heart."

She took the ring Annani handed her and slipped it over his finger. "Orion, son of Toven, you are mine forever, and I am yours."

As Orion gazed at Alena, his eyes shone enough light to illuminate the entire ship.

"Alena, from the very first moment I heard you sing, I knew you were destined to be mine, and when I first gazed into your eyes, I knew I would do everything I could to win you over. Today, I stand before you humbled and honored to be your chosen one. I vow to protect and cherish the love we've built, to be your anchor in the stormiest of seas and your compass if you ever feel lost. I vow to be your partner, your confidant, and your best friend, to share in every high and low and to walk beside you every step of the way. I vow to honor and celebrate the history you carry, the family you have raised, and to build a future that pays homage to both of our pasts. And most importantly, I vow to love you, deeply and truly, for all the days of our eternal lives and beyond."

He took the ring from Annani and slipped it on Alena's finger. "Alena, daughter of Annani, you are mine, and I am yours."

Her gaze locked onto her mate's, Alena's eyes glistened with tears, and he, usually so composed, seemed overcome with emotion. His hand trembled slightly as he lifted Alena's, pressing a gentle kiss to the back of her hand.

As the dining hall erupted in applause, cheers, and whistles, the couple turned to face their guests. Annani took the opportunity to step down from the podium.

Her heart was heavy with a mixture of happiness and sorrow. Watching her eldest daughter basking in the love of her mate and her clan was bittersweet. Somehow, Annani had never expected Alena to leave her side, and letting go of her was more difficult than it had been with her younger siblings.

Syssi placed a reassuring hand on her shoulder. "It's hard, isn't it?" she whispered. "Seeing your children grow, change, and choose their own paths no matter their age."

Annani nodded, her gaze still fixed on the joyous couple. "Every parent's dream is to see their child happy. But parting, even for the best of reasons, is never easy."

Syssi smiled gently, "Alena is not going far, and soon she will have another child for you to dote over. These are happy times, Clan Mother."

"Indeed." Annani patted her daughter-in-law's hand. "You are wise beyond your years, my child from another mother."

Syssi laughed. "Don't let my mother hear you say that. She'll get jealous."

Annani patted Syssi's hand again. "Perhaps it will inspire her to retire and move into the village to be near you."

"Not a chance." Syssi smiled sadly. "I learned to let go of that hope a long time ago."

Dagor

༄

"That was so beautiful." Frankie dabbed at her eyes with the napkin.

Dagor didn't know whether she was referring to the goddess's speech or the vows the couple had exchanged. The truth was that he was a little moved himself.

The ceremony was very different from the ones he'd witnessed on Anumati. Over there, an oracle always presided over the wedding, giving the couple her vision of their future. They were also done with much more pomp and ceremony. Gods invested heavily in the wedding parties for their children. After all, most were lucky to have one offspring, so one wedding celebration was all they would ever get to have. There was also the issue of good luck, which many believed was tied to how grand the party was and for how long guests talked about it—a silly superstition that was probably propagated by the owners of wedding venues.

"Indeed." Gabi lifted her champagne goblet. "It puts pressure on us to come up with even lovelier vows."

Aru arched a brow. "No need because we are not getting married."

"Why not?"

"Because I'm not getting mated without my family, and since they can't come to our celebration, we can't have one. We will just need to stay unmarried."

Gabi gaped at him. "Where did that come from? I thought you were happy staying on Earth so we could be together."

"I am. But do you really need a ceremony to make our love official?"

Gabi deflated. "I guess not." She rose to her feet. "I should spend some time with my family." She gave him a tight smile before walking away.

Even Dagor knew that Aru had messed up, and he wasn't an authority on females, not by a long shot.

Negal shook his head. "You shouldn't have said that. Some things are better left unsaid."

Dagor couldn't agree more. Turning to Frankie, he extended his hand. "Would you like to dance?"

"I thought you would never ask." She took his offered hand and let him pull her up. "Do you even know how to dance?" she whispered in his ear. "Or did you just want to escape the argument between Aru and Negal?"

"I can dance," he dodged the answer. "I am a god."

She laughed. "That doesn't mean that you can move. Do they have dances on Anumati?"

"Of course." He pulled her into his arms and started swaying in place. "You see? This is not difficult."

"That's a slow dance," she murmured as she melted into his embrace. "What are you going to do when they change the beat?"

He hoped they wouldn't do that anytime soon. Holding Frankie felt incredibly good, and he was reluctant to let go of her. "I've been to clubs. I can emulate what I've seen."

Resting her cheek on his chest, she put her hand right over his heart as if guarding it so it wouldn't jump out. "I like being with you, Dagor. And it has nothing to do with you being a god. I would have liked you even if you were human."

Dagor froze as her words resonated through him, causing an earthquake and cracking his armor. The truth was that he liked being with Frankie as well, and he would have liked her whether she was human, immortal, or a goddess.

But he couldn't allow himself to feel that way. He wouldn't change his eternal life trajectory just because he'd met a female he liked.

It didn't matter that he felt more comfortable with her than with any of the goddesses he'd dated and that being with her was as easy as breathing. It didn't matter that she made him smile and eased the tightness in his chest.

"I like you a lot, too." He gently rubbed her back through the bodice of her dress. "Especially when you are naked and under me."

It wasn't a lie, but it wasn't the entire truth either.

He liked her in bed and outside of it.

Frankie stiffened for a moment, and Dagor wondered if he'd offended her by his comment about liking her in bed. It hadn't been one of his finest moments, and he regretted resorting to such an immature statement to guard himself against his own feelings for her.

But as the music continued to play, and he held her close, she relaxed against him again. The steady rhythm of her heartbeat was like his but not as strong, and it made him think of her humanity, her fragility, and the transient nature of her existence. There was a vast chasm between their worlds, unbridgeable, and the differences in their lifespans weren't even the most critical part of it.

When the melody changed, becoming more upbeat, Dagor felt a moment of panic. He hadn't lied about being able to dance, but he wasn't in some random club where no one knew him, and he didn't want to make a fool of himself by moving too much or too little.

Frankie looked up at him with amusement dancing in her eyes. "Don't worry. Give me your hand and follow my lead."

As soon as he did as she'd instructed, she spun them around and faced Dagor. Placing one hand on her hip, she extended the other, beckoning him to follow. With a playful twirl, she moved to the beat, her feet tracing intricate patterns on the floor, which was truly an acrobatic achievement given the size of her heels.

Dagor followed her lead effortlessly, mimicking her moves. After all, he might not be a good dancer when pitted against other gods, but he could hold his own against immortals and humans.

Frankie moved closer and took his hand, guiding it to her waist, and with her other, she directed his movements, teaching him without words. Her steps were fluid and confident, and soon Dagor was dancing as if he had known those movements since he was in the cradle. Frankie transitioned into more complex moves, spinning under Dagor's outstretched arm and pulling him into a series of gyrations that had their bodies popping and locking in sync with the beat.

The laughter and chatter around them faded as they lost themselves in the dance, their movements becoming more synchronized with each step. She was a great teacher, telegraphing her next steps so he had no problem adjusting his accordingly.

Dancing with her felt natural, instinctive.

When the song ended, Frankie was breathless, her face flushed with the exhilaration of the dance. Dagor looked down into her eyes and was about to lean in for a kiss when Negal's voice interrupted them.

"That was quite the performance, Dagor."

"You should compliment Frankie. Without her, I wouldn't have known which foot went where."

She laughed. "Not true. You are a natural. All you needed was just a little guidance."

Dagor smiled. "Don't be modest, Francesca. You are an inspired dancer. Did you take lessons?"

"Yes, I did." She looked proud as she squared her shoulders. "I owe my fabulous posture to the ballet classes I took throughout elementary and middle school."

"What happened to make you stop?"

She laughed. "Boys. There were none in my ballet classes."

Frankie

As the music took on a mellow tone, signaling the winding down of the night, the dancers began to exit the floor. Some made their way to the bar for a final drink, while others lingered by the dessert table.

Frankie took Dagor's hand and led him off the dance floor.

"Where are we going?" he asked when she stopped by their table to snatch her purse.

"The Lido deck."

"Why? They are still serving drinks at the bar."

She rolled her eyes. "I want some fresh air."

"Oh." He let her drag him along.

Dagor's romantic intelligence needed some nurturing. It was funny that a god interested in engineering had the same emotional issues as a human interested in the same topics.

Evidently, Toven was right, and there was little difference between humans, immortals, and gods. It made sense since the gods had used their genetic material to create humans.

As they reached the Lido deck, it became apparent that they weren't the only people who had thought about strolling in the fresh air after the party started winding down. Still, thankfully, the place was far from crowded.

"It's beautiful," Frankie said, leaning on the railing and gazing at the vast expanse of the ocean stretching out before her.

The moonlight bathed the gentle waves in a soft glow, making it look magical.

"Yes, you are."

She turned to him and smiled. "You are such a flatterer."

"I mean it." He cupped her cheek and dipped his head to take her lips in a gentle kiss. "I've had more fun today with you than I can remember ever having."

That was such a sweet lie. He was probably ancient, and spending time with a mere human was meh compared to the gorgeous goddesses on his home planet.

Arching a brow, Frankie looked at Dagor from under lowered lashes and asked the question she'd been too chicken to ask until now. "How old are you?"

He frowned. "There is no straightforward answer. It depends on your frame of reference. I'm very young for a god."

"What's considered young? Two hundred years, three hundred?"

"I'm sixty-nine, not counting the time I spent in stasis. That adds several hundred years to my lifespan."

"Sixty-nine," she repeated. "You lived for sixty-nine years, and you call yourself very young."

"That's right."

She shook her head. "The way you regard the passage of time will take some adjusting to."

As worry crossed his eyes, he tightened his arm around her waist. "Are you feeling faint?"

"I'm fine." She put her hand on his chest. "I'm no longer shocked by what I learn, so I don't get dizzy. I'm twenty-seven, but since in human years, I've depleted about one-third of my lifespan, I'm much older than you. It's like we count dogs' age differently than human age. For every human year, we count seven dog years."

Smiling, he put a finger on her lips. "Please, stop. It's irrelevant how old we are compared to each other. What matters is that we enjoy each other's company. Right?"

"Right." She looked into his piercing blue eyes. "For the duration of the cruise."

He nodded. "That's all we can have."

Frankie wasn't sure of that, but Dagor wasn't ready to hear that perhaps they could have more.

Cupping his cheek, she forced a smile. "Whatever happens, I want you to know that what we have is real, even if it can only last nine more days. For me, it's not just about the physical attraction or the novelty of being with a god. I feel a connection to you. We are good together."

Dagor took a deep breath, "Frankie, I..."

She placed a finger on his lips, silencing him. "It's okay," she whispered, "you don't need to say anything."

Sometimes, it was better to leave things unsaid and let Fate or circumstances pave the road ahead.

Frankie turned her gaze back to the ocean, the rhythmic lapping of waves against the ship's hull providing a comforting backdrop to the words they had just exchanged.

The moon's silvery glow made the waters shimmer, and it occurred to her that the beauty of the night seemed to encapsulate the fleeting nature of their relationship.

Dagor's hand found hers, their fingers intertwining. "In my world, time has a different meaning. Decades and centuries pass differently for us. But these moments with you are real."

She smiled wistfully. "For humans, every moment is precious. We learn to treasure the time we have because it's limited."

"It might not be for you. You can become immortal."

"Maybe I can, and maybe I cannot." She turned around and leaned her back against the railing. "I don't even know if I want to be immortal."

The truth was that she didn't believe she was indeed a Dormant, and convincing herself that she wasn't sure that she wanted to become immortal was easier than discovering that she could not.

Dagor looked at her, a hint of sadness in his eyes. "Do you regret it?"

"Regret what?"

"Meeting me, knowing that our time has an expiration date."

Frankie sighed. "Life is full of chance encounters and fleeting moments that can change the course of our lives. I don't regret meeting you even if the ten days of this cruise are all we will have. I'll cherish this time with you forever, but I won't lie by saying that it doesn't make me a little sad that something so wonderful has to end. I would have liked to see where it could lead."

Dagor pulled her close, dipped his head, and rested his forehead against hers. "The future is uncertain, and the present is all that matters. We will make each minute of each day count."

She wrapped her arms around him, pulling him into a tight embrace. "I just wish we had more time."

Dagor kissed the top of her head. "Time is a construct, Frankie. What matters is how we spend it. And I intend to spend every moment I have with you, making memories that will last me an eternity."

She pulled back slightly. "Promise me something?"

"Anything."

"When this cruise ends, and we go our separate ways, you won't forget me."

Dagor cupped her face, his thumb gently wiping away a tear that had escaped the corner of her eye. "I could never forget you, Frankie. You've left a permanent impression on my heart."

She chuckled. "A good one, I hope."

"The best."

Ani

As the giant red sun of Anumati cast its dimming radiance upon the city, Queen Ani's hovercraft glided smoothly toward the Temple of the Supreme Oracle. The sprawling capital, constantly buzzing with life and energy, seemed to quieten as people raised their heads to follow the royal craft on its unscheduled journey.

It was not her usual once-a-month visit to the temple. People must be wondering why she was making the journey today. Still, Ani had made unexpected visits to the Supreme before, so it was not entirely out of character.

Looking out through the shimmering dome of her craft, Ani wondered about the cryptic message from her friend, inviting her for a fortune reading.

Had Sofringhati seen something without being asked to part the veil of destiny?

That was different from how an oracle's visions usually worked, but sometimes she gleaned information while fulfilling petitioners' requests, and perhaps she had something of value to impart.

As the hovercraft descended, Ani watched the temple attendants assemble on its steps to welcome her. Their ceremonial robes seemed to shimmer in the dying light, and the long semi-sheer veils covering their faces fluttered in the ever-present wind.

As the craft touched down gently on the temple's landing platform, the queen's guard disembarked first, forming two formidable rows to shield her even though there had never been an attempt on her life. But then, perhaps no one had ever dared because of the diligence of her personal guard and the rumors of their ferocity.

Once the guards were in place, half of her attendants disembarked ahead of her, and as she descended the steps, the other half trailed behind her. The pomp and ceremony were one of the many costs of queenly life, one that Ani was so used to that she hardly noticed it anymore.

The vast doors of the temple opened silently, revealing the antechamber to the inner sanctum where the Supreme awaited and where Ani could enjoy an hour or two of privacy with her old friend without anyone watching every move and every expression she made.

As she traversed the courtyard, the weight of countless decisions, hopes and fears pressed in on her, but in the presence of the Supreme, she would not only find insight into the tapestry of fate, but also the respite of friendship with no strings attached.

The temple of the Supreme Oracle was an architectural marvel, a testament to the grandeur of Anumati's ancient civilization. As Ani stepped inside, she lifted her eyes to the grand vaulted ceiling soaring above. It seemed to touch the heavens, with the intricate carvings of stars and planets symbolizing the Supreme's connection to the universe.

Each colossal column had been carved from a single block of luminescent alludium and etched with spiral scripts running their lengths. The scripts represented pivotal prophecies given by one Supreme Oracle or another, and thousands of them had been collected since the temple had been erected.

The torchlight cast shifting shadows on the columns, making the spirals seem alive, moving, writhing, their words changing with the passing epochs, but it was an illusion.

The scripts never changed; only their interpretations did.

Lowering her gaze to the mosaic floor of azure and gold tiles that were arranged in patterns mirroring constellations in Anumati's night sky, Ani took a moment to appreciate the workmanship before lifting her eyes toward the back of the chamber where the Oracle sat on her throne-like chair.

Elevated by three steps, the podium was made of delludim, the dark light-absorbing stone contrasting starkly with the alludium columns. Upon it sat the Oracle, and behind her hung an enormous tapestry depicting the Tree of Life, its branches and roots intertwined with symbols of past, present, and future.

On either side of the podium, large bronze braziers burned, filled with fragrant herbs. The scent permeated the chamber, a mix of aromatic herbs inducing a sense of calm and reverence and a bit of something else that most petitioners were not aware of.

The Supreme possessed an incredible power—the ability to peer into past and future and even pierce the veil between worlds, but she had some tricks up her sleeve to make the experience even more epic for the petitioners and increase the level of their contributions.

Her other trick was the complete privacy of the grand chamber.

No modern technology was allowed, not even electricity, and the walls, made of smooth gray stone, absorbed sound.

Ani's entourage, a mix of guards, advisors, and ladies-in-waiting, followed in precise formation, their movements practiced and synchronized.

The Oracle, draped in deep indigo robes, met Ani's gaze with an inscrutable expression. Until they were alone in the chamber, they had to follow protocol and ceremonial formalities.

It was a dance the Oracle and the queen had performed countless times.

Respectful words of greeting were exchanged while the attendants watched with bated breath, always vigilant, always trying to catch hidden meanings.

Ani knew that her husband had spies among them, and she knew precisely who they were, but she pretended that she did not.

Then, as the last formalities and rituals were concluded, a silent signal from Ani sent the attendants retreating to the edges of the chamber and out its doors.

Once the vast doors closed with a soft thud, leaving the two most powerful women on Anumati alone in the heart of the temple, the air between them grew charged.

The Oracle's stern demeanor softened, and Ani's shoulders relaxed ever so slightly.

They approached each other, not as monarch and seer, but as old friends.

"Ani," Sofri whispered as she pulled her into her arms. "Oh, Ani."

"What is it?" Ani leaned away and looked astonished at her friend's tear-stricken face.

"I have good news."

As they pulled apart, Sofringhati's eyes communicated layers of emotions without words.

"Why are you crying?" Ani asked.

Sofri took her hand and led her to a stack of cushions. "My heart is overflowing with emotion," she said, her eyes glistening as she brushed away a tear with the edge of her robe. "There are revelations that change the course of destinies. Brace yourself, Ani, for what I am about to tell you is this. Your son had a daughter, and she is alive and well on Earth."

COMING UP NEXT
The Children of the Gods Book 78
Dark Voyage Matters of the Mind

*To read the first 3 chapters JOIN the VIP club
at ITLUCAS.COM —To find out what's
included in your free membership, click HERE or
flip to the last page.*

As conflicting expectations strain Dagor and Frankie's
budding relationship, they join a shore excursion to the

ruins of Tehuacalo, where an ancient map of dubious origins claims a powerful amulet is buried. Despite Kian's reservation about the danger of entering cartel territory, Kalugal is set on leading the group of immortals, gods, and one human on an adventure and promises they will be back in time for Amanda and Dalhu's wedding.

When the leisurely archeological quest turns into a deadly conflict, the group stumbles upon a much more precious treasure than the amulet they have set out to uncover.

Coming up next in the
PERFECT MATCH SERIES
THE VALKYRIE & THE WITCH

A treat for fans of *The Wheel of Time*.

After breaking up with my boyfriend, I vow never to date a physician again and avoid workplace romances like the plague. Seeking an escape from bad memories and hospital politics, I apply for a job at the Perfect Match Virtual Fantasy Studios, where I hope to explore fantastical scenarios and beta-test new experiences.

I have no intention of entering a new relationship anytime soon, but it is difficult to ignore Kayden, a fellow trainee who's good-looking and charming but regrettably has aspirations of becoming a physician.

Hoping never to get paired with him to beta test an experience, I choose the Valkyrie adventure. It seems like a safe bet to avoid a guy like him, who would never select an experience where the female is the kick-ass heroine and the man only gets a supporting role. However, the algorithm has other plans in store for us. It seems to think that we are a perfect match.

Dear reader,

I hope Dark Voyage Matters of the Heart have added a little joy to your day. If you have a moment to add some to mine, you can help spread the word about the Children Of The Gods series by telling your friends and penning a review. Your recommendations are the most powerful way to inspire new readers to explore the series.

Thank you,

Isabell

Join the VIP Club

To find out what's included in your free membership,
flip to the last page.

Also by I. T. Lucas

The Children of the Gods Series Sets

Books 1-3: Dark Stranger trilogy— Includes a bonus short story: **The Fates take a Vacation**

Books 4-6: Dark Enemy Trilogy —Includes a bonus short story—**The Fates' Post-Wedding Celebration**

Books 7-10: Dark Warrior Tetralogy

Books 11-13: Dark Guardian Trilogy

Books 14-16: Dark Angel Trilogy

Books 17-19: Dark Operative Trilogy

Books 20-22: Dark Survivor Trilogy

Books 23-25: Dark Widow Trilogy

Books 26-28: Dark Dream Trilogy

Books 29-31: Dark Prince Trilogy

Books 32-34: Dark Queen Trilogy

Books 35-37: Dark Spy Trilogy

Books 38-40: Dark Overlord Trilogy

CHECK OUT THE SPECIALS ON
ITLUCAS.COM
(https://itlucas.com/specials)

FOR EXCLUSIVE PEEKS AT UPCOMING RELEASES &
A FREE I. T. LUCAS COMPANION BOOK

JOIN MY *VIP CLUB* AND GAIN ACCESS TO THE VIP PORTAL AT ITLUCAS.COM

TO JOIN, GO TO:
http://eepurl.com/blMTpD

Find out more details about what's included with your free membership on the book's last page.

TRY THE CHILDREN OF THE GODS SERIES ON
<u>AUDIBLE</u>
2 FREE audiobooks with your new Audible subscription!

Published by Evening Star Press

EveningStarPress.com

ISBN-13: 978-1-962067-08-9

FOR EXCLUSIVE PEEKS AT UPCOMING RELEASES & A FREE COMPANION BOOK

JOIN MY *VIP CLUB* AND GAIN ACCESS TO THE VIP PORTAL AT ITLUCAS.COM
TO JOIN, GO TO:
http://eepurl.com/blMTpD

INCLUDED IN YOUR FREE MEMBERSHIP:

YOUR VIP PORTAL

- READ PREVIEW CHAPTERS OF UPCOMING RELEASES.
- LISTEN TO GODDESS'S CHOICE NARRATION BY CHARLES LAWRENCE
- EXCLUSIVE CONTENT OFFERED ONLY TO MY VIPs.

FREE I.T. LUCAS COMPANION INCLUDES:

- GODDESS'S CHOICE PART I
- PERFECT MATCH: VAMPIRE'S CONSORT (A STANDALONE NOVELLA)
- INTERVIEW Q & A
- CHARACTER CHARTS

IF YOU'RE ALREADY A SUBSCRIBER, AND YOU ARE NOT GETTING MY EMAILS, YOUR PROVIDER IS

SENDING THEM TO YOUR JUNK FOLDER, AND YOU ARE MISSING OUT ON **IMPORTANT UPDATES, SIDE CHARACTERS' PORTRAITS, ADDITIONAL CONTENT, AND OTHER GOODIES.** TO FIX THAT, ADD isabell@itlucas.com TO YOUR EMAIL CONTACTS OR YOUR EMAIL VIP LIST.

Check out the specials at
https://www.itlucas.com/specials

Made in the USA
Las Vegas, NV
13 November 2023

80818938R00223